FOUR EYES

VOLUME TWO

HEARTS OF FIRE

WRITER
JOE KELLY

COVER ARTIST   ILLUSTRATOR   FLOURISHER
(CHAPTERS 1 & 4)
MAX FIUMARA

ILLUSTRATOR
(CHAPTERS 2 & 3)
RAFAEL ORTIZ

ART ASSISTANT
(CHAPTER 2)
JUAN CRUZ RODRIGUEZ

LETTERING & DESIGN
THOMAS MAUER

CREATED BY
JOE KELLY & MAX FIUMARA

www.manofaction.tv

FOUR EYES, VOL. 2: HEARTS OF FIRE

ISBN: 978-1-63215-806-2
July 2016. First Printing. Published by Image Comics, Inc.
Office of publication: 2001 Center Street, Sixth Floor, Berkeley, CA 94704.

For information regarding the CPSIA on this printed material call: 203-595-3636 and provide reference #RICH-690202.

For international rights, contact:
foreignlicensing@imagecomics.com

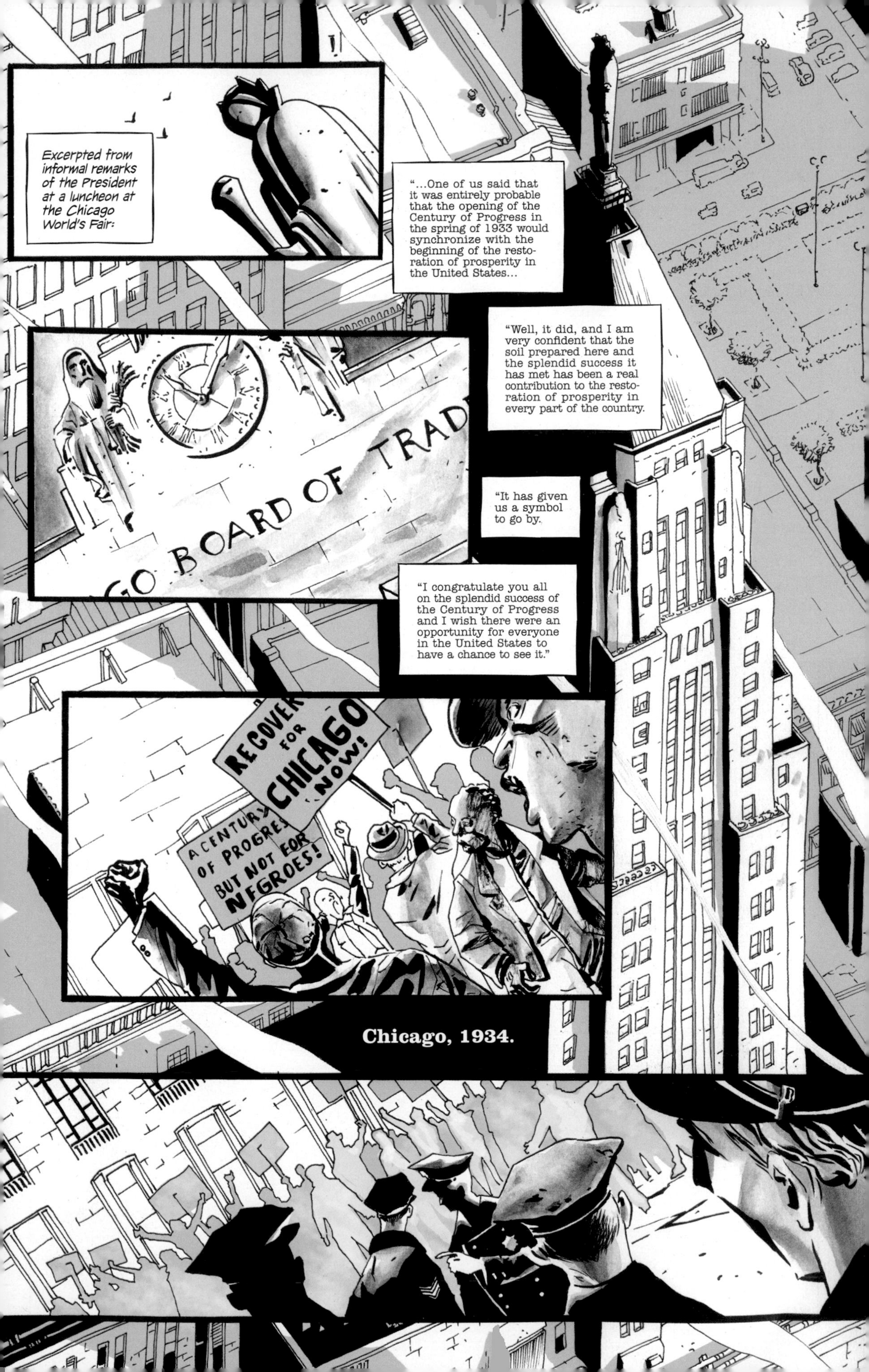
Excerpted from informal remarks of the President at a luncheon at the Chicago World's Fair:
"...One of us said that it was entirely probable that the opening of the Century of Progress in the spring of 1933 would synchronize with the beginning of the restoration of prosperity in the United States...
GO BOARD OF TRAD
"Well, it did, and I am very confident that the soil prepared here and the splendid success it has met has been a real contribution to the restoration of prosperity in every part of the country.
"It has given us a symbol to go by.
"I congratulate you all on the splendid success of the Century of Progress and I wish there were an opportunity for everyone in the United States to have a chance to see it."
RECOVER FOR CHICAGO NOW!
A CENTURY OF PROGRES BUT NOT FOR NEGROES!
Chicago, 1934.

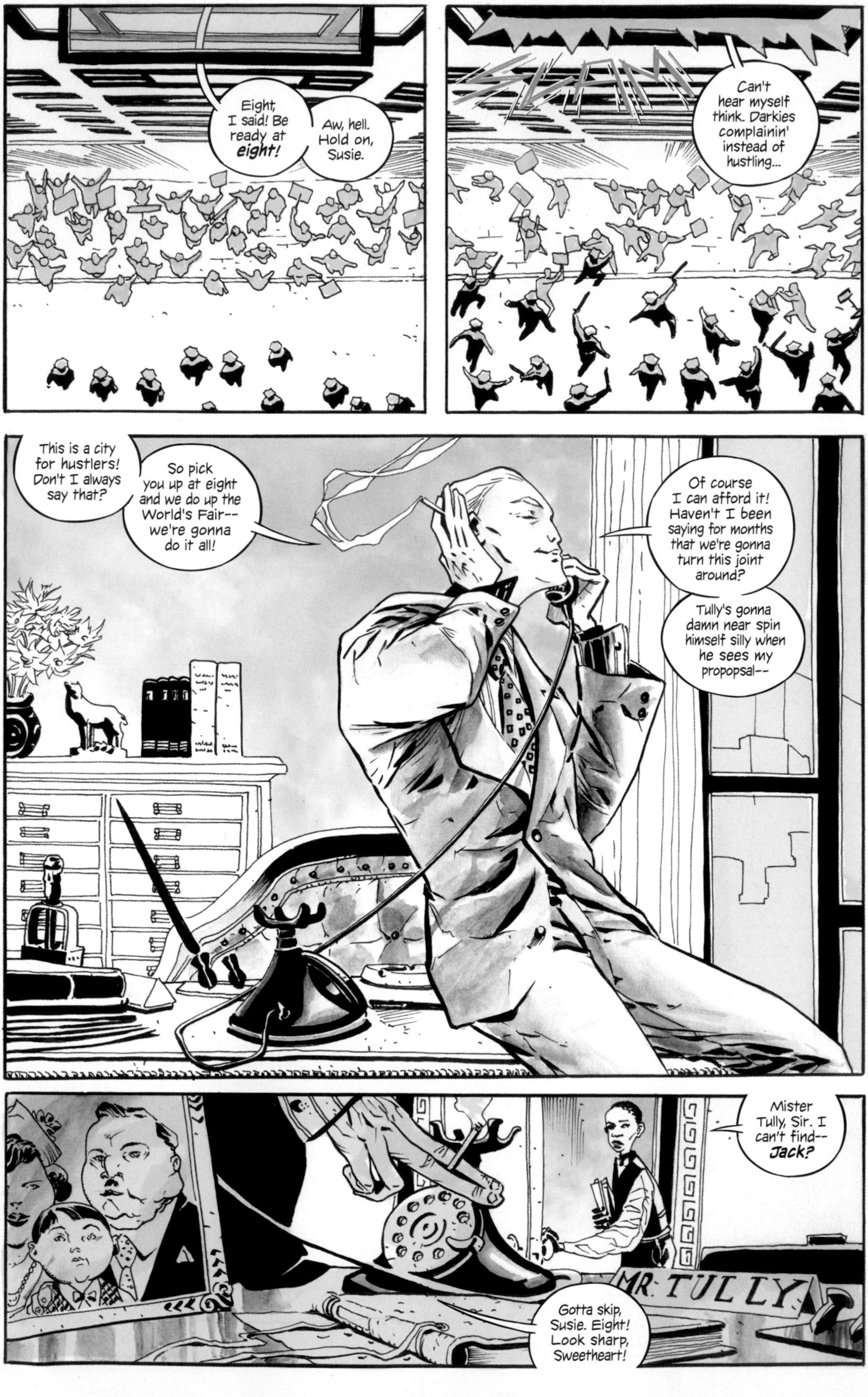

Eight, I said! Be ready at eight!
Aw, hell. Hold on, Susie.
SLAM
Can't hear myself think. Darkies complainin' instead of hustling...
This is a city for hustlers! Don't I always say that?
So pick you up at eight and we do up the World's Fair--we're gonna do it all!
Of course I can afford it! Haven't I been saying for months that we're gonna turn this joint around?
Tully's gonna damn near spin himself silly when he sees my propopsal--
Mister Tully, Sir. I can't find-- Jack?
MR. TULLY
Gotta skip, Susie. Eight! Look sharp, Sweetheart!

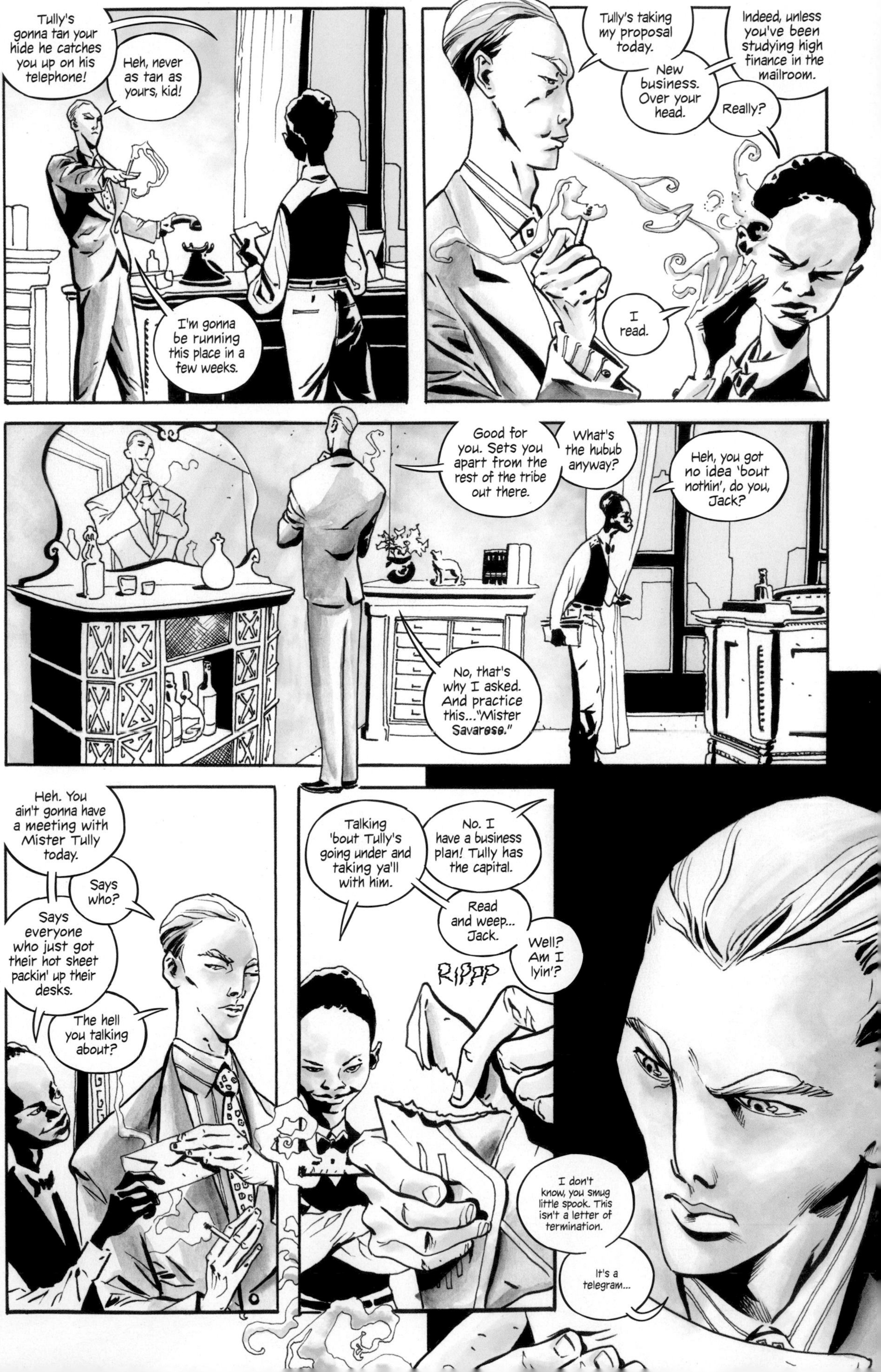
Tully's gonna tan your hide he catches you up on his telephone!
Heh, never as tan as yours, kid!
I'm gonna be running this place in a few weeks.
Tully's taking my proposal today.
New business. Over your head.
Indeed, unless you've been studying high finance in the mailroom.
Really?
I read.
Good for you. Sets you apart from the rest of the tribe out there.
What's the hubub anyway?
Heh, you got no idea 'bout nothin', do you, Jack?
No, that's why I asked. And practice this..."Mister Savarese."
Heh. You ain't gonna have a meeting with Mister Tully today.
Says who?
Says everyone who just got their hot sheet packin' up their desks.
The hell you talking about?
Talking 'bout Tully's going under and taking ya'll with him.
No. I have a business plan! Tully has the capital.
Read and weep... Jack.
Well? Am I lyin'?
RIPP
I don't know, you smug little spook. This isn't a letter of termination.
It's a telegram...

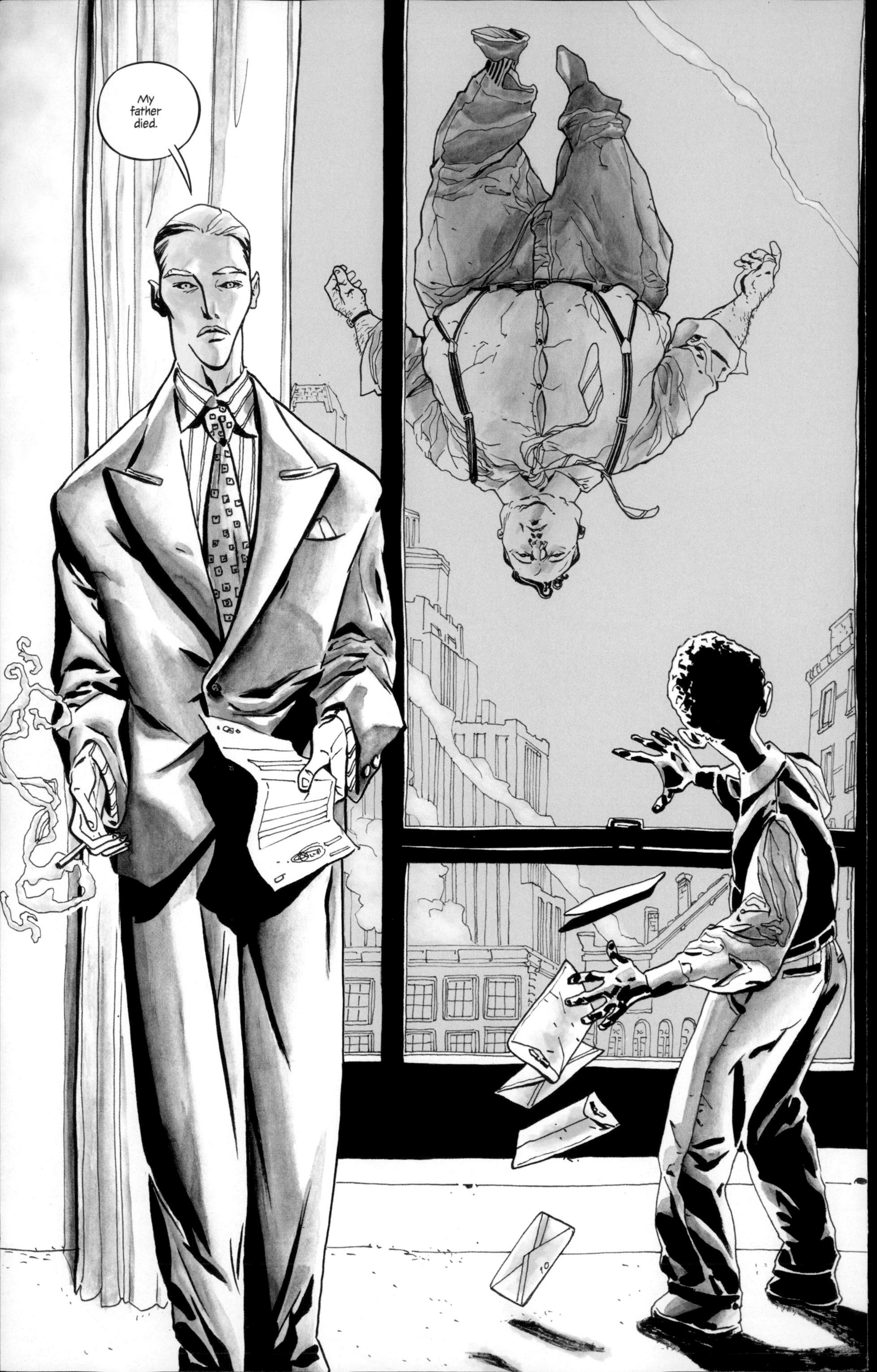
My father died.

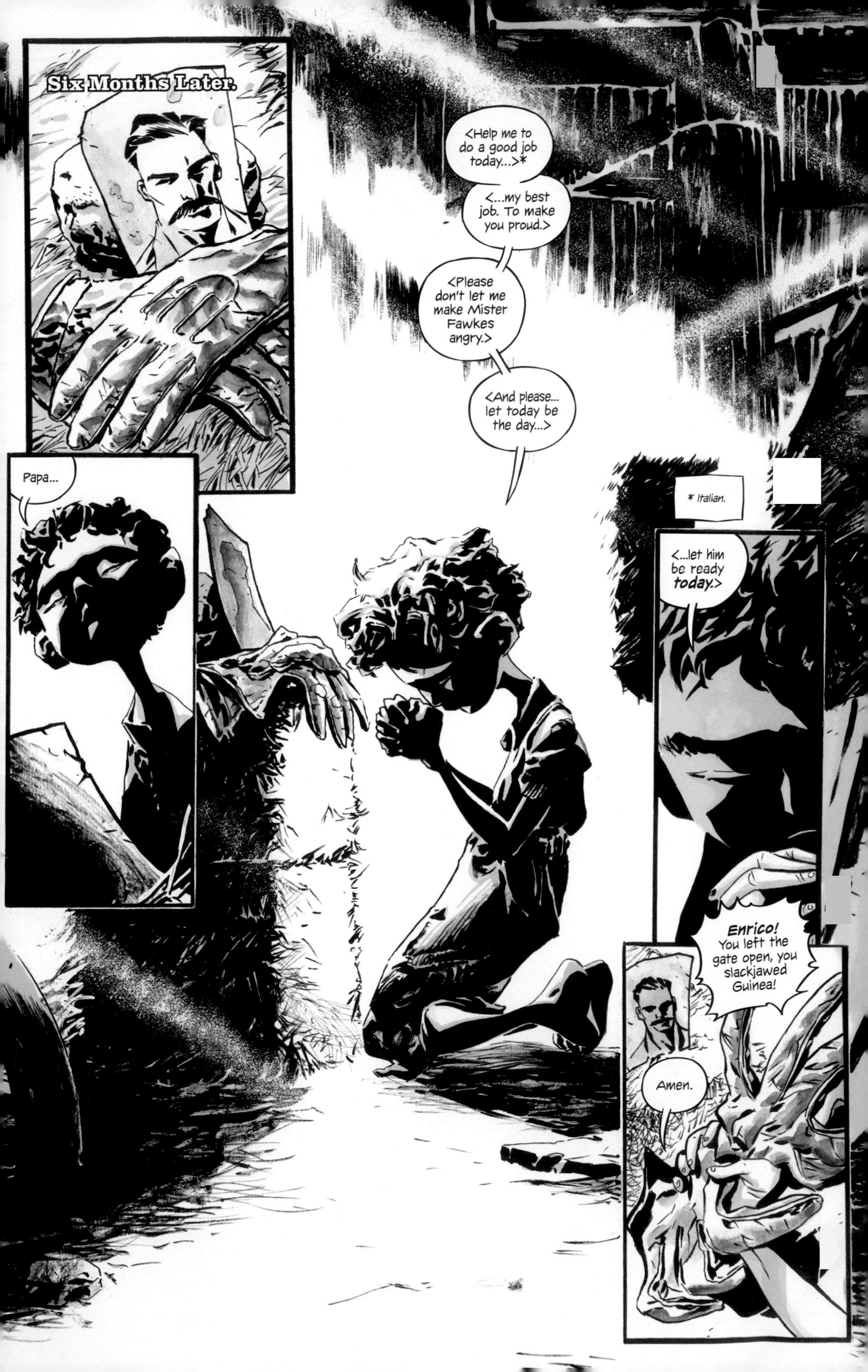
Six Months Later.
<Help me to do a good job today...>*
<...my best job. To make you proud.>
<Please don't let me make Mister Fawkes angry.>
<And please... let today be the day...>
Papa...
* Italian.
<...let him be ready today.>
Enrico! You left the gate open, you slackjawed Guinea!
Amen.

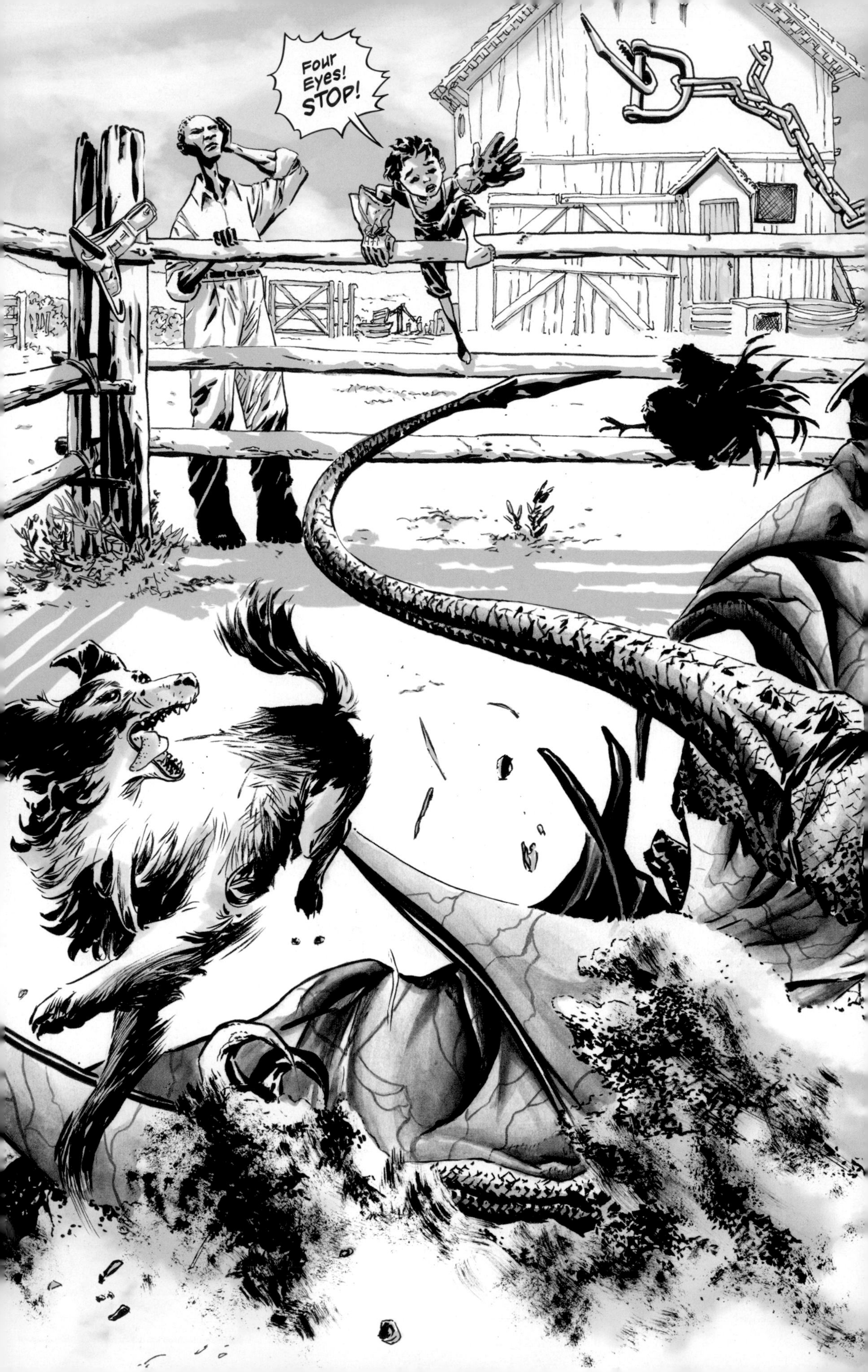
Four Eyes! STOP!

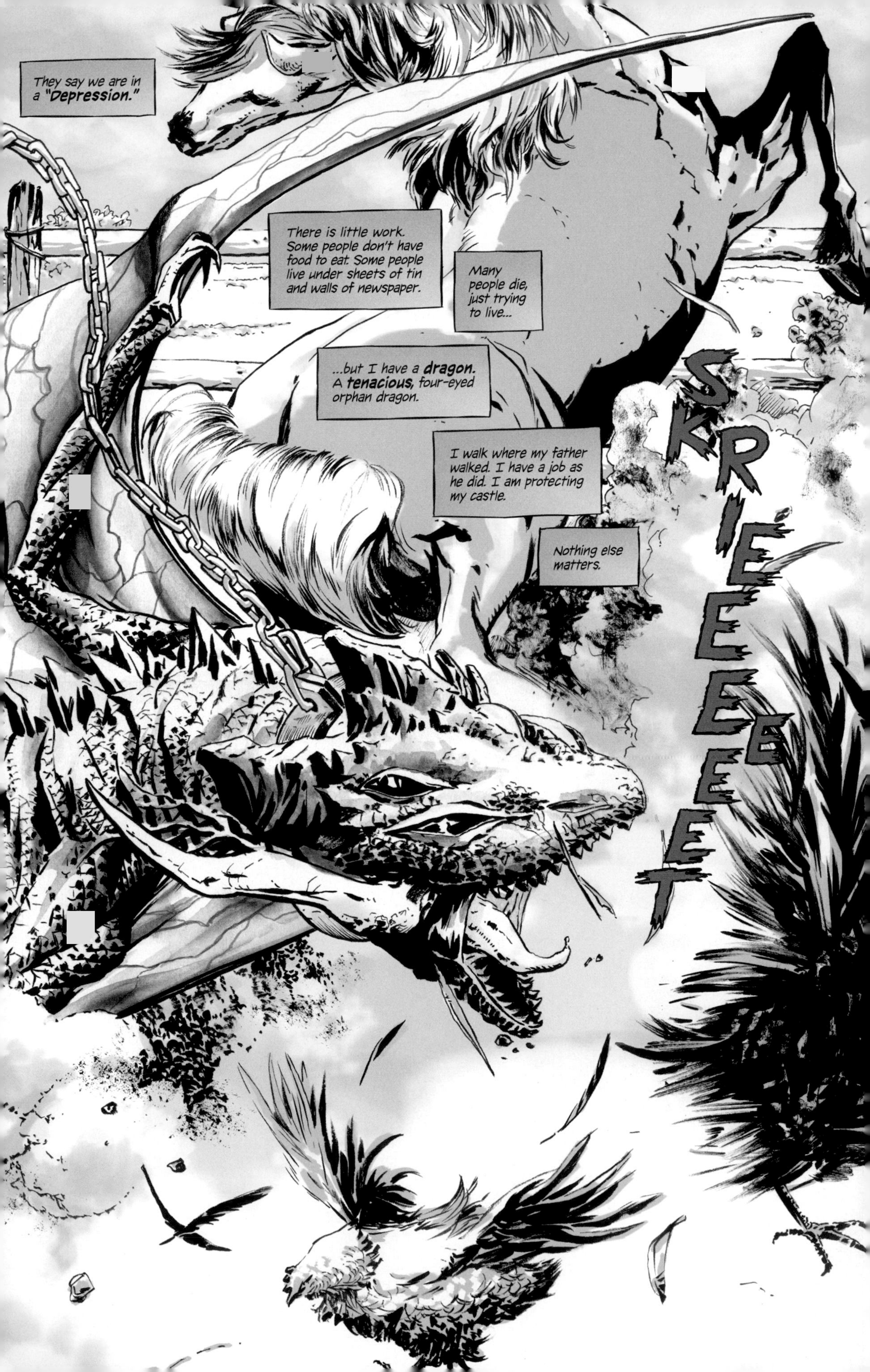
They say we are in a "Depression."
There is little work. Some people don't have food to eat. Some people live under sheets of tin and walls of newspaper.
Many people die, just trying to live...
...but I have a dragon. A tenacious, four-eyed orphan dragon.
I walk where my father walked. I have a job as he did. I am protecting my castle.
Nothing else matters.
SKRIEEEEEET

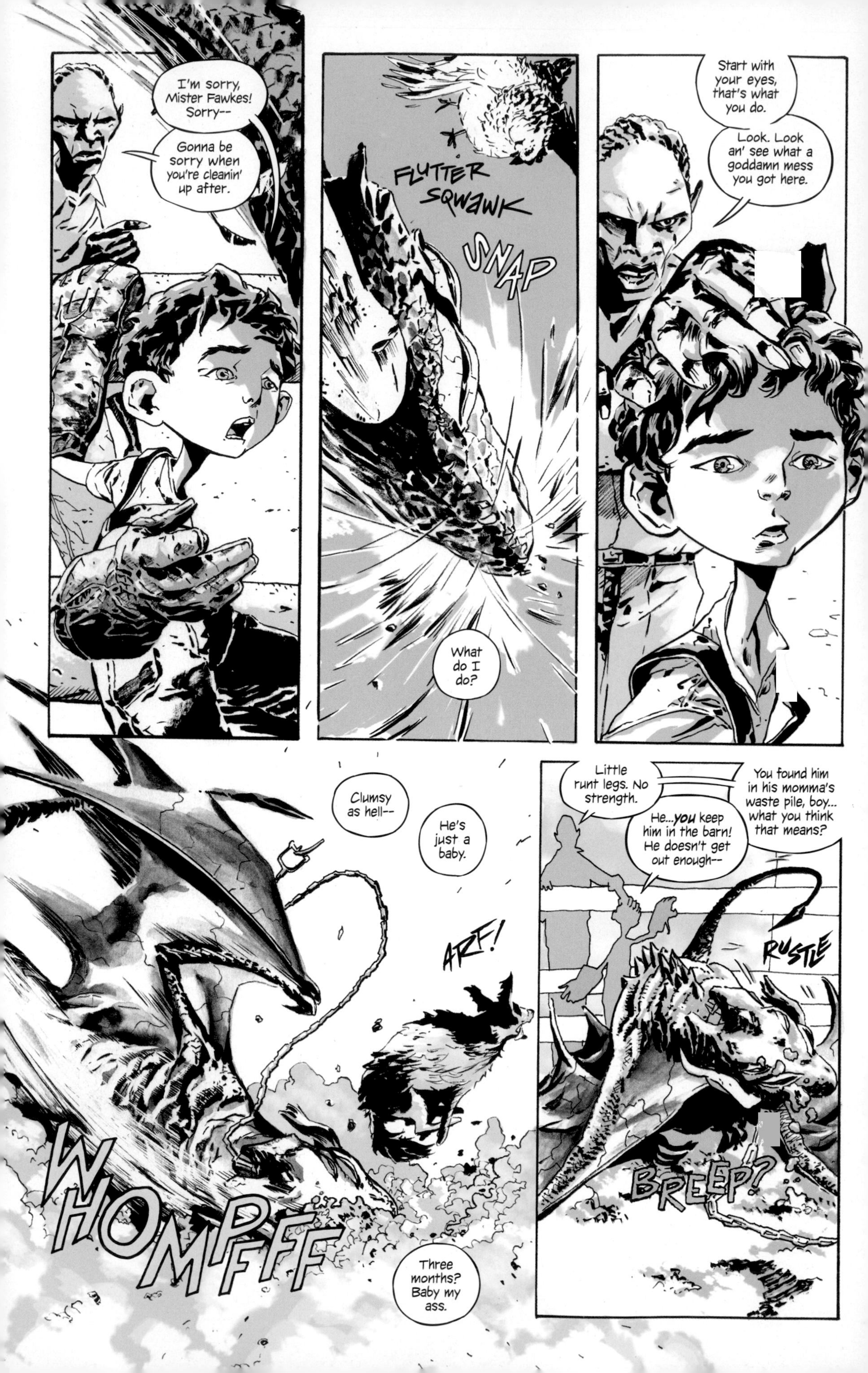

I'm sorry, Mister Fawkes! Sorry--
Gonna be sorry when you're cleanin' up after.
FLUTTER SQWAWK
SNAP
What do I do?
Start with your eyes, that's what you do.
Look. Look an' see what a goddamn mess you got here.
Clumsy as hell--
He's just a baby.
ARF!
WHOMPFFF
Three months? Baby my ass.
Little runt legs. No strength.
He...you keep him in the barn! He doesn't get out enough--
You found him in his momma's waste pile, boy... what you think that means?
RUSTLE
BREEP?

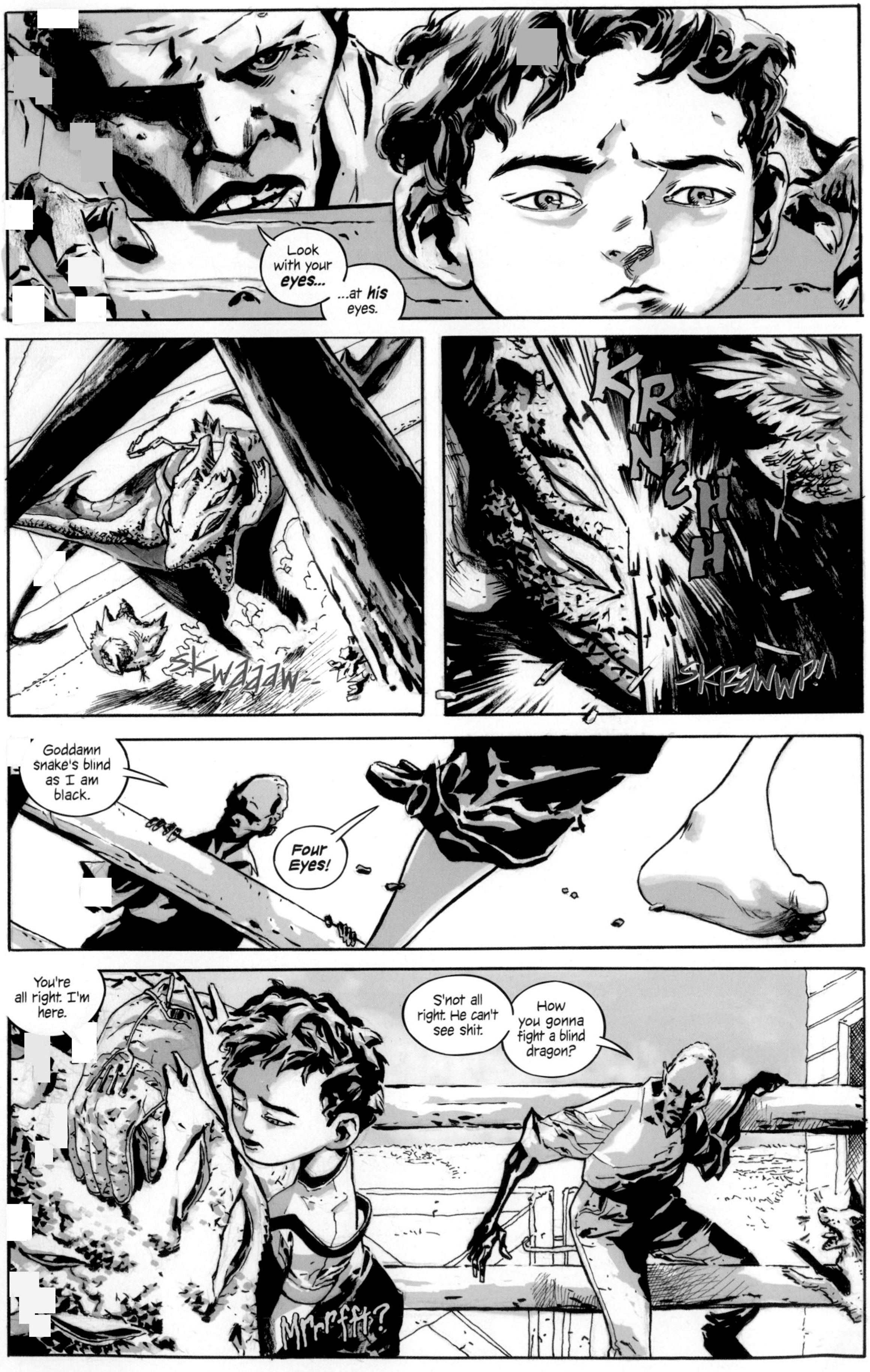

Look with your *eyes...*
...at *his* eyes.
SKWAAAW--
KRNCHHH
SKRAWWP!
Goddamn snake's blind as I am black.
Four Eyes!
You're all right. I'm here.
S'not all right. He can't see shit.
How you gonna fight a blind dragon?
Mrrrfft?

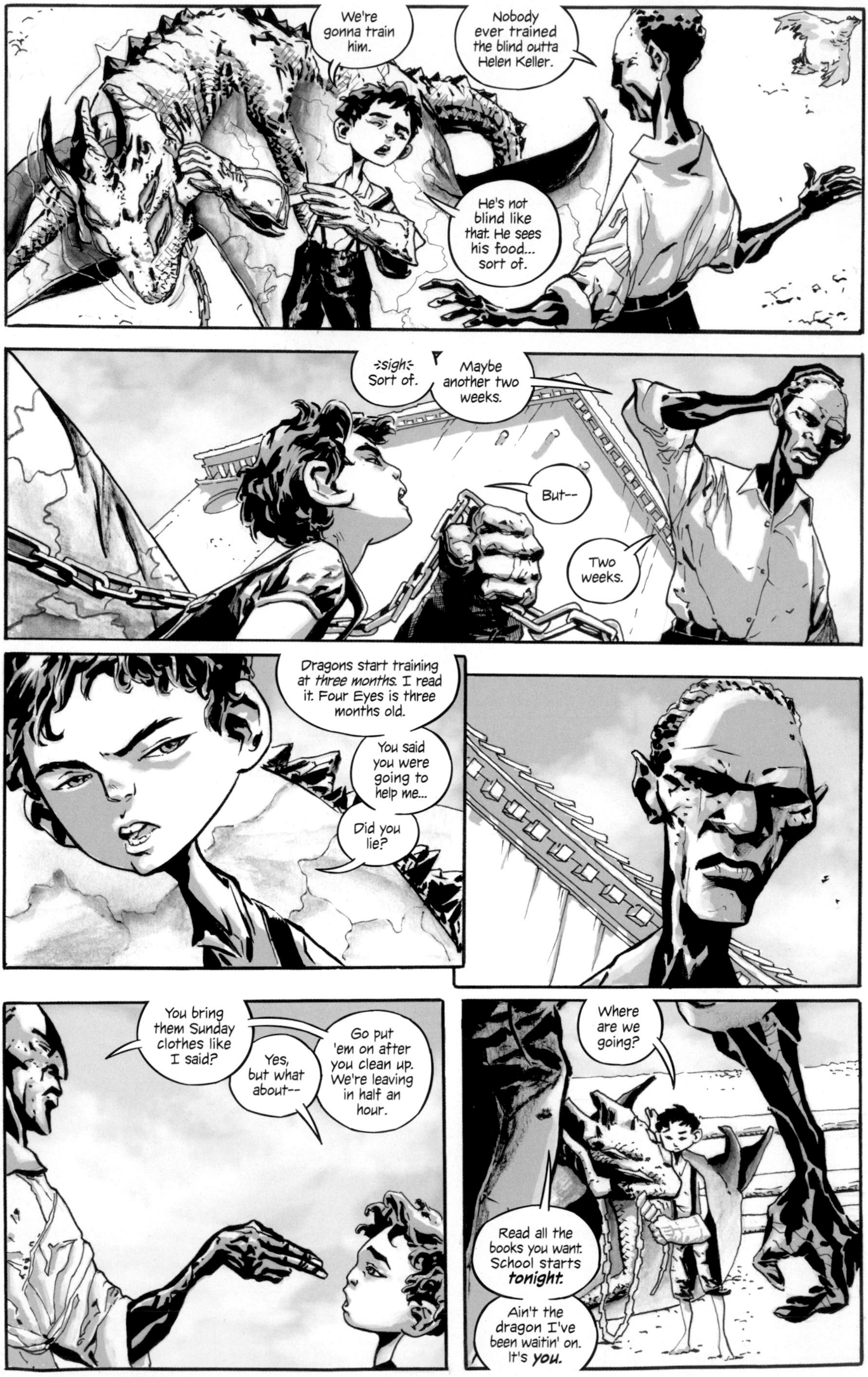
We're gonna train him.
Nobody ever trained the blind outta Helen Keller.
He's not blind like that. He sees his food... sort of.
-sigh- Sort of.
Maybe another two weeks.
But--
Two weeks.
Dragons start training at *three months.* I read it. Four Eyes is three months old.
You said you were going to help me...
Did you lie?
You bring them Sunday clothes like I said?
Yes, but what about--
Go put 'em on after you clean up. We're leaving in half an hour.
Where are we going?
Read all the books you want. School starts ***tonight.***
Ain't the dragon I've been waitin' on. It's ***you.***

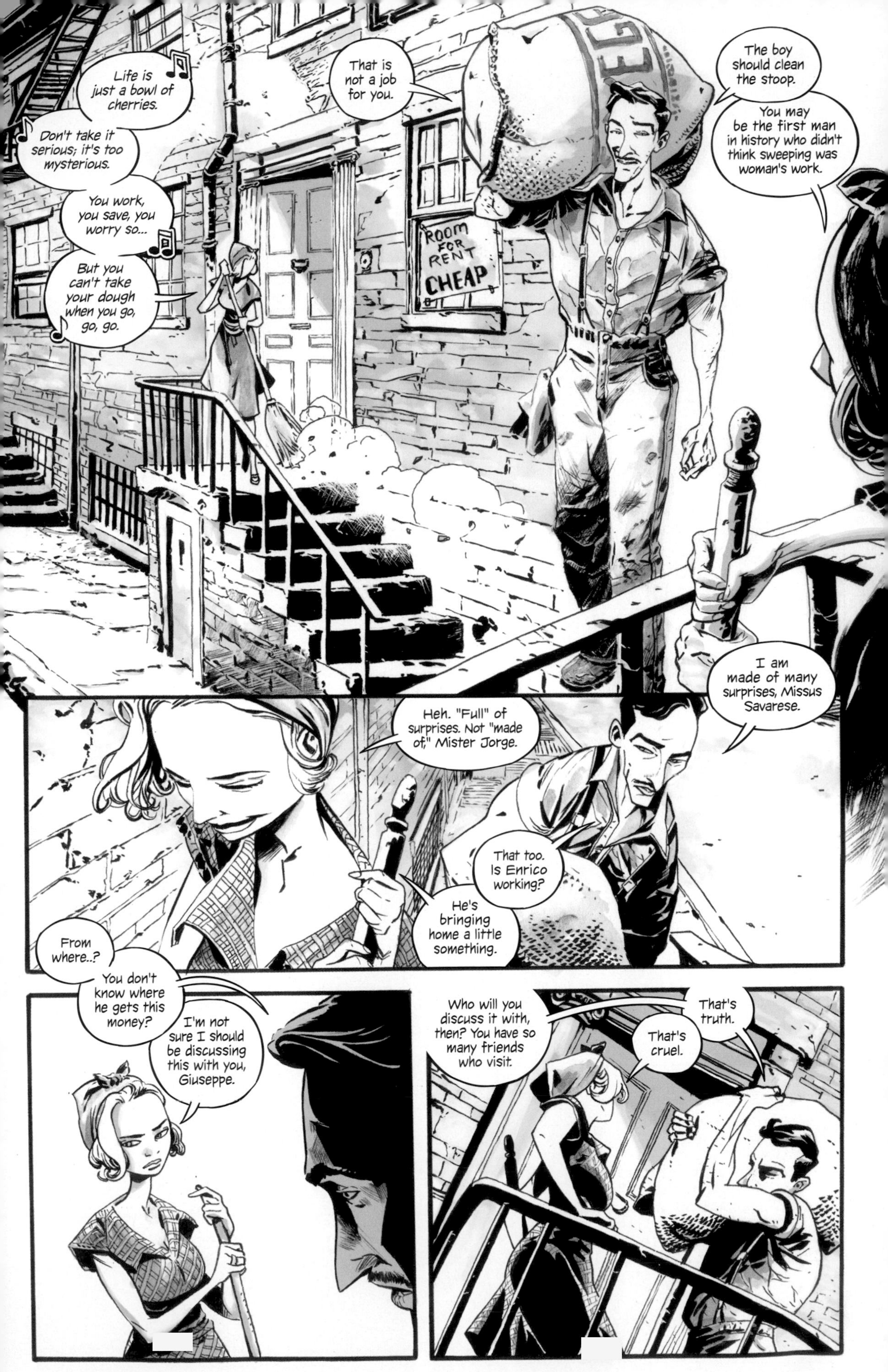
Life is just a bowl of cherries.
Don't take it serious; it's too mysterious.
You work, you save, you worry so...
But you can't take your dough when you go, go, go.
That is not a job for you.
The boy should clean the stoop.
You may be the first man in history who didn't think sweeping was woman's work.
ROOM FOR RENT CHEAP
I am made of many surprises, Missus Savarese.
Heh. "Full" of surprises. Not "made of," Mister Jorge.
That too. Is Enrico working?
He's bringing home a little something.
From where..?
You don't know where he gets this money?
I'm not sure I should be discussing this with you, Giuseppe.
Who will you discuss it with, then? You have so many friends who visit.
That's truth.
That's cruel.

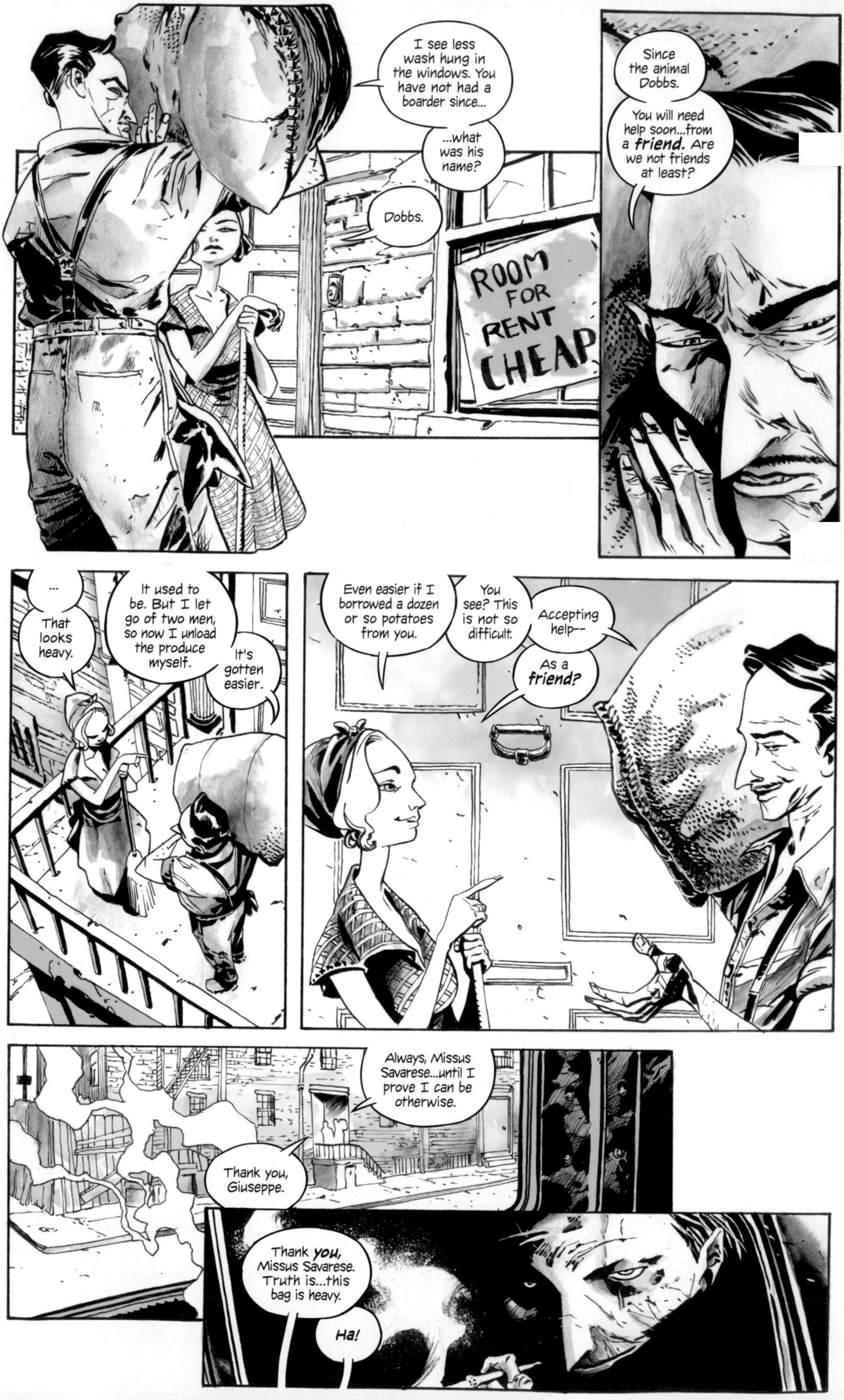

I see less wash hung in the windows. You have not had a boarder since...
...what was his name?
Dobbs.
ROOM FOR RENT CHEAP
Since the animal Dobbs.
You will need help soon...from a *friend.* Are we not friends at least?
...
That looks heavy.
It used to be. But I let go of two men, so now I unload the produce myself.
It's gotten easier.
Even easier if I borrowed a dozen or so potatoes from you.
You see? This is not so difficult.
Accepting help--
As a *friend?*
Always, Missus Savarese...until I prove I can be otherwise.
Thank you, Giuseppe.
Thank *you,* Missus Savarese. Truth is...this bag is heavy.
Ha!

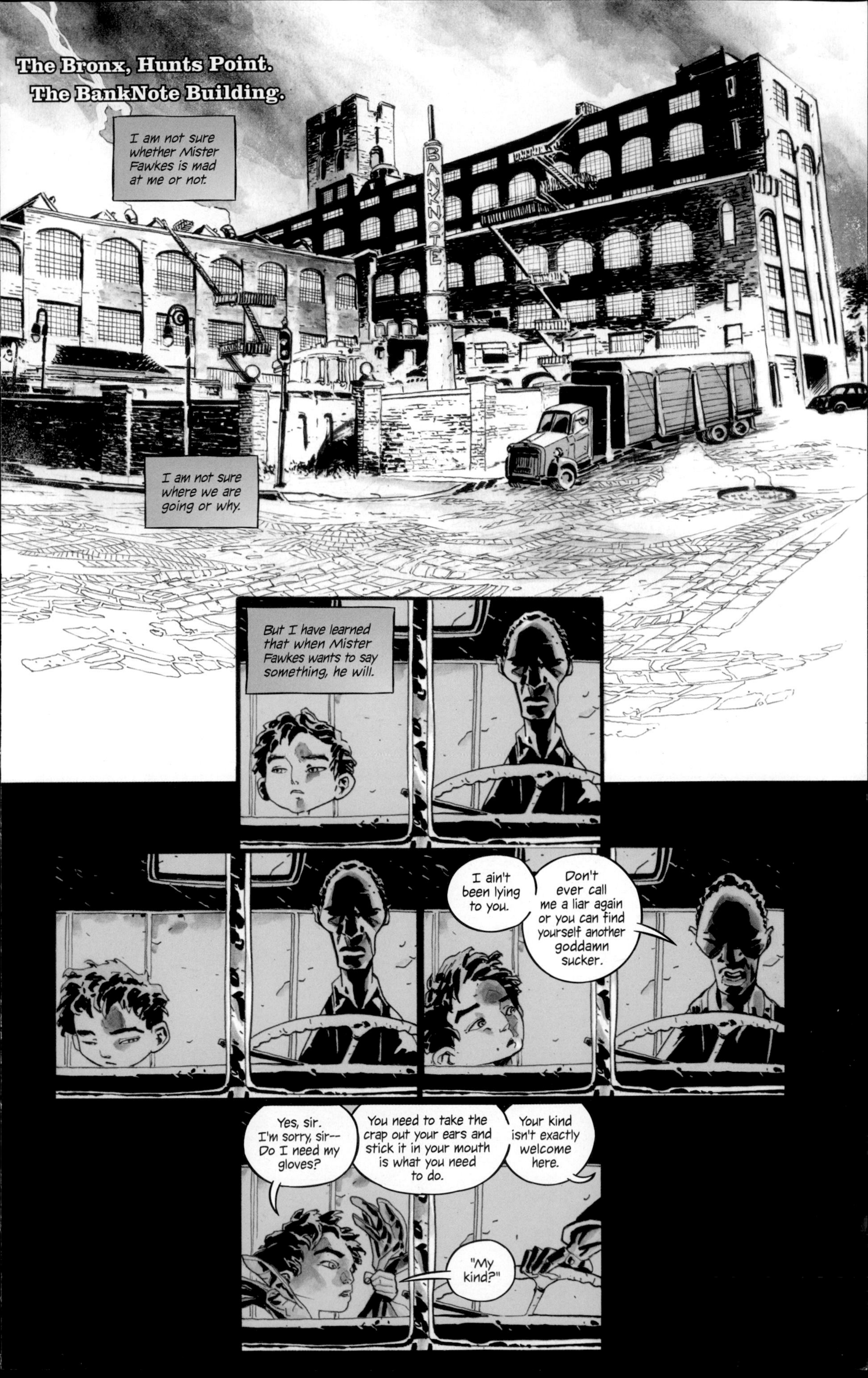
The Bronx, Hunts Point.
The BankNote Building.
I am not sure whether Mister Fawkes is mad at me or not.
BANKNOTE
I am not sure where we are going or why.
But I have learned that when Mister Fawkes wants to say something, he will.
I ain't been lying to you.
Don't ever call me a liar again or you can find yourself another goddamn sucker.
Yes, sir. I'm sorry, sir-- Do I need my gloves?
You need to take the crap out your ears and stick it in your mouth is what you need to do.
Your kind isn't exactly welcome here.
"My kind?"

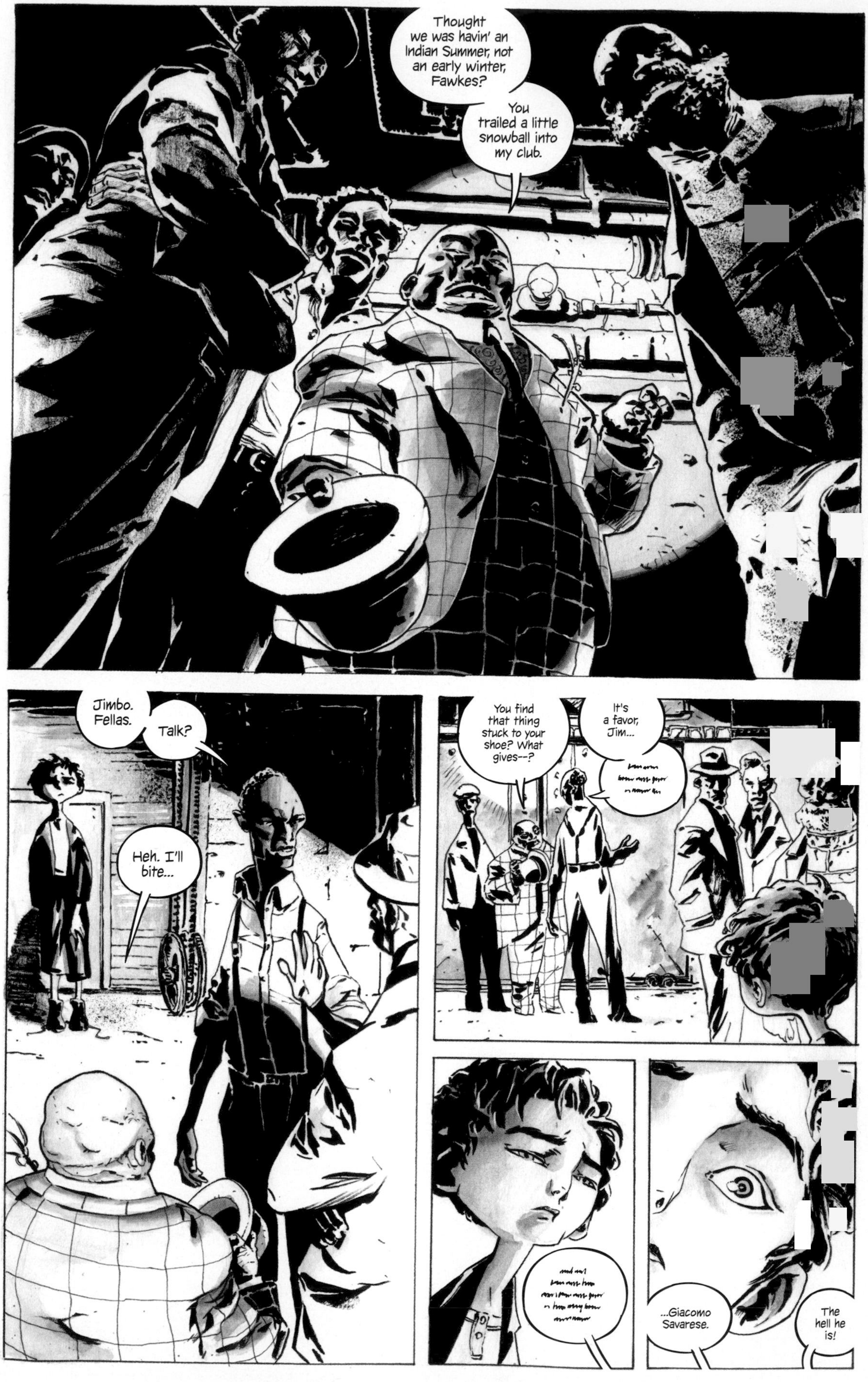
Thought we was havin' an Indian Summer, not an early winter, Fawkes?
You trailed a little snowball into my club.
Jimbo. Fellas.
Talk?
Heh. I'll bite...
You find that thing stuck to your shoe? What gives--?
It's a favor, Jim...
...Giacomo Savarese.
The hell he is!

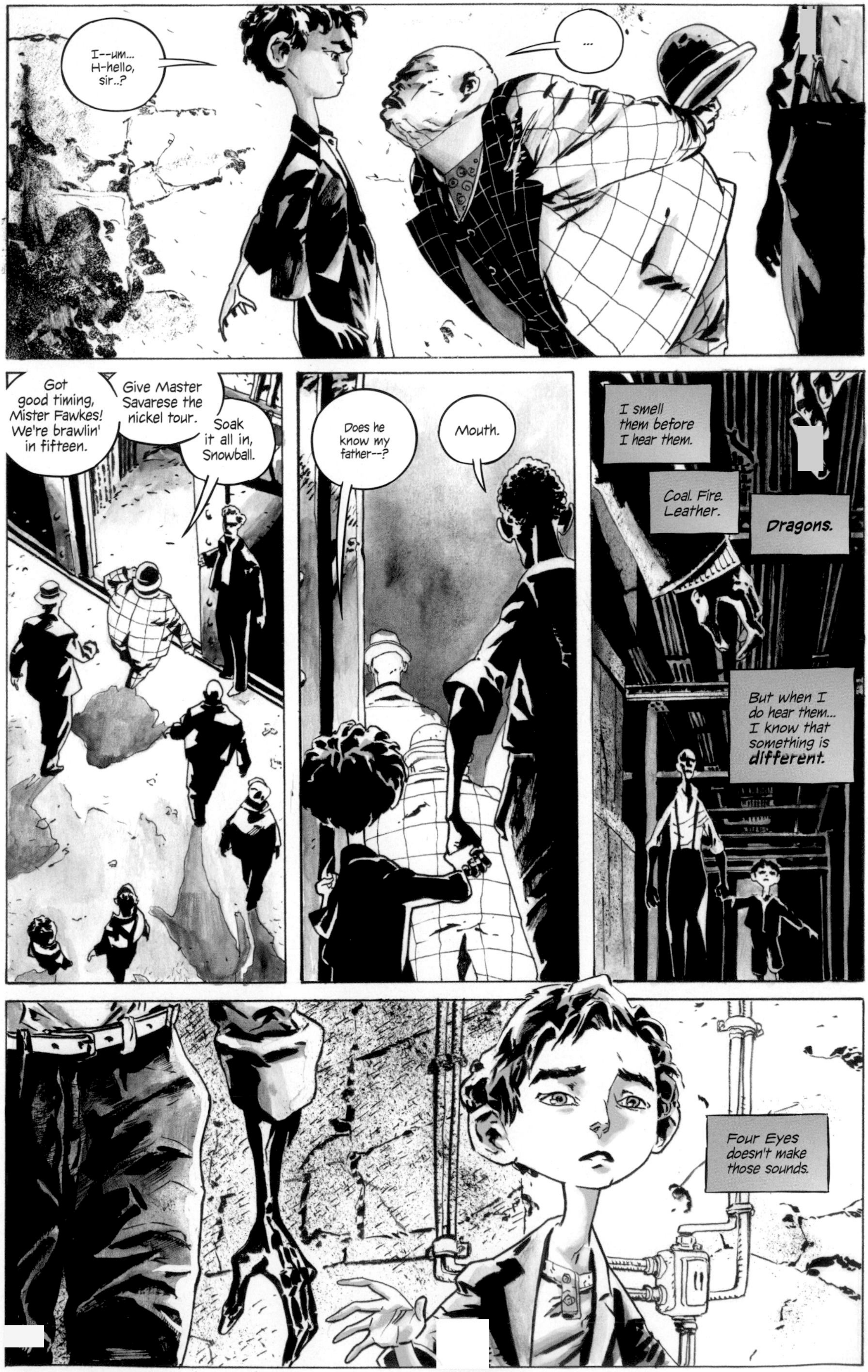

I--um... H-hello, sir..?
...
Got good timing, Mister Fawkes! We're brawlin' in fifteen.
Give Master Savarese the nickel tour.
Soak it all in, Snowball.
Does he know my father--?
Mouth.
I smell them before I hear them.
Coal. Fire. Leather.
Dragons.
But when I do hear them... I know that something is different.
Four Eyes doesn't make those sounds.

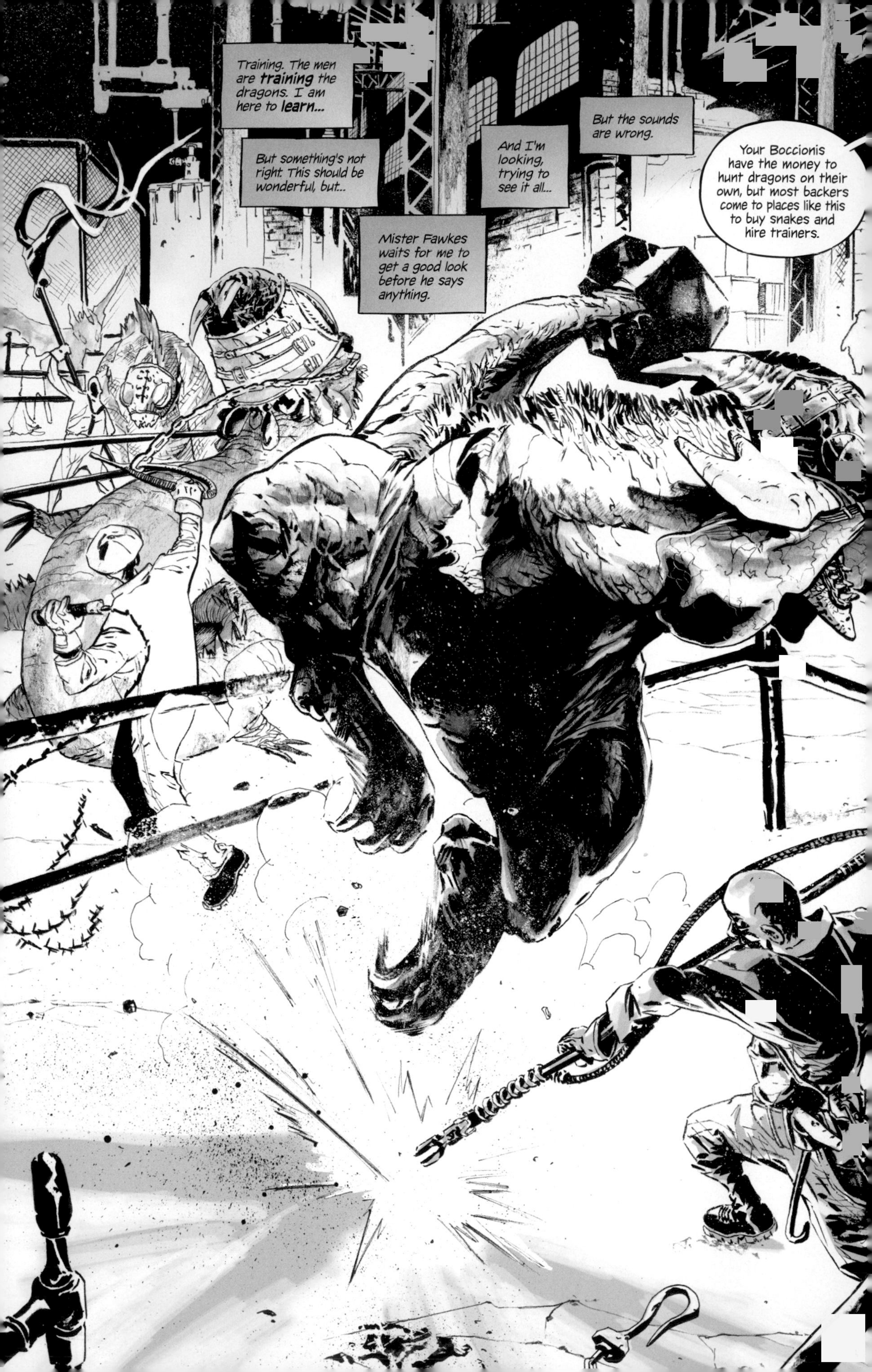
Training. The men are training the dragons. I am here to learn...
But something's not right. This should be wonderful, but...
And I'm looking, trying to see it all...
But the sounds are wrong.
Mister Fawkes waits for me to get a good look before he says anything.
Your Boccionis have the money to hunt dragons on their own, but most backers come to places like this to buy snakes and hire trainers.

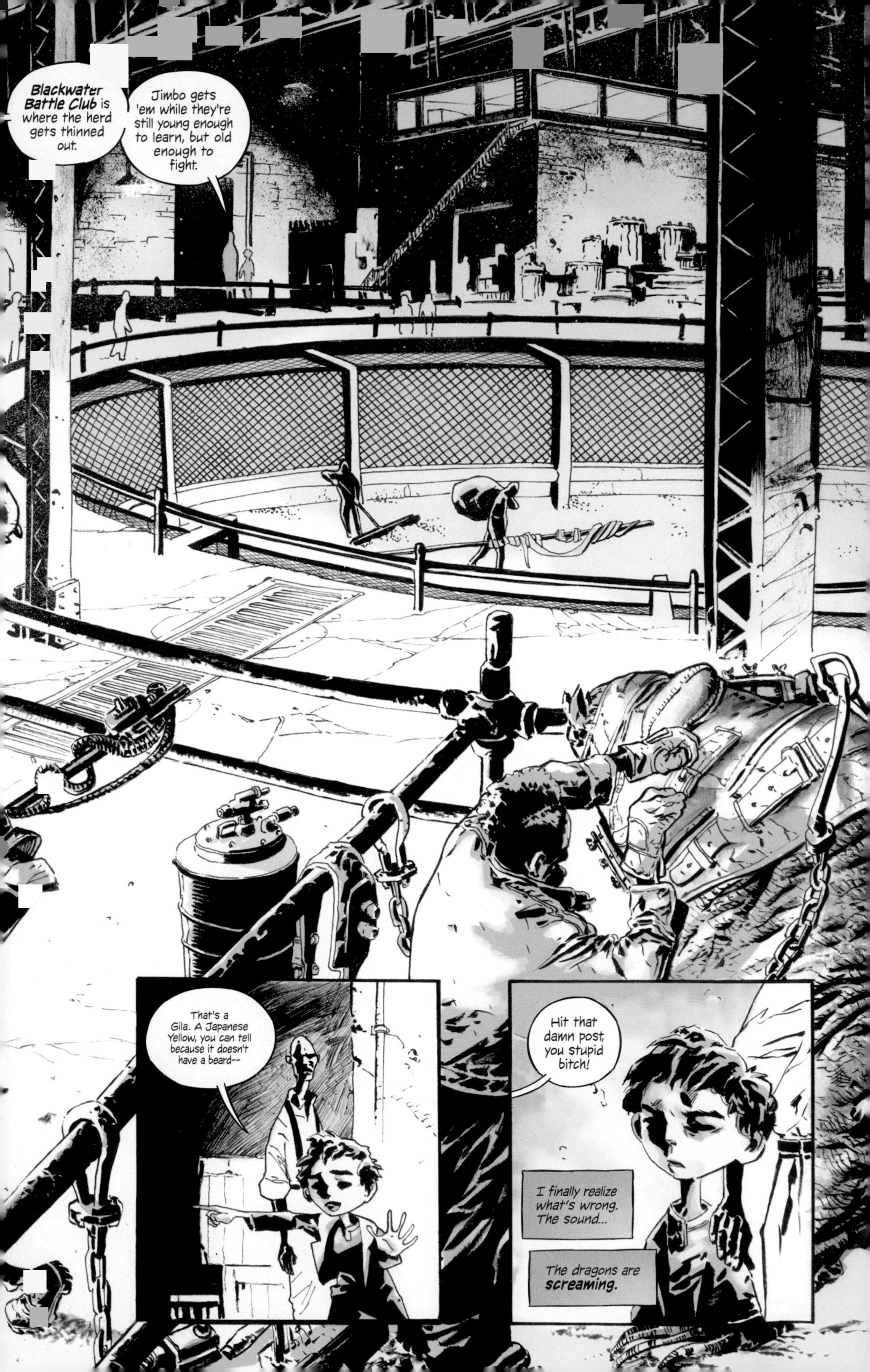
Blackwater Battle Club is where the herd gets thinned out.
Jimbo gets 'em while they're still young enough to learn, but old enough to fight.
That's a Gila. A Japanese Yellow, you can tell because it doesn't have a beard--
Hit that damn post, you stupid bitch!
I finally realize what's wrong. The sound...
The dragons are screaming.

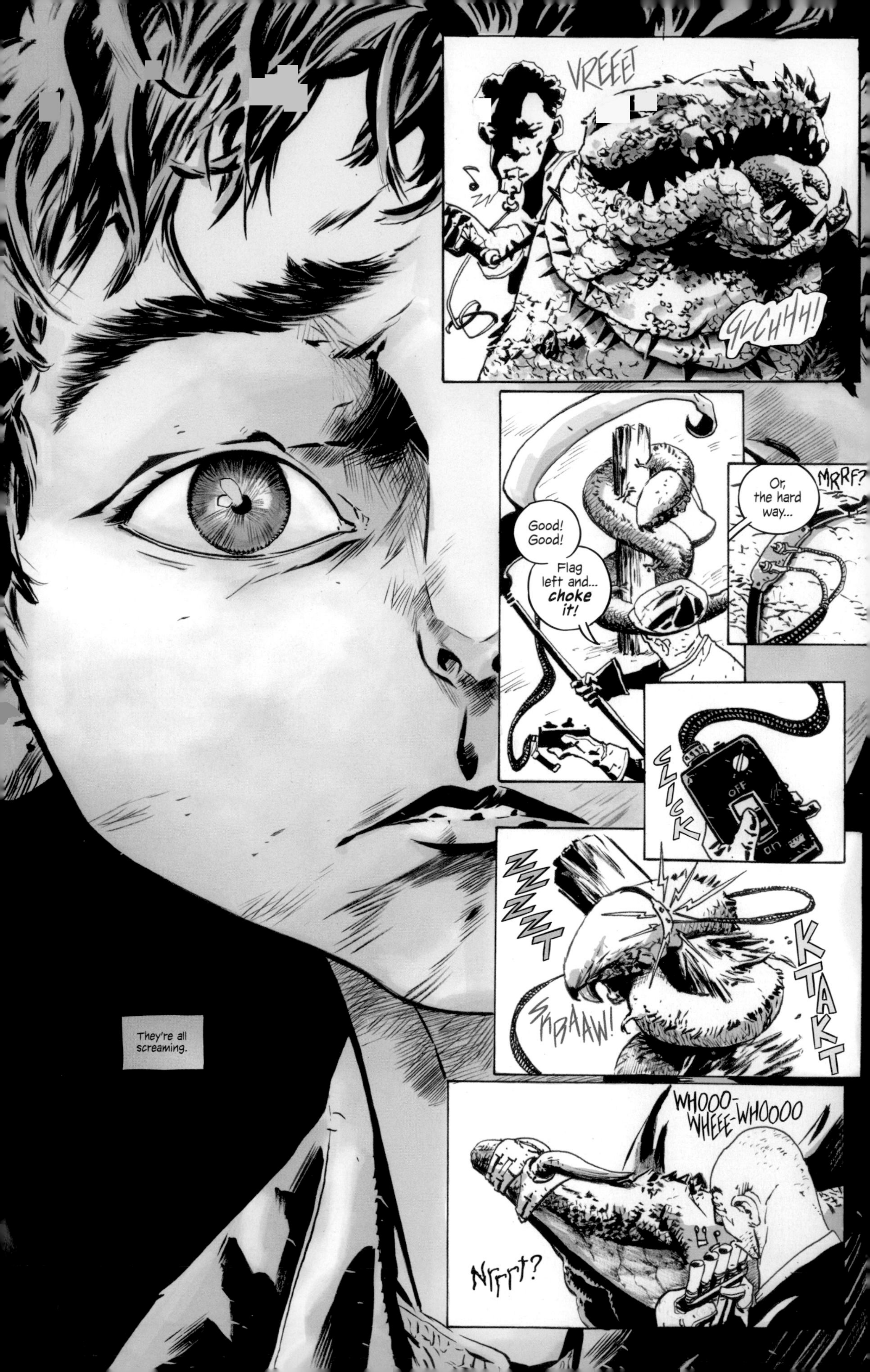
VREEET
GLCHHH!
Good! Good!
Flag left and... **choke it!**
Or, the hard way...
MRRF?
CLICK
OFF
ON
NNNNT
KTAKT
SKRAAW!
They're all screaming.
WHOOO-WHEEE-WHOOOO
Nrrrt?

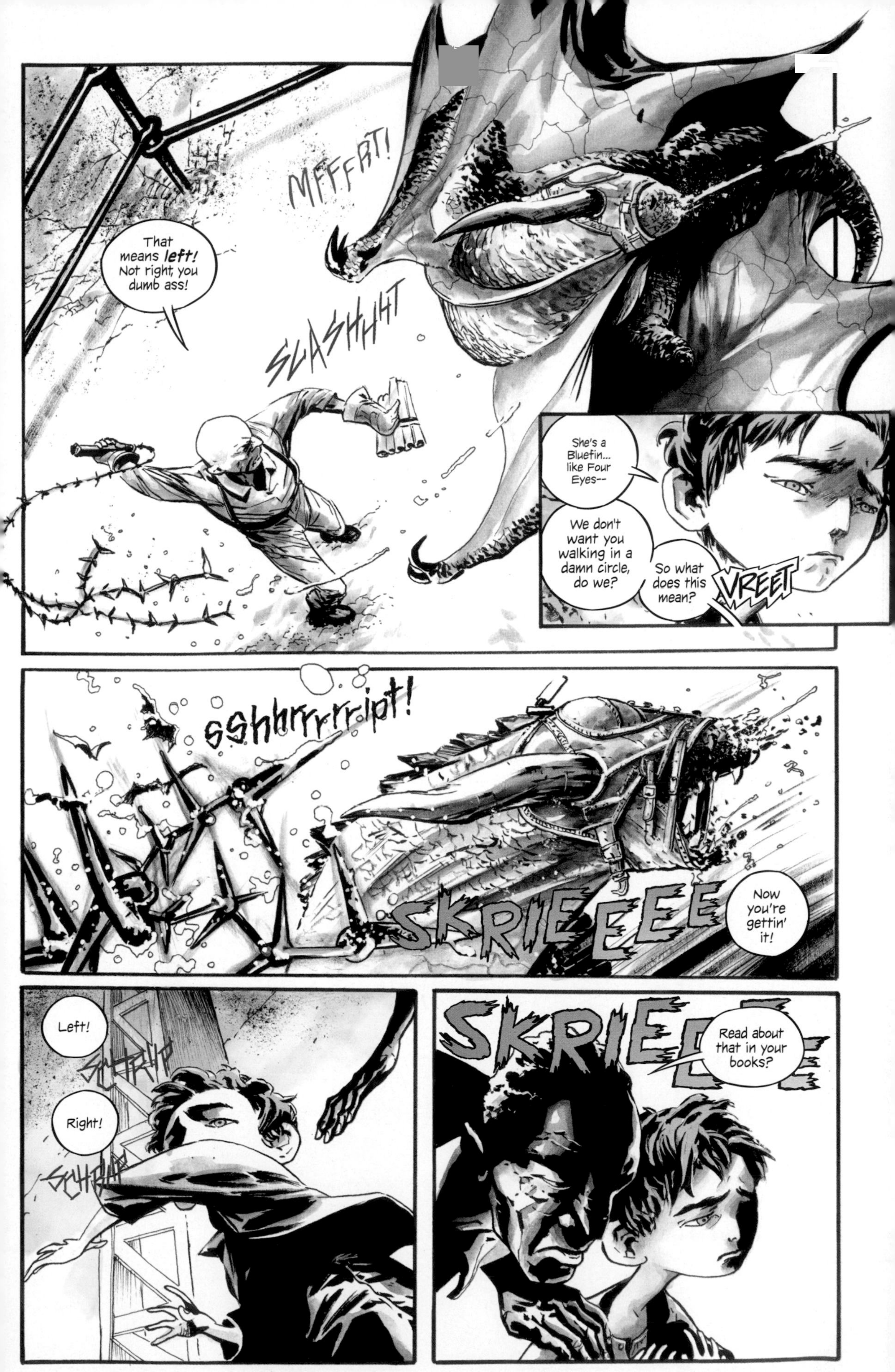
MFFFRT!
That means left! Not right, you dumb ass!
SLASHHHT
She's a Bluefin... like Four Eyes--
We don't want you walking in a damn circle, do we?
So what does this mean?
VREET
sshhrrrript!
SKRIEEEEE
Now you're gettin' it!
Left!
SCHRIP
Right!
SCHRIP
SKRIEEEE
Read about that in your books?

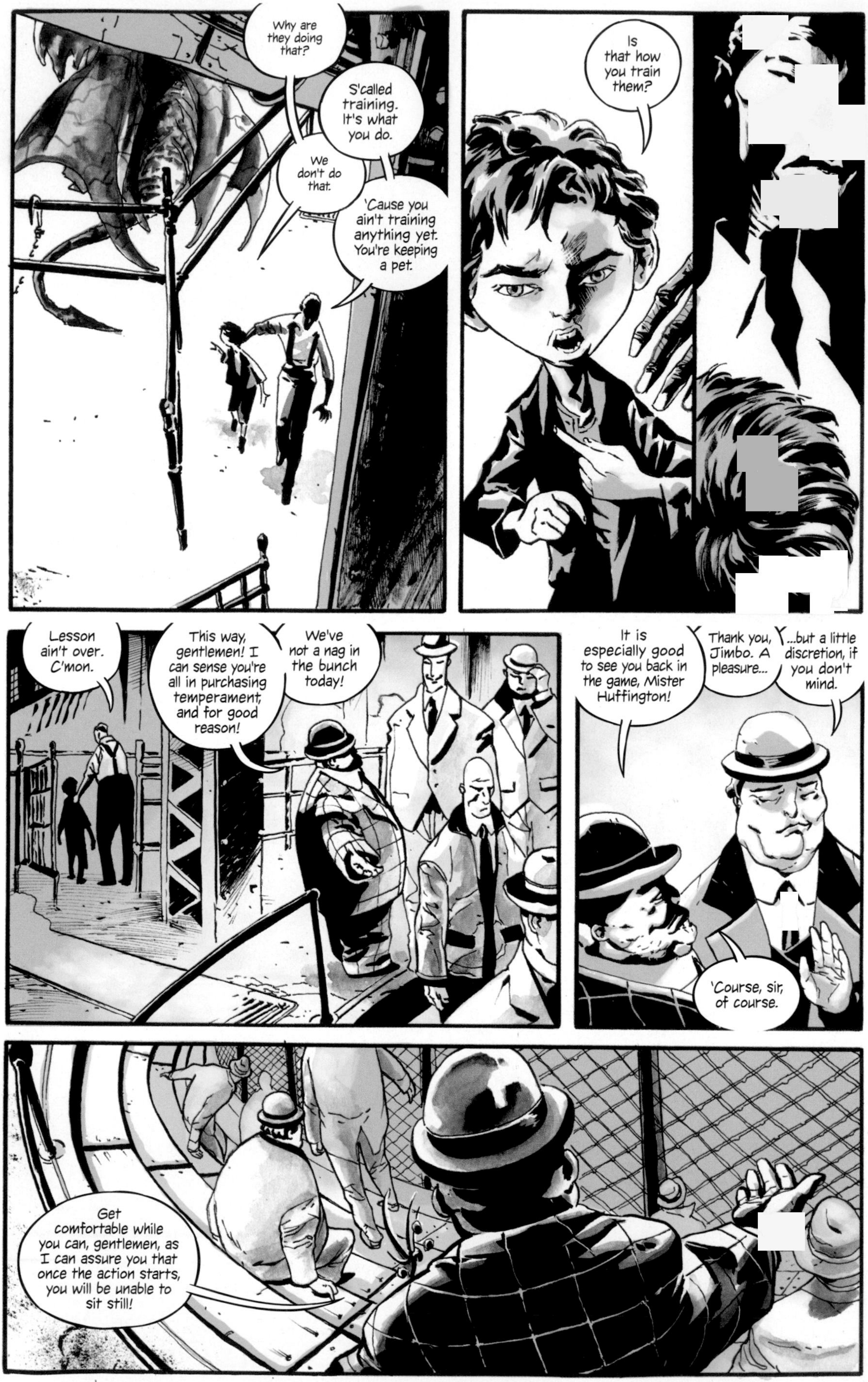
Why are they doing that?
S'called training. It's what you do.
We don't do that.
'Cause you ain't training anything yet. You're keeping a pet.
Is that how you train them?
Lesson ain't over. C'mon.
This way, gentlemen! I can sense you're all in purchasing temperament, and for good reason!
We've not a nag in the bunch today!
It is especially good to see you back in the game, Mister Huffington!
Thank you, Jimbo. A pleasure...
...but a little discretion, if you don't mind.
'Course, sir, of course.
Get comfortable while you can, gentlemen, as I can assure you that once the action starts, you will be unable to sit still!

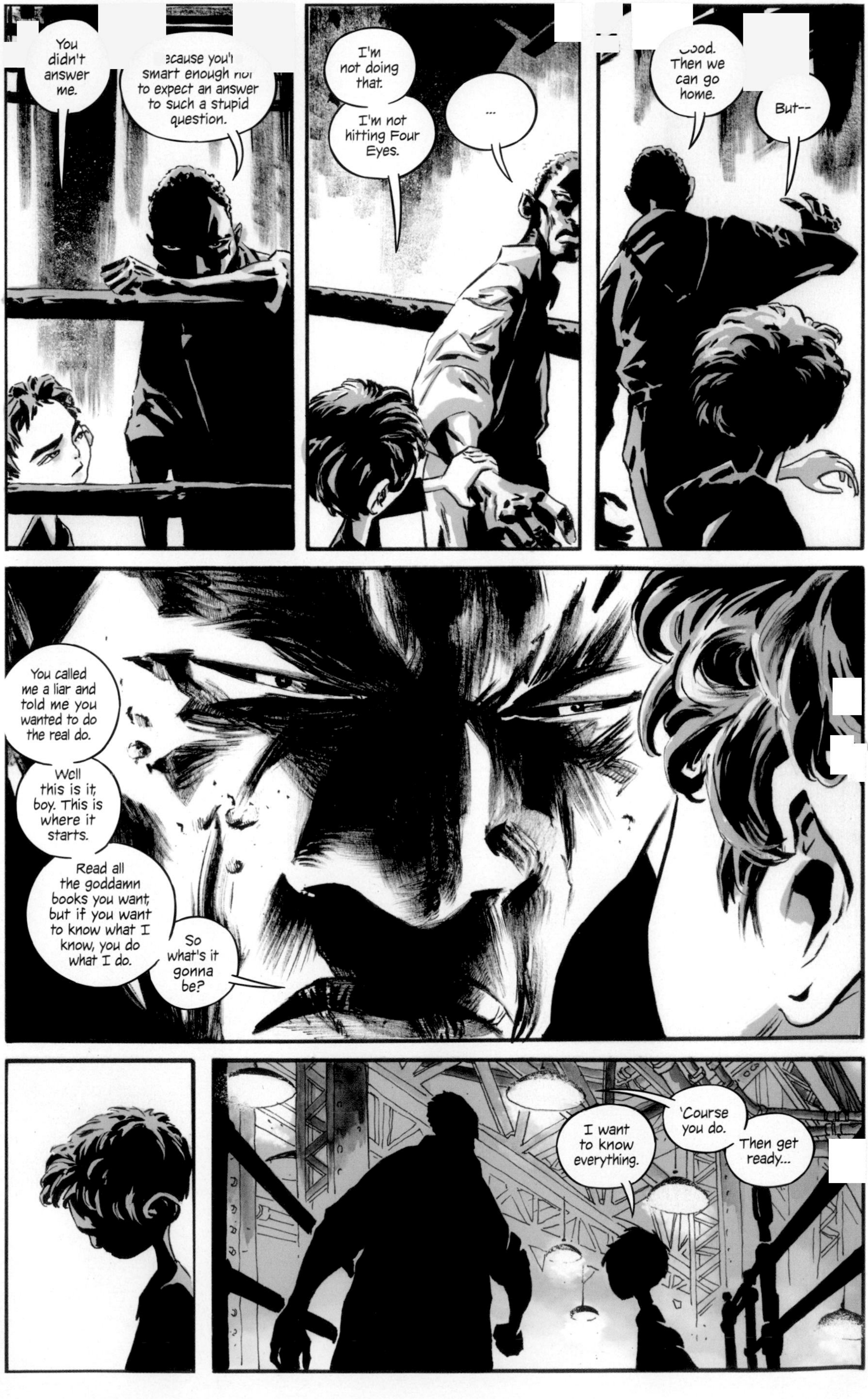
You didn't answer me.
ecause you'r smart enough not to expect an answer to such a stupid question.
I'm not doing that.
I'm not hitting Four Eyes.
...
ood. Then we can go home.
But--
You called me a liar and told me you wanted to do the real do.
Well this is it, boy. This is where it starts.
Read all the goddamn books you want, but if you want to know what I know, you do what I do.
So what's it gonna be?
I want to know everything.
'Course you do.
Then get ready...

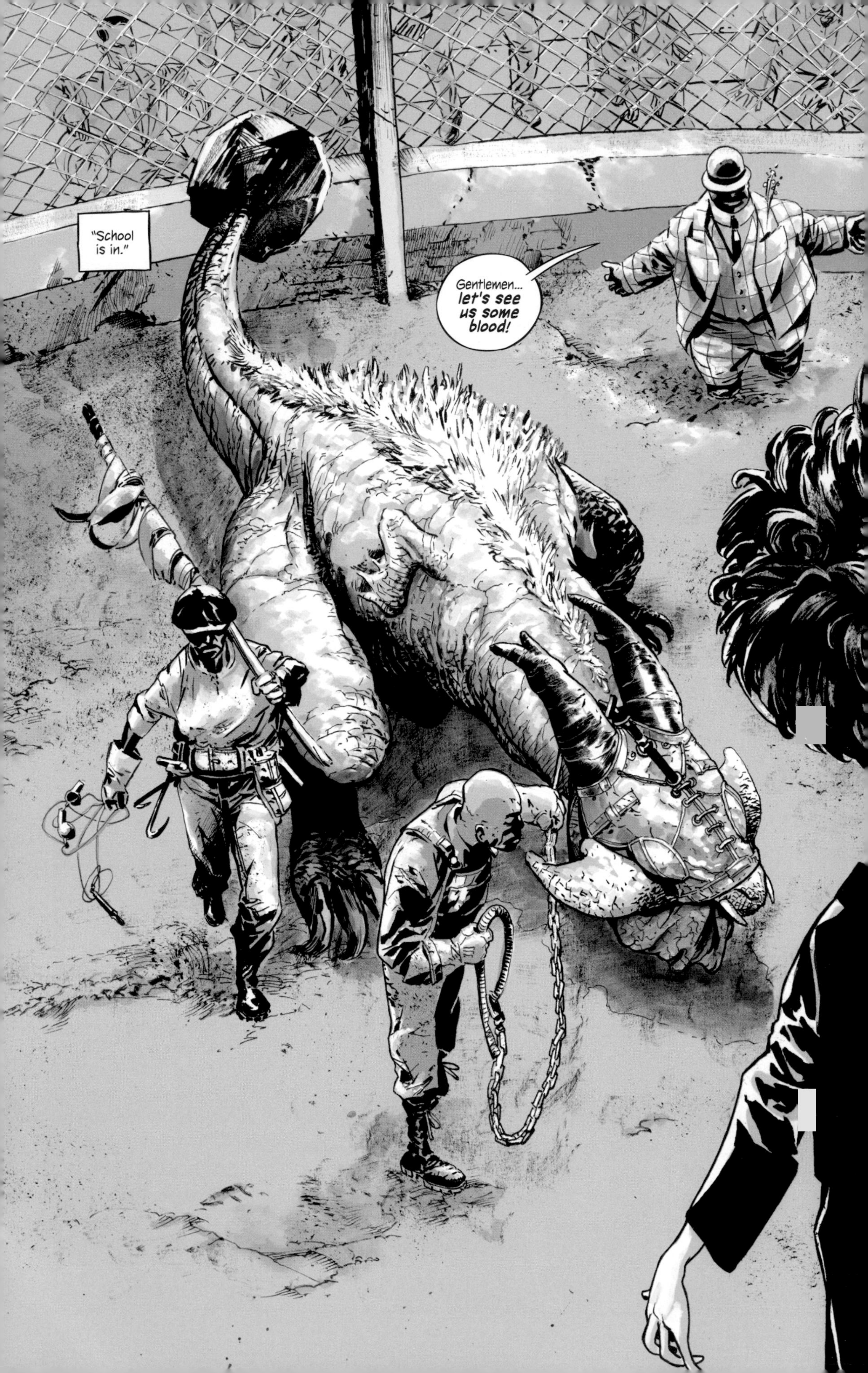
"School is in."
Gentlemen... let's see us some blood!

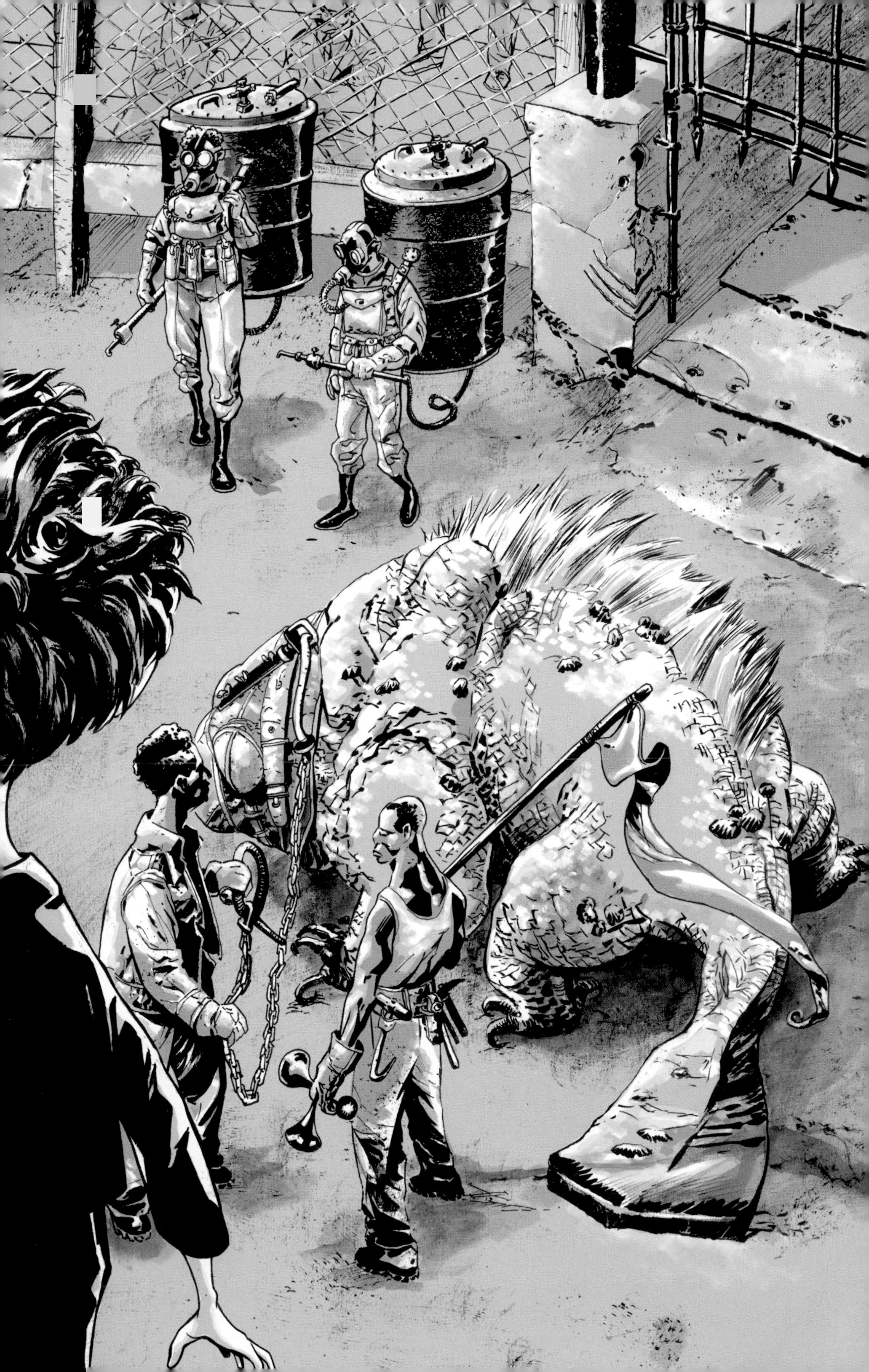

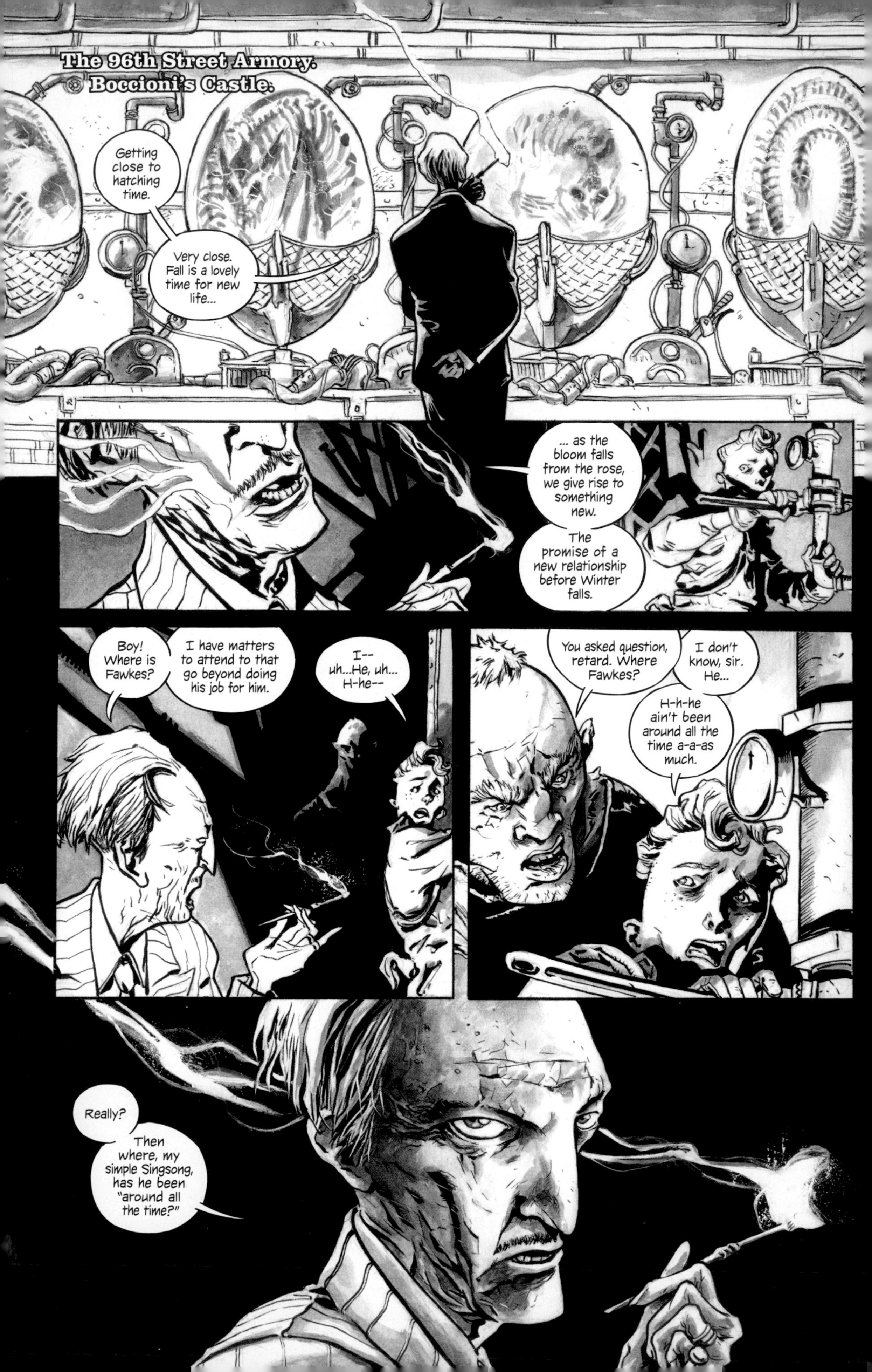
The 96th Street Armory. Boccioni's Castle.
Getting close to hatching time.
Very close. Fall is a lovely time for new life...
... as the bloom falls from the rose, we give rise to something new.
The promise of a new relationship before Winter falls.
Boy! Where is Fawkes?
I have matters to attend to that go beyond doing his job for him.
I-- uh...He, uh... H-he--
You asked question, retard. Where Fawkes?
I don't know, sir. He...
H-h-he ain't been around all the time a-a-as much.
Really?
Then where, my simple Singsong, has he been "around all the time?"

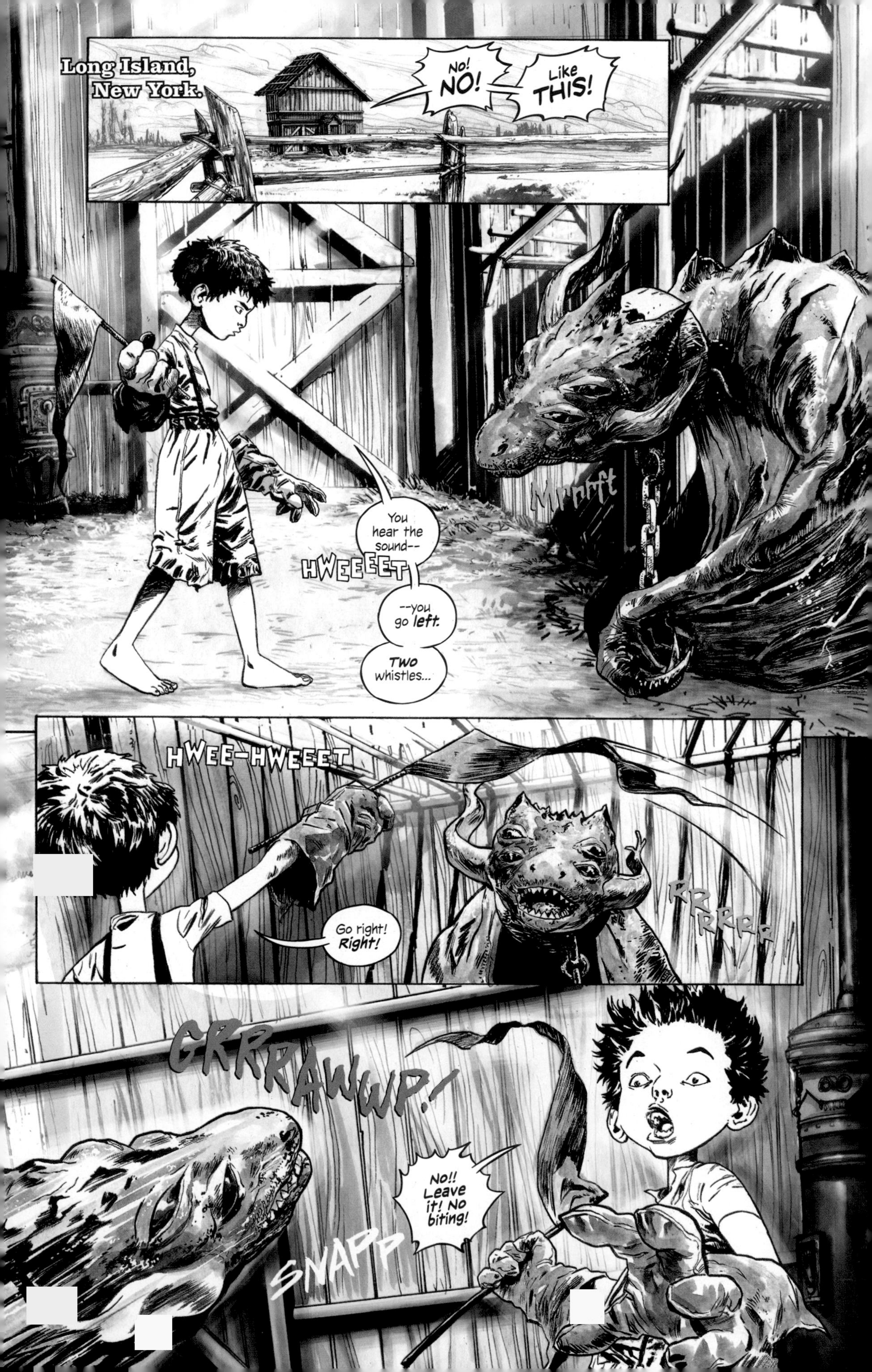
Long Island, New York.
No! NO!
Like THIS!
Mrrrft
You hear the sound--
HWEEEET
--you go left.
Two whistles...
HWEE-HWEEET
Go right! Right!
RRRRRRA
GRRRAWWP!
No!! Leave it! No biting!
SNAPP

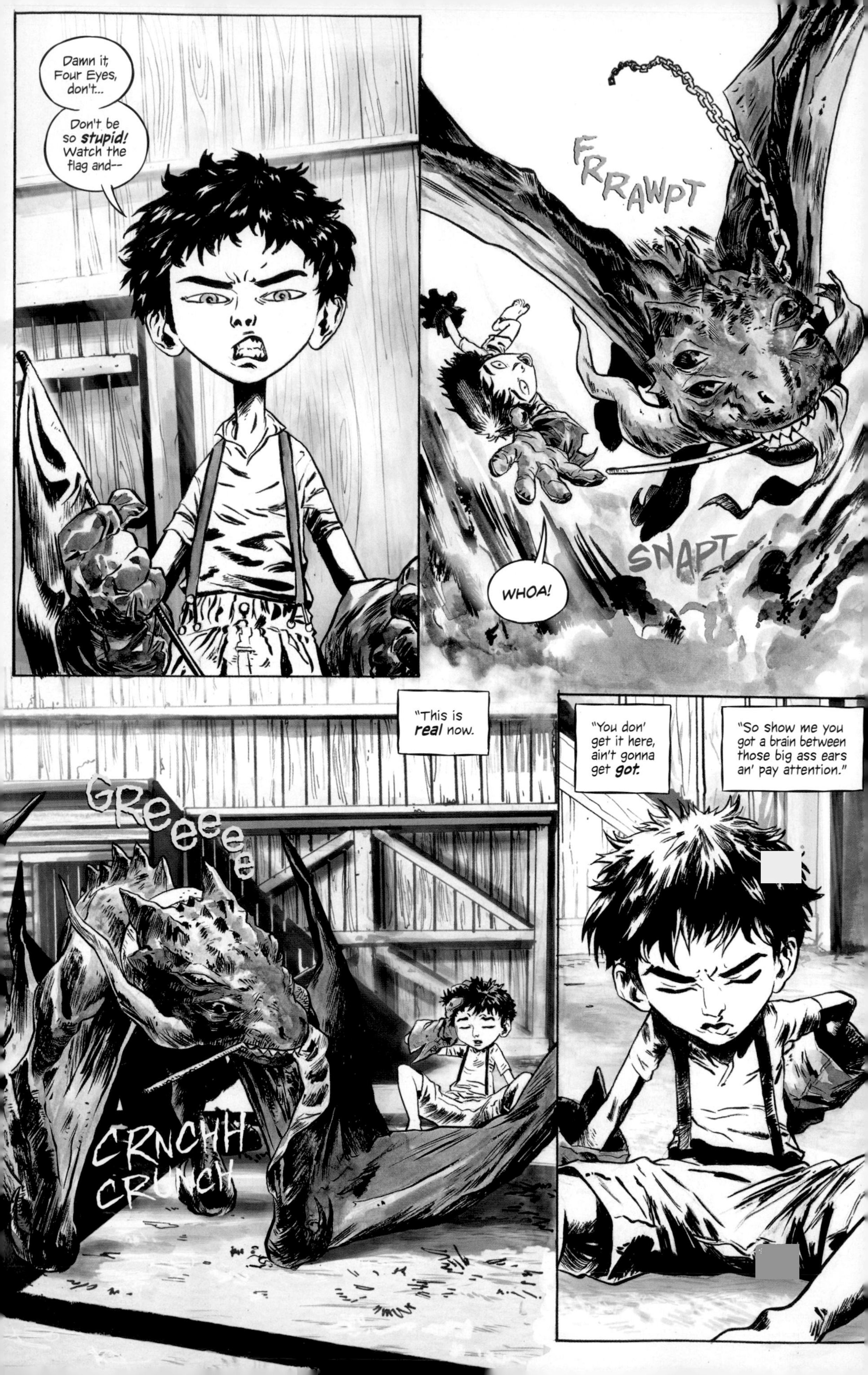
Damn it, Four Eyes, don't...
Don't be so ***stupid!*** Watch the flag and--
FRRAWPT
SNAPT
WHOA!
"This is ***real*** now.
GREeeeee
CRNCHH CRUNCH
"You don' get it here, ain't gonna get ***got.***
"So show me you got a brain between those big ass ears an' pay attention."

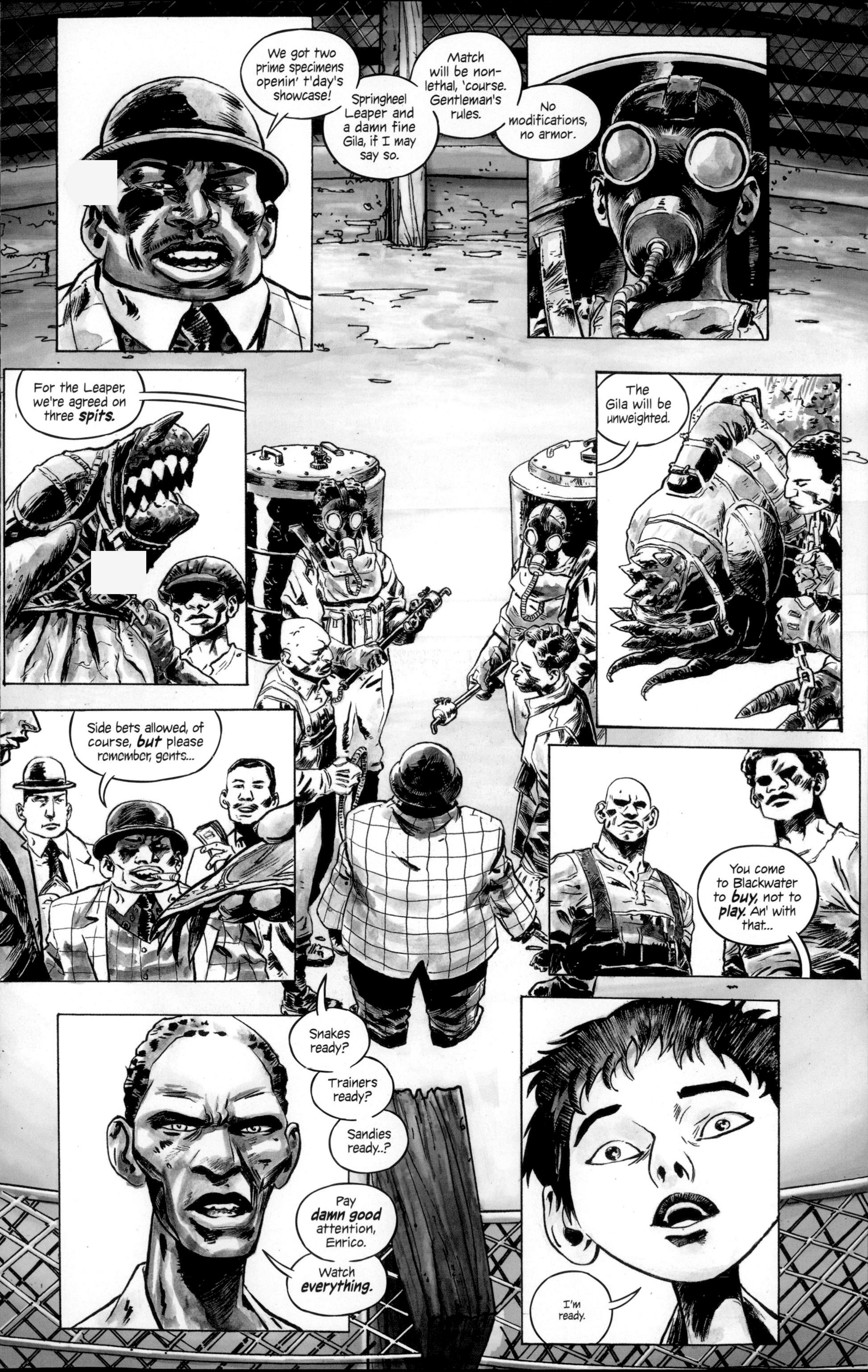
We got two prime specimens openin' t'day's showcase!
Springheel Leaper and a damn fine Gila, if I may say so.
Match will be non-lethal, 'course. Gentleman's rules.
No modifications, no armor.
For the Leaper, we're agreed on three **spits.**
The Gila will be unweighted.
Side bets allowed, of course, **but** please remember, gents...
You come to Blackwater to **buy,** not to **play.** An' with that...
Snakes ready?
Trainers ready?
Sandies ready..?
Pay **damn good** attention, Enrico.
Watch **everything.**
I'm ready.

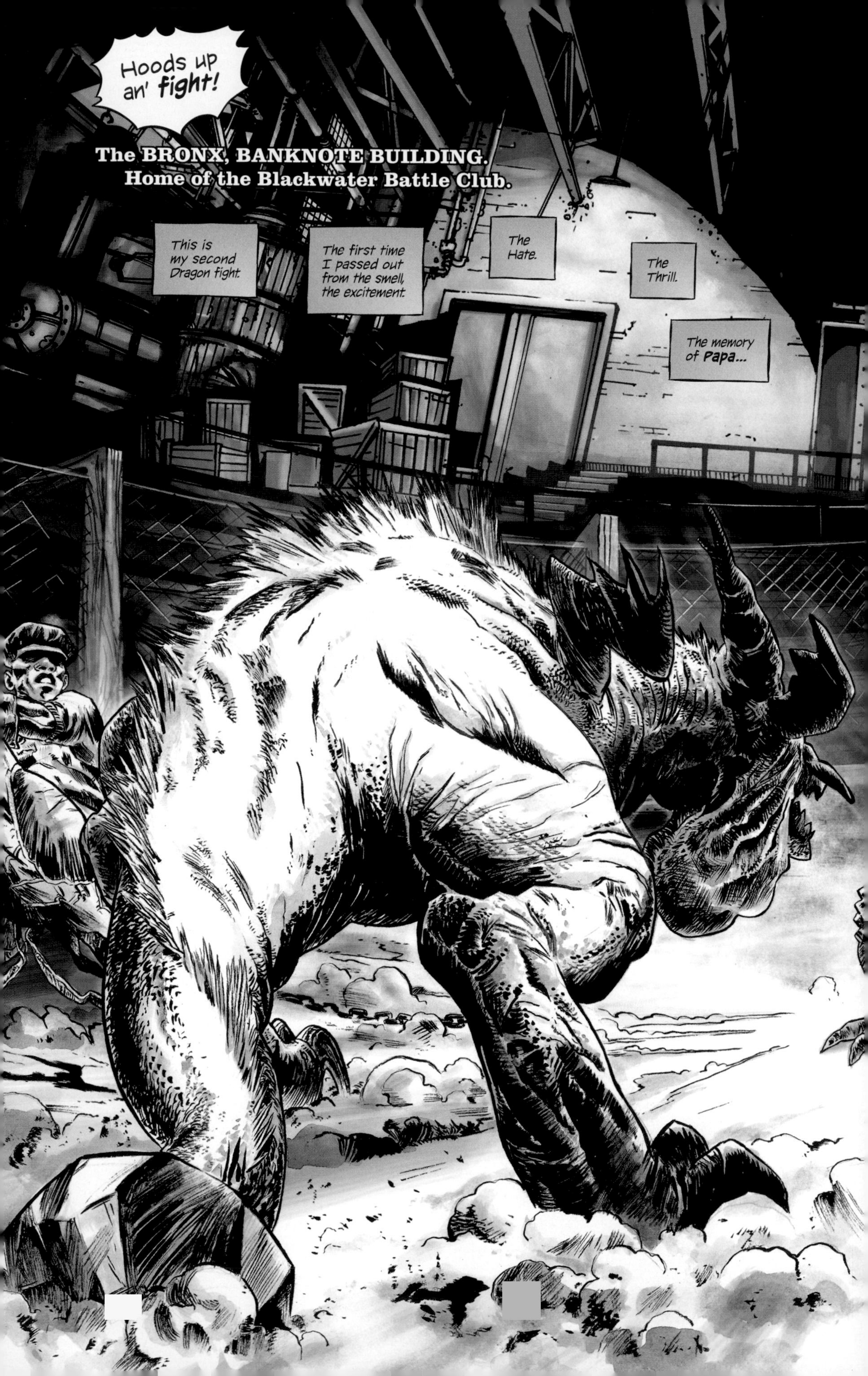
Hoods up an' fight!
The BRONX, BANKNOTE BUILDING. Home of the Blackwater Battle Club.
This is my second Dragon fight.
The first time I passed out from the smell, the excitement.
The Hate.
The Thrill.
The memory of Papa...

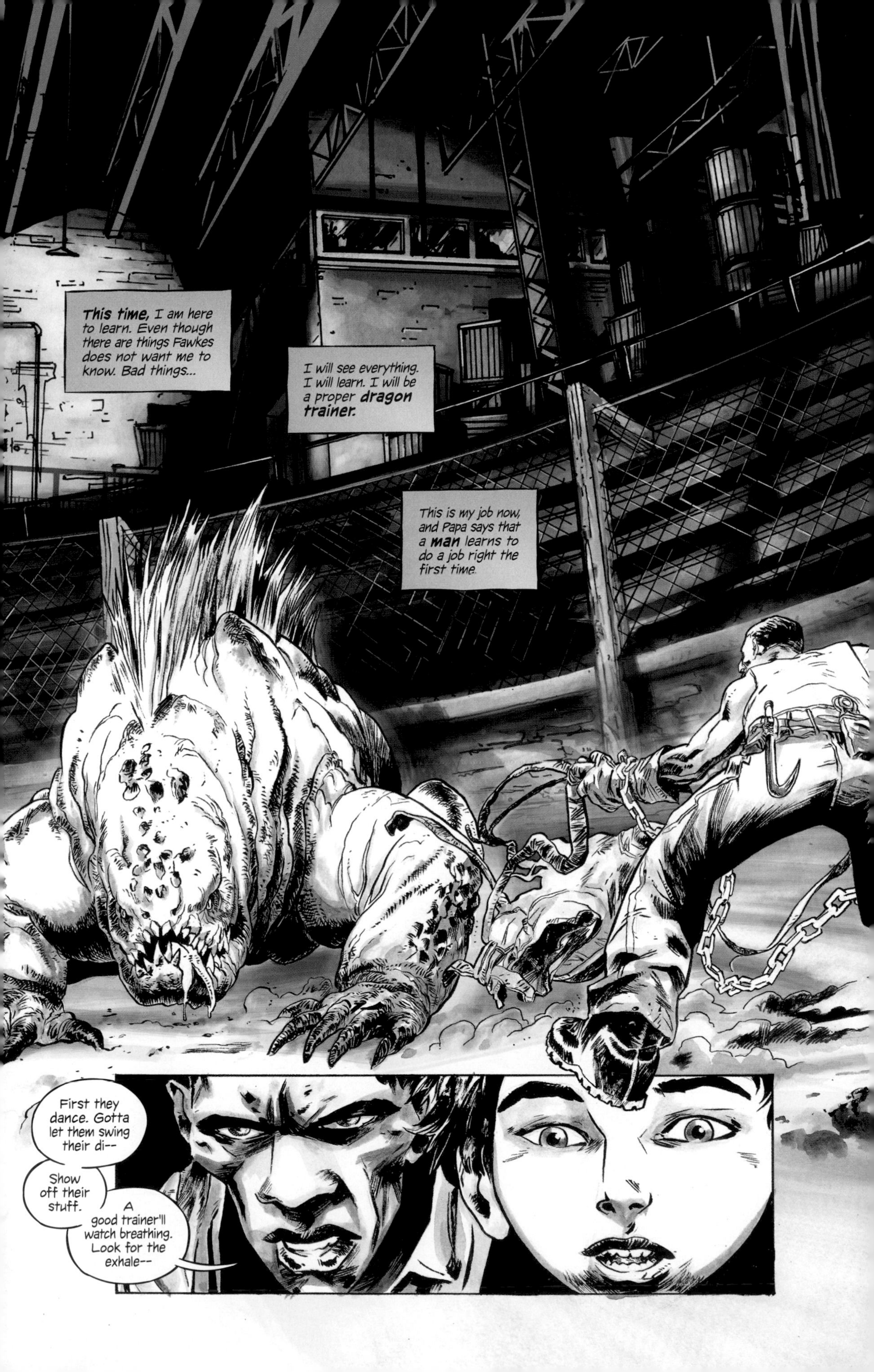
This time, I am here to learn. Even though there are things Fawkes does not want me to know. Bad things...
I will see everything. I will learn. I will be a proper dragon trainer.
This is my job now, and Papa says that a man learns to do a job right the first time.
First they dance. Gotta let them swing their di--
Show off their stuff.
A good trainer'll watch breathing. Look for the exhale--

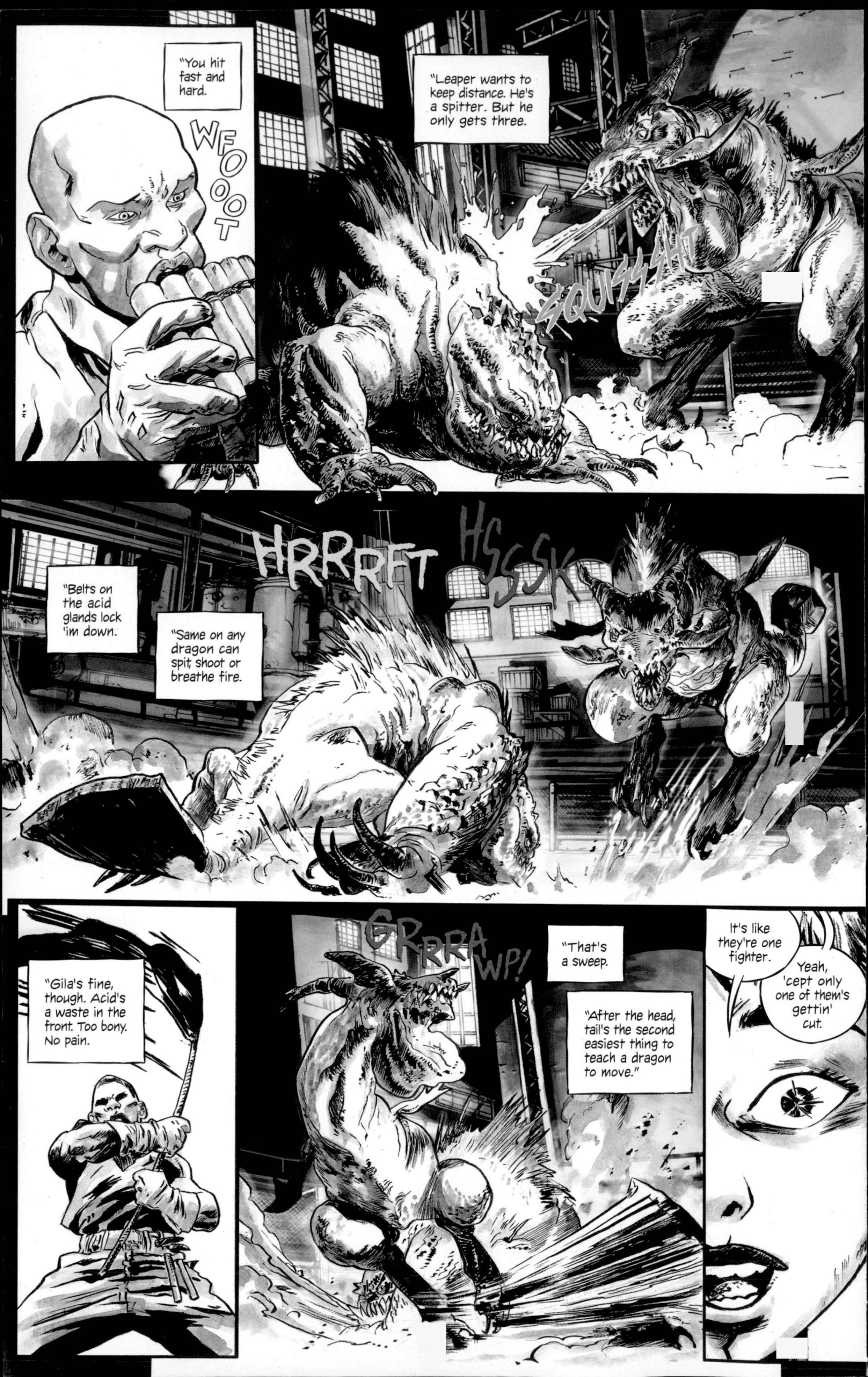
"You hit fast and hard.
WFOOOT
"Leaper wants to keep distance. He's a spitter. But he only gets three.
SQUISSSHT
HRRRFT
HSSSK
"Belts on the acid glands lock 'im down.
"Same on any dragon can spit, shoot or breathe fire.
"Gila's fine, though. Acid's a waste in the front. Too bony. No pain.
GRRRAWP!
"That's a sweep.
"After the head, tail's the second easiest thing to teach a dragon to move."
It's like they're one fighter.
Yeah, 'cept only one of them's gettin' cut.

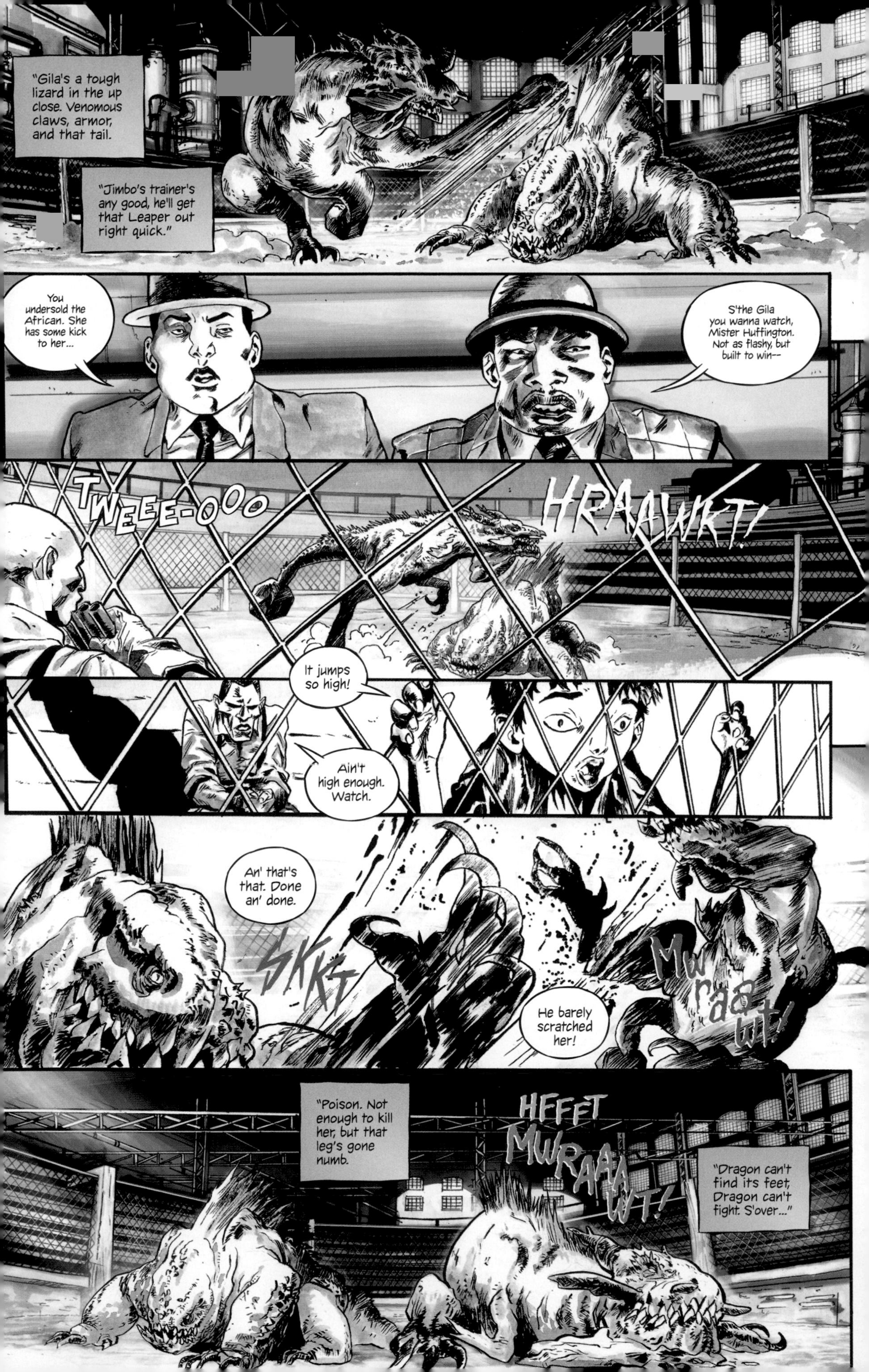
"Gila's a tough lizard in the up close. Venomous claws, armor, and that tail.
"Jimbo's trainer's any good, he'll get that Leaper out right quick."
You undersold the African. She has some kick to her...
S'the Gila you wanna watch, Mister Huffington. Not as flashy, but built to win--
TWEEE-OOO
HRAAAWKT!
It jumps so high!
Ain't high enough. Watch.
An' that's that. Done an' done.
SKKT
He barely scratched her!
Mwraawt!
"Poison. Not enough to kill her, but that leg's gone numb.
HFFFT
MURAAAWT!
"Dragon can't find its feet, Dragon can't fight. S'over..."

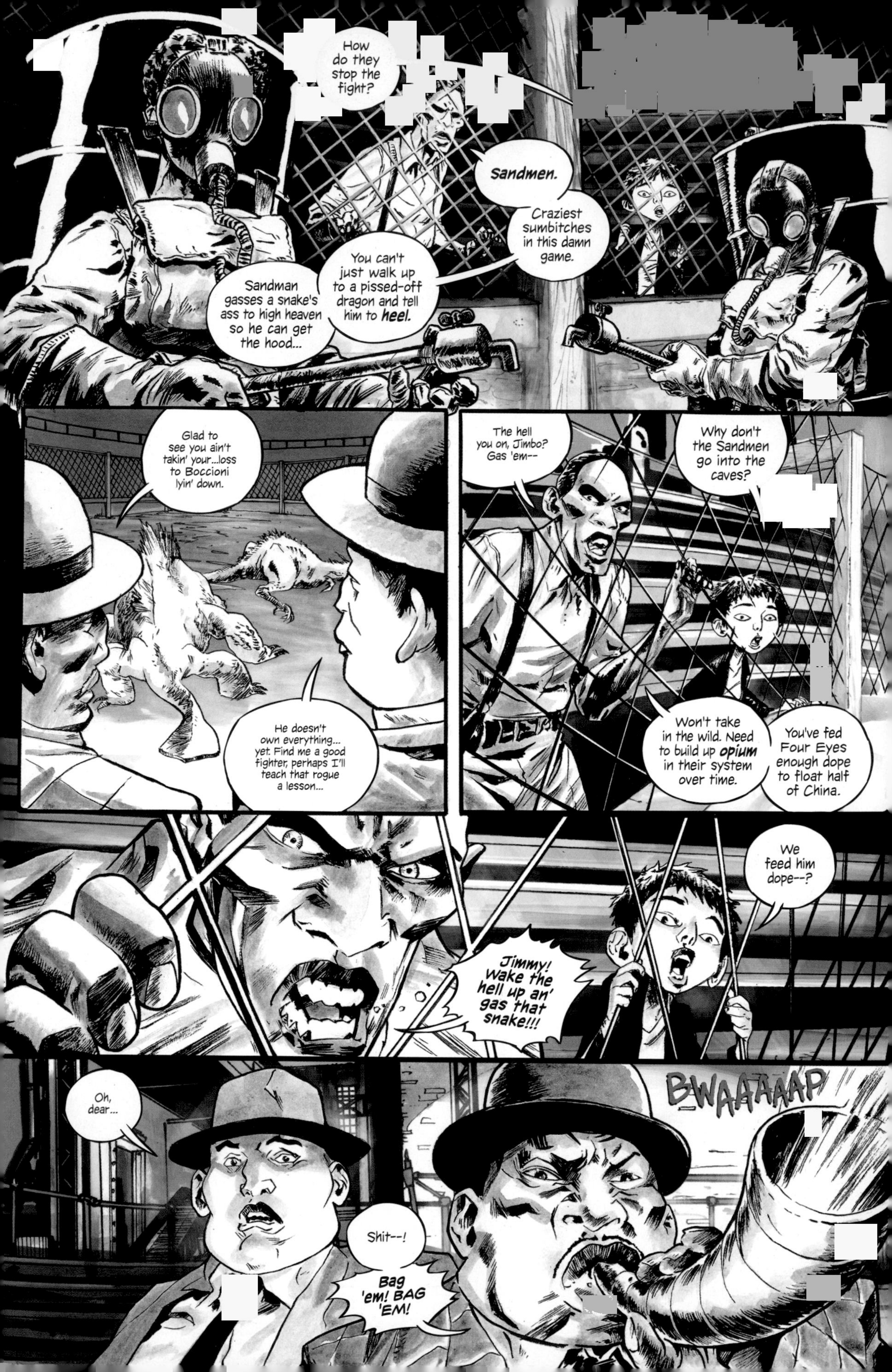
How do they stop the fight?
Sandmen.
Craziest sumbitches in this damn game.
You can't just walk up to a pissed-off dragon and tell him to heel.
Sandman gasses a snake's ass to high heaven so he can get the hood...
Glad to see you ain't takin' your...loss to Boccioni lyin' down.
He doesn't own everything... yet. Find me a good fighter, perhaps I'll teach that rogue a lesson...
The hell you on, Jimbo? Gas 'em--
Why don't the Sandmen go into the caves?
Won't take in the wild. Need to build up opium in their system over time.
You've fed Four Eyes enough dope to float half of China.
We feed him dope--?
Jimmy! Wake the hell up an' gas that snake!!!
Oh, dear...
BWAAAAAP
Shit--!
Bag 'em! BAG 'EM!

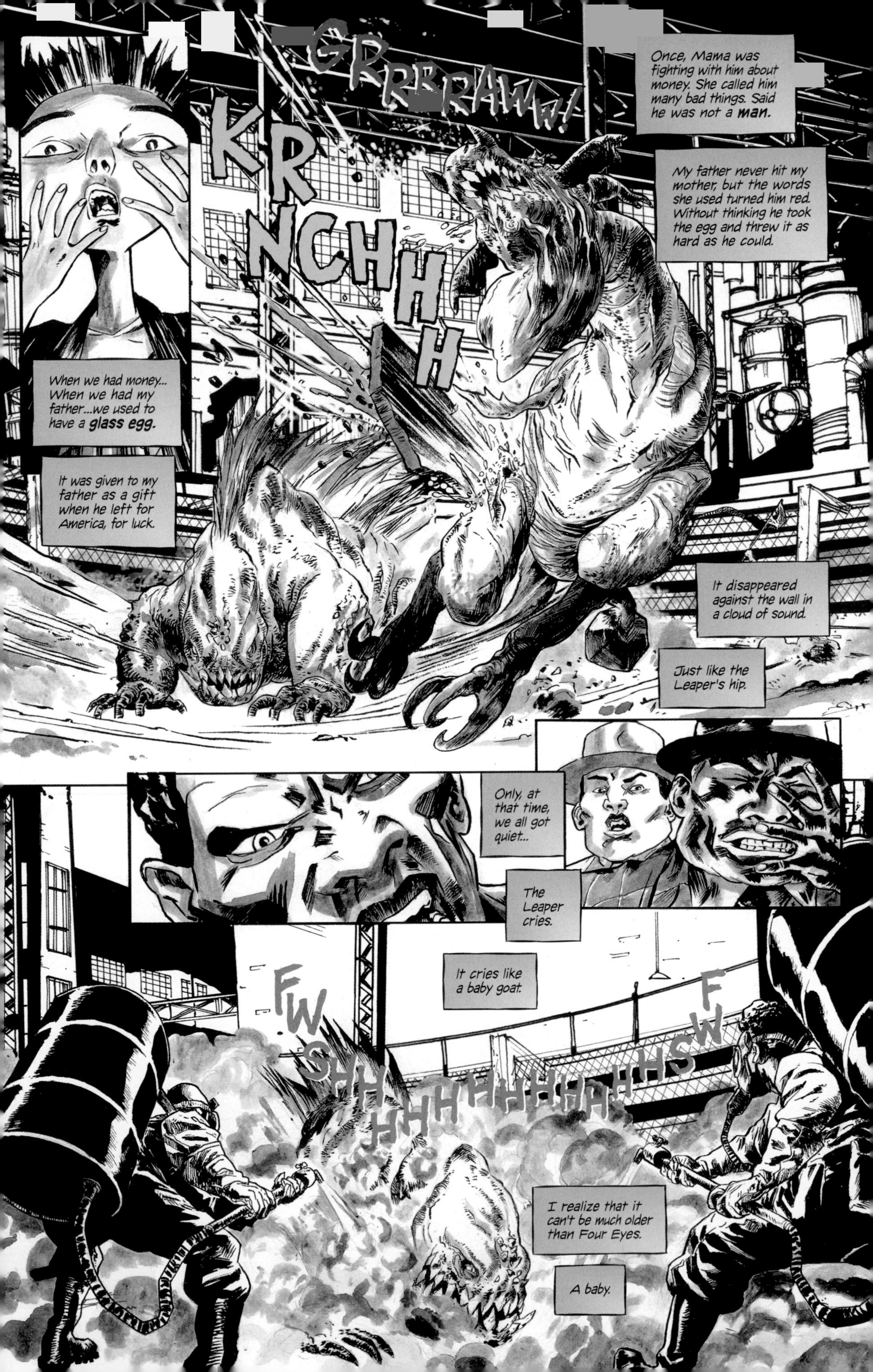

When we had money... When we had my father...we used to have a **glass egg.**
It was given to my father as a gift when he left for America, for luck.
Once, Mama was fighting with him about money. She called him many bad things. Said he was not a **man.**
My father never hit my mother, but the words she used turned him red. Without thinking he took the egg and threw it as hard as he could.
GRRBRRAWW!
KRNCHHH
It disappeared against the wall in a cloud of sound.
Just like the Leaper's hip.
Only, at that time, we all got quiet...
The Leaper cries.
It cries like a baby goat.
FWSHHHHHHHHHHHHHSWF
I realize that it can't be much older than Four Eyes.
A baby.

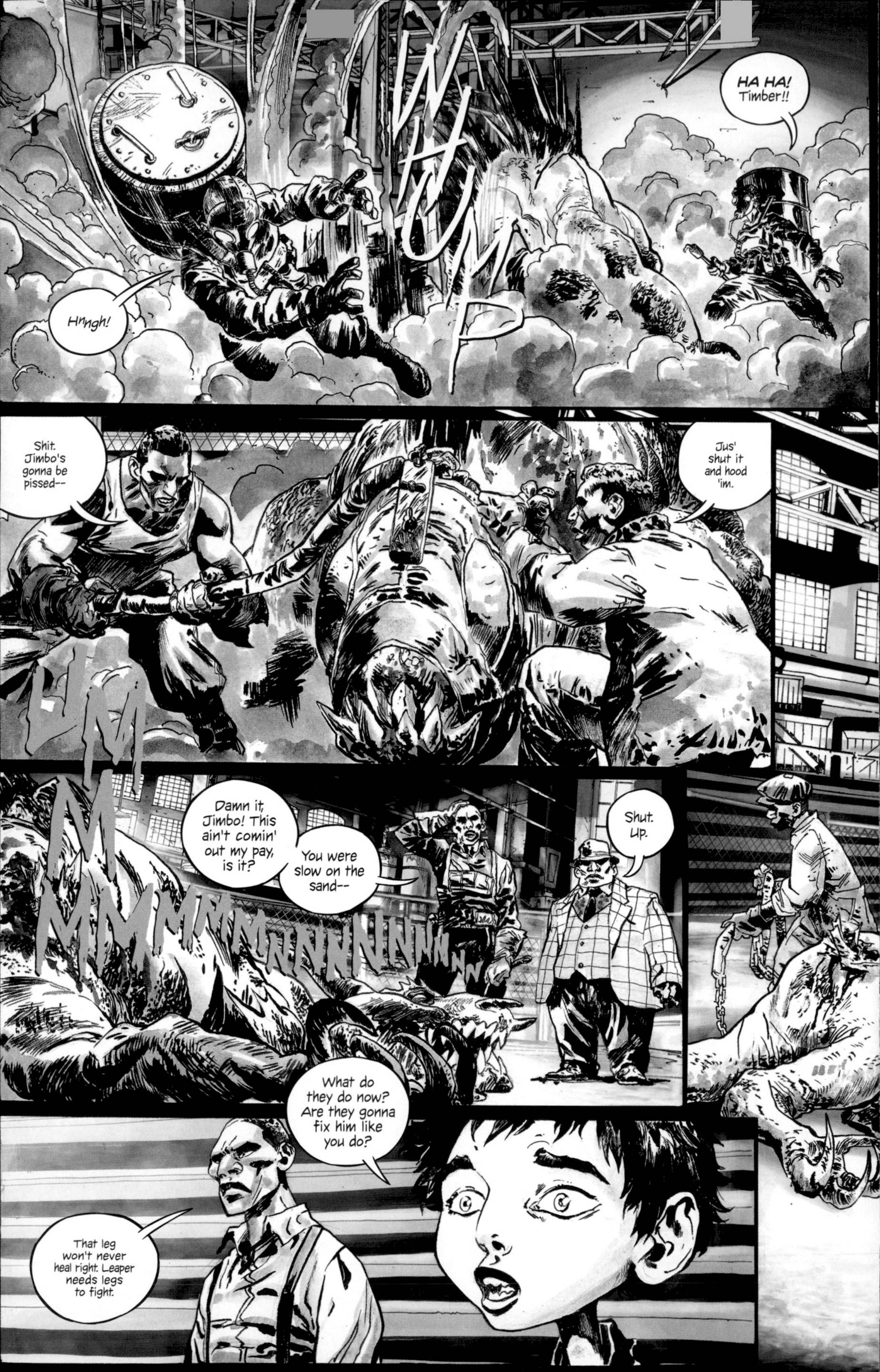
WHUMP
HA HA! Timber!!
Hnngh!
Shit. Jimbo's gonna be pissed--
Jus' shut it and hood 'im.
UMMMMMMMMNNNNNNNNNN
Damn it, Jimbo! This ain't comin' out my pay, is it?
You were slow on the sand--
Shut. Up.
What do they do now? Are they gonna fix him like you do?
That leg won't never heal right. Leaper needs legs to fight.

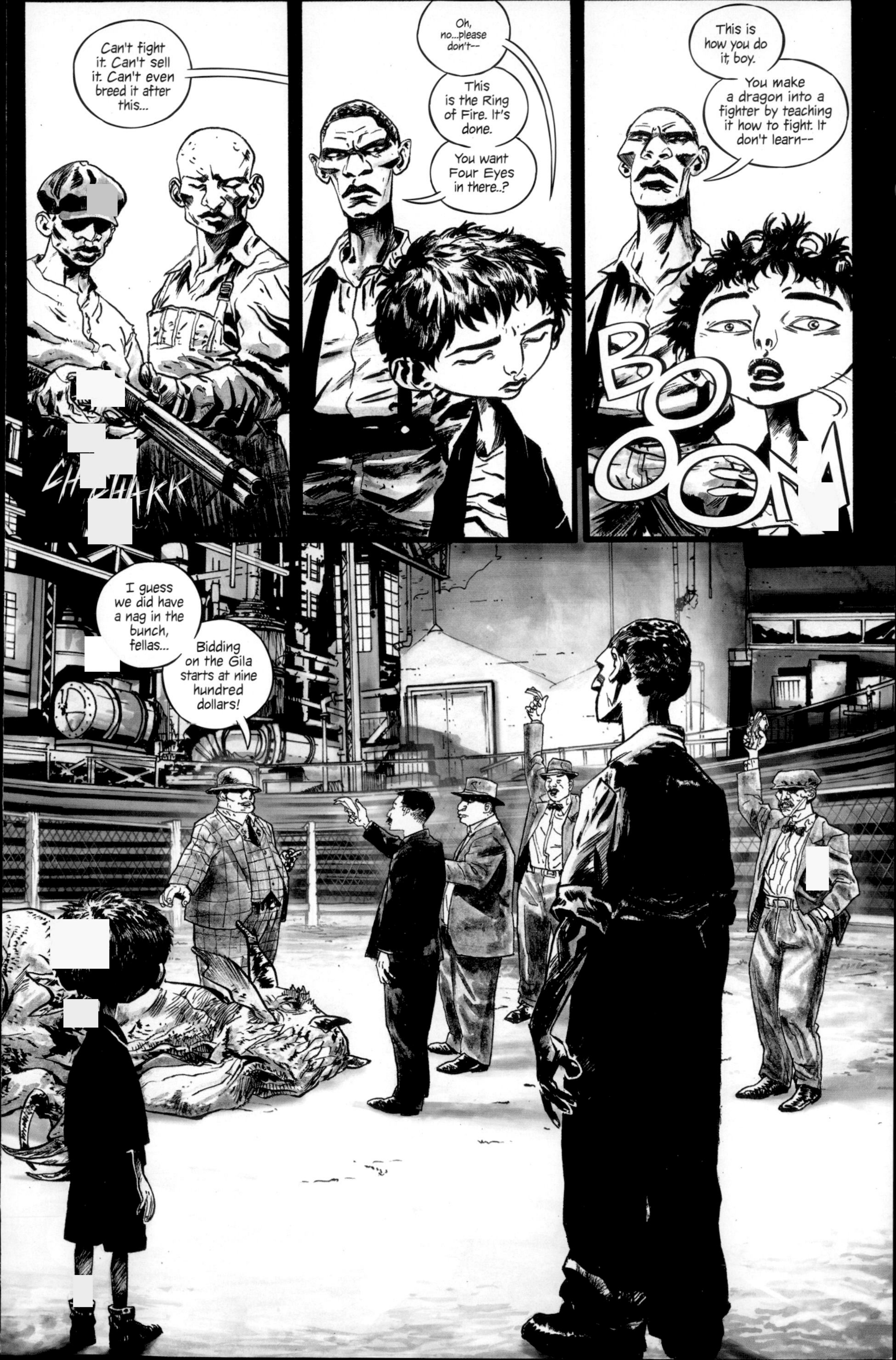
Can't fight it. Can't sell it. Can't even breed it after this...
Oh, no...please don't--
This is the Ring of Fire. It's done.
You want Four Eyes in there..?
This is how you do it, boy.
You make a dragon into a fighter by teaching it how to fight. It don't learn--
BOOOOM
I guess we did have a nag in the bunch, fellas...
Bidding on the Gila starts at nine hundred dollars!

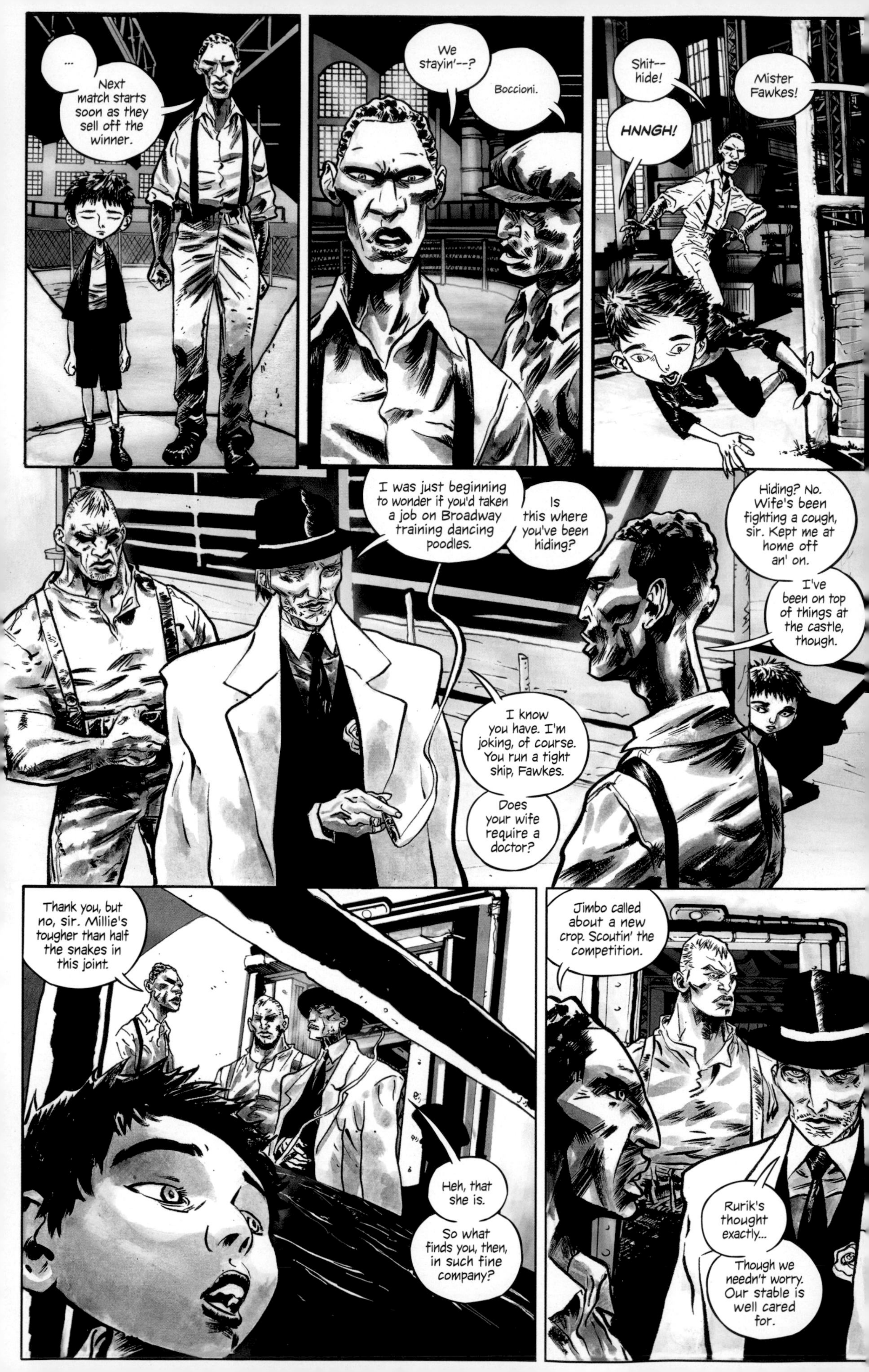
...
Next match starts soon as they sell off the winner.
We stayin'--?
Boccioni.
Shit-- hide!
HNNGH!
Mister Fawkes!
I was just beginning to wonder if you'd taken a job on Broadway training dancing poodles.
Is this where you've been hiding?
Hiding? No. Wife's been fighting a cough, sir. Kept me at home off an' on.
I've been on top of things at the castle, though.
I know you have. I'm joking, of course. You run a tight ship, Fawkes.
Does your wife require a doctor?
Thank you, but no, sir. Millie's tougher than half the snakes in this joint.
Heh, that she is.
So what finds you, then, in such fine company?
Jimbo called about a new crop. Scoutin' the competition.
Rurik's thought exactly...
Though we needn't worry. Our stable is well cared for.

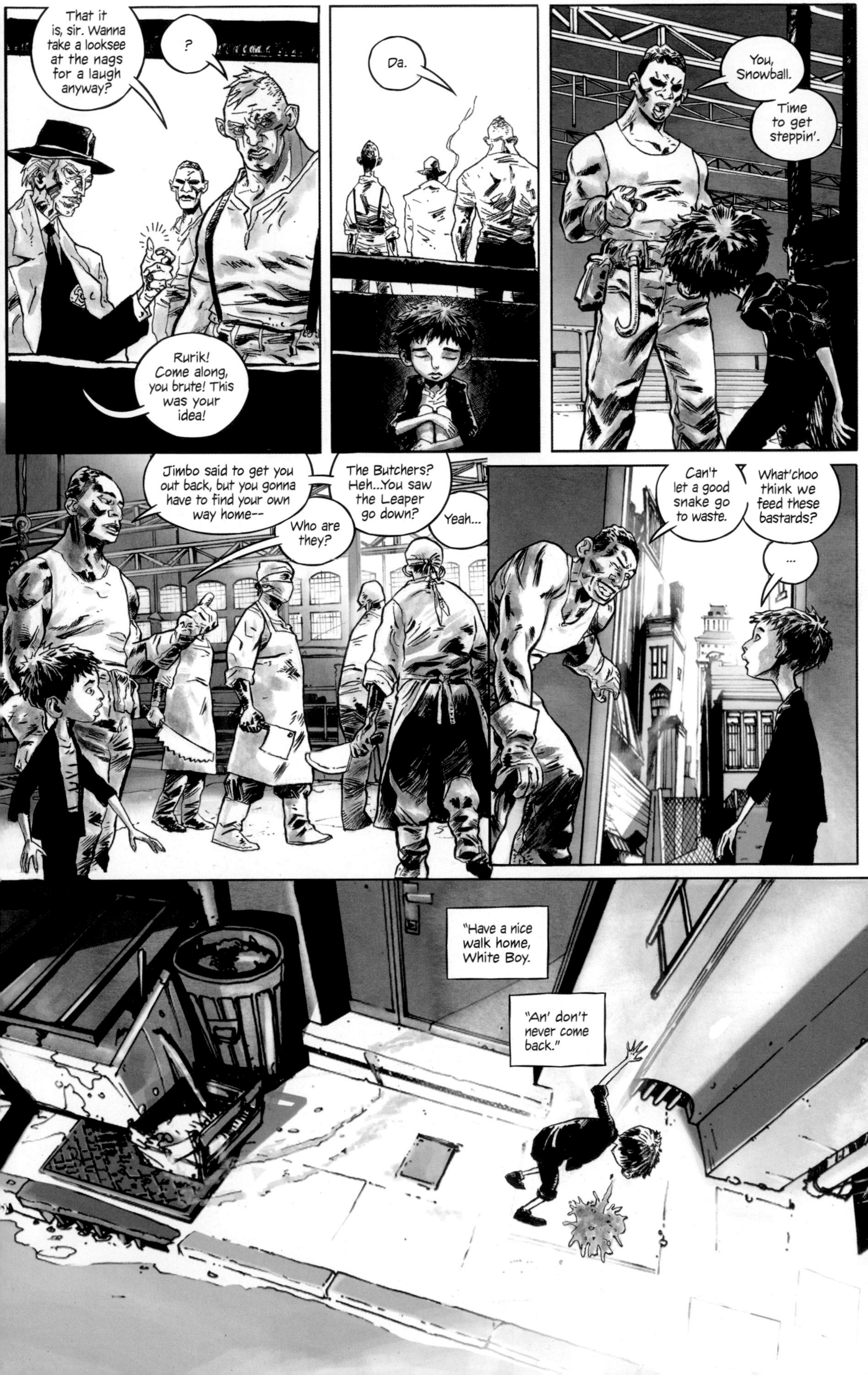
That it is, sir. Wanna take a looksee at the nags for a laugh anyway?
?
Rurik! Come along, you brute! This was your idea!
Da.
You, Snowball.
Time to get steppin'.
Jimbo said to get you out back, but you gonna have to find your own way home--
Who are they?
The Butchers? Heh...You saw the Leaper go down?
Yeah...
Can't let a good snake go to waste.
What'choo think we feed these bastards?
...
"Have a nice walk home, White Boy.
"An' don't never come back."

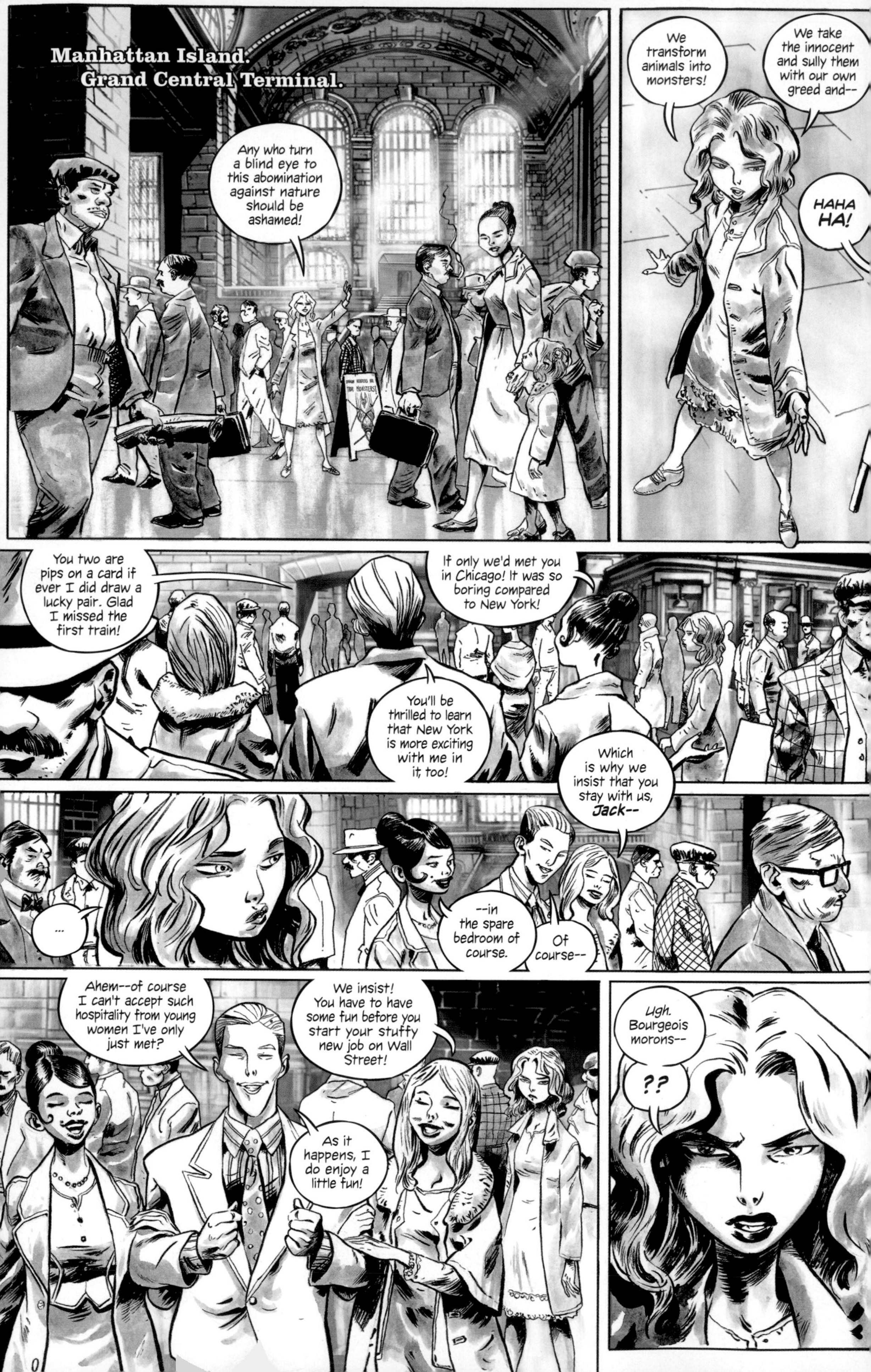
Manhattan Island.
Grand Central Terminal.
Any who turn a blind eye to this abomination against nature should be ashamed!
We transform animals into monsters!
We take the innocent and sully them with our own greed and--
HAHA HA!
You two are pips on a card if ever I did draw a lucky pair. Glad I missed the first train!
If only we'd met you in Chicago! It was so boring compared to New York!
You'll be thrilled to learn that New York is more exciting with me in it, too!
Which is why we insist that you stay with us, Jack--
...
--in the spare bedroom of course.
Of course--
Ahem--of course I can't accept such hospitality from young women I've only just met?
We insist! You have to have some fun before you start your stuffy new job on Wall Street!
As it happens, I do enjoy a little fun!
Ugh. Bourgeois morons--
??

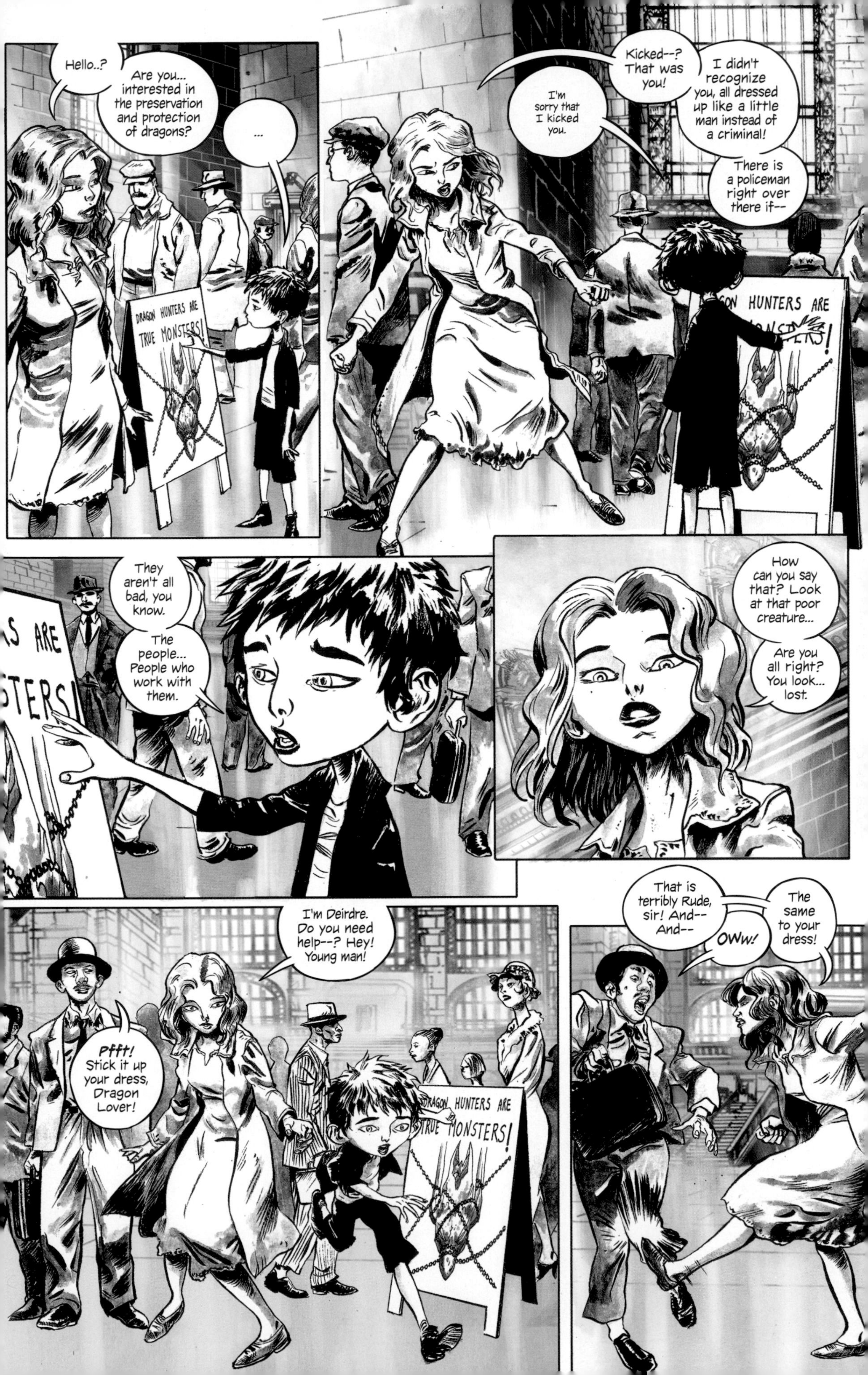
Hello..?
Are you... interested in the preservation and protection of dragons?
...
DRAGON HUNTERS ARE TRUE MONSTERS!
Kicked--? That was you!
I'm sorry that I kicked you.
I didn't recognize you, all dressed up like a little man instead of a criminal!
There is a policeman right over there if--
They aren't all bad, you know.
The people... People who work with them.
How can you say that? Look at that poor creature...
Are you all right? You look... lost.
I'm Deirdre. Do you need help--? Hey! Young man!
Pfft! Stick it up your dress, Dragon Lover!
DRAGON HUNTERS ARE TRUE MONSTERS!
That is terribly Rude, sir! And-- And--
OWW!
The same to your dress!

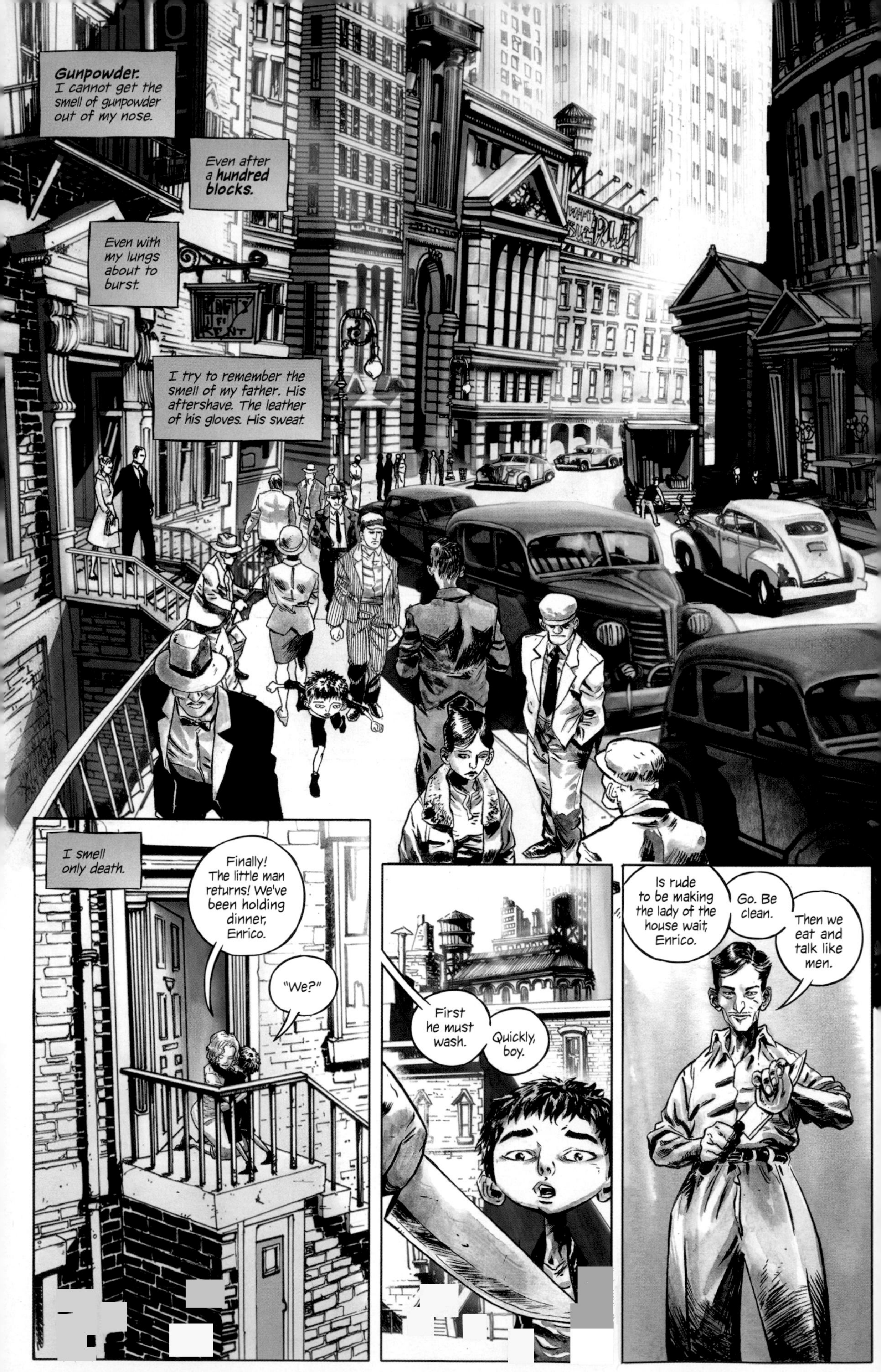

Gunpowder. I cannot get the smell of gunpowder out of my nose.
Even after a **hundred blocks.**
Even with my lungs about to burst.
I try to remember the smell of my father. His aftershave. The leather of his gloves. His sweat.
I smell only death.
Finally! The little man returns! We've been holding dinner, Enrico.
"We?"
First he must wash.
Quickly, boy.
Is rude to be making the lady of the house wait, Enrico.
Go. Be clean.
Then we eat and talk like men.

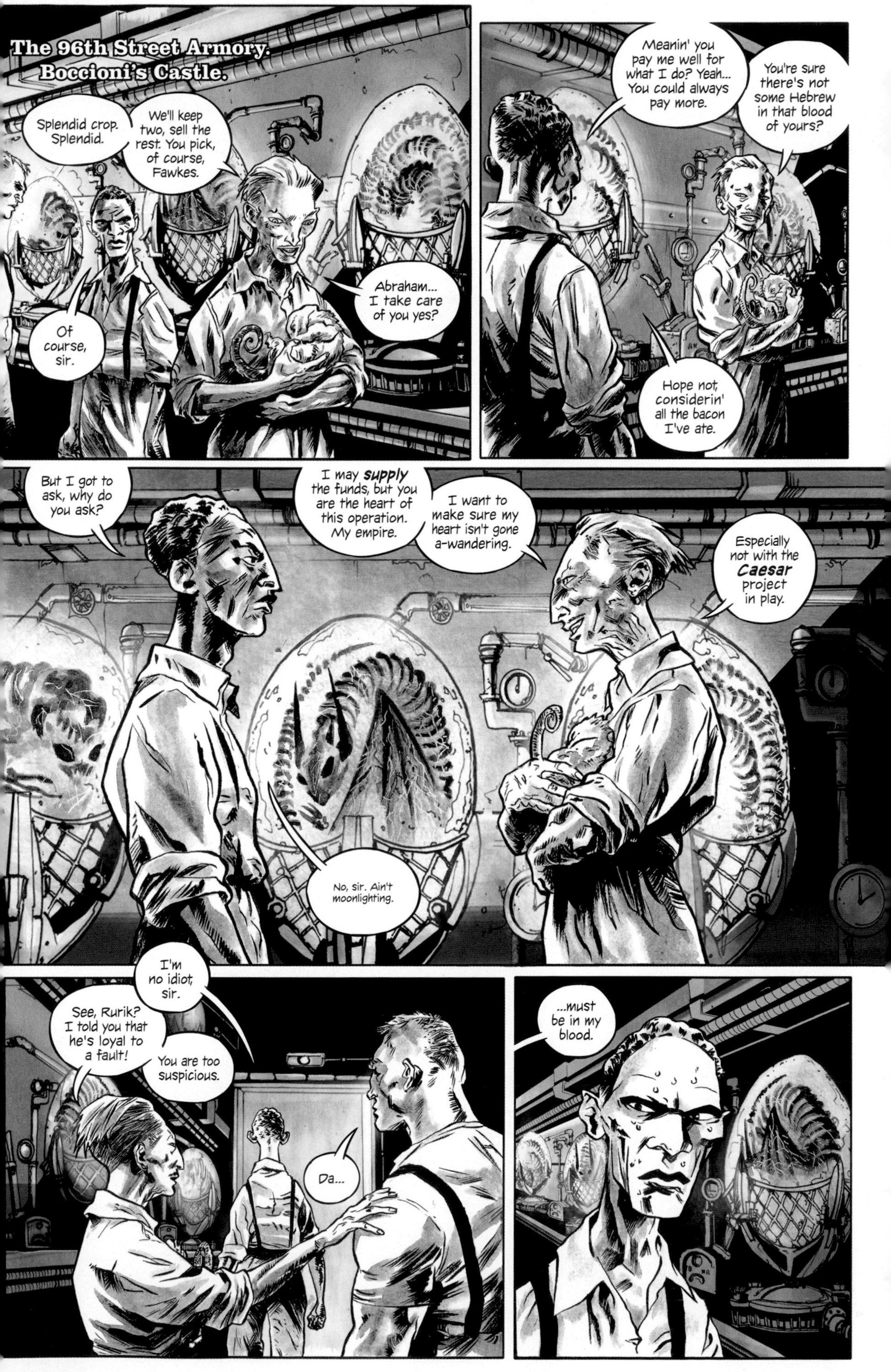
The 96th Street Armory. Boccioni's Castle.
Splendid crop. Splendid.
We'll keep two, sell the rest. You pick, of course, Fawkes.
Of course, sir.
Abraham... I take care of you yes?
Meanin' you pay me well for what I do? Yeah... You could always pay more.
You're sure there's not some Hebrew in that blood of yours?
Hope not, considerin' all the bacon I've ate.
But I got to ask, why do you ask?
I may supply the funds, but you are the heart of this operation. My empire.
I want to make sure my heart isn't gone a-wandering.
Especially not with the Caesar project in play.
No, sir. Ain't moonlighting.
I'm no idiot, sir.
See, Rurik? I told you that he's loyal to a fault!
You are too suspicious.
Da...
...must be in my blood.

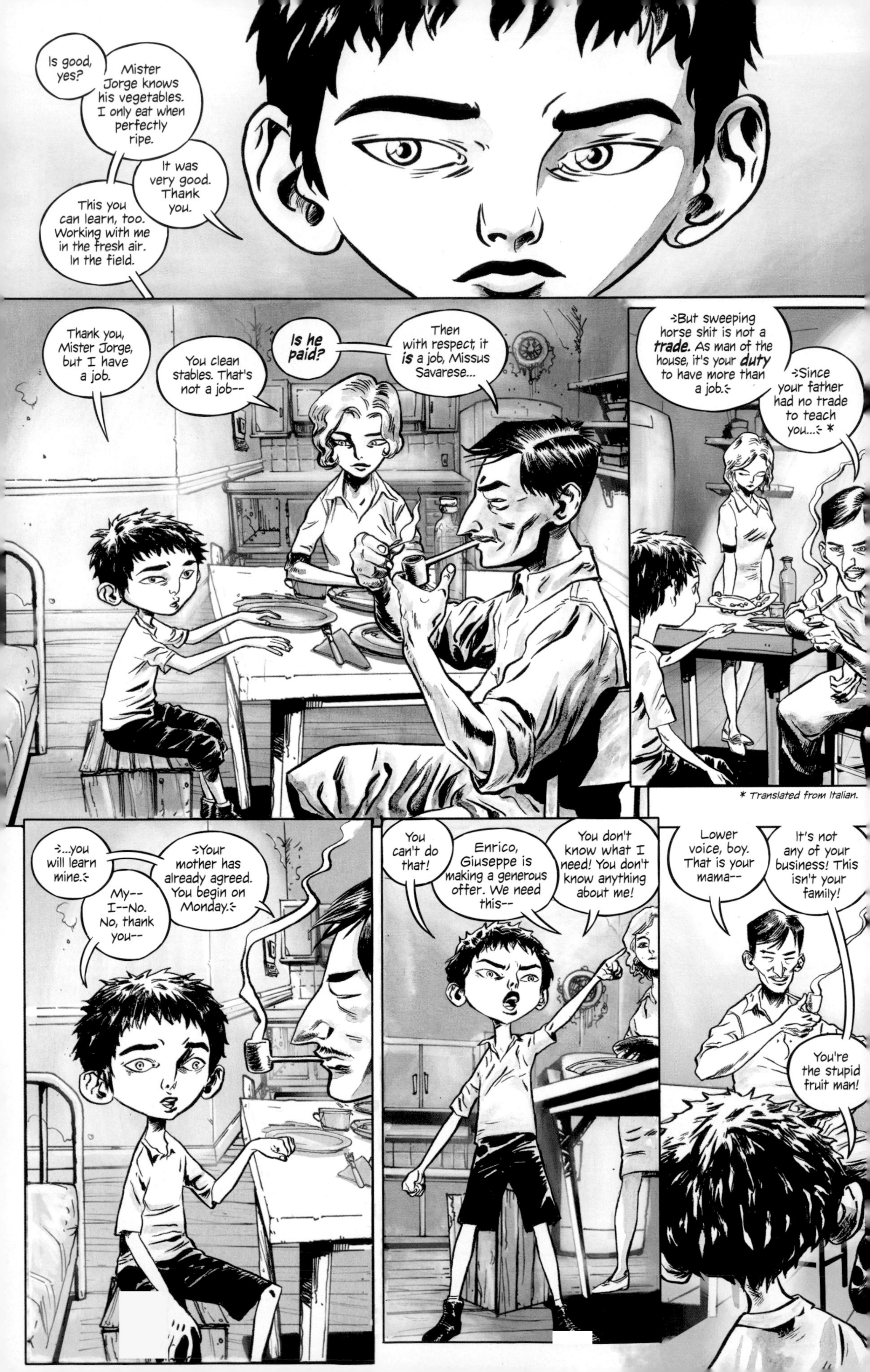
Is good, yes?
Mister Jorge knows his vegetables. I only eat when perfectly ripe.
It was very good. Thank you.
This you can learn, too. Working with me in the fresh air. In the field.
Thank you, Mister Jorge, but I have a job.
You clean stables. That's not a job--
Is he paid?
Then with respect, it is a job, Missus Savarese...
But sweeping horse shit is not a trade. As man of the house, it's your duty to have more than a job.
Since your father had no trade to teach you... *
* Translated from Italian.
...you will learn mine.
Your mother has already agreed. You begin on Monday.
My-- I--No. No, thank you--
You can't do that!
Enrico, Giuseppe is making a generous offer. We need this--
You don't know what I need! You don't know anything about me!
Lower voice, boy. That is your mama--
It's not any of your business! This isn't your family!
You're the stupid fruit man!

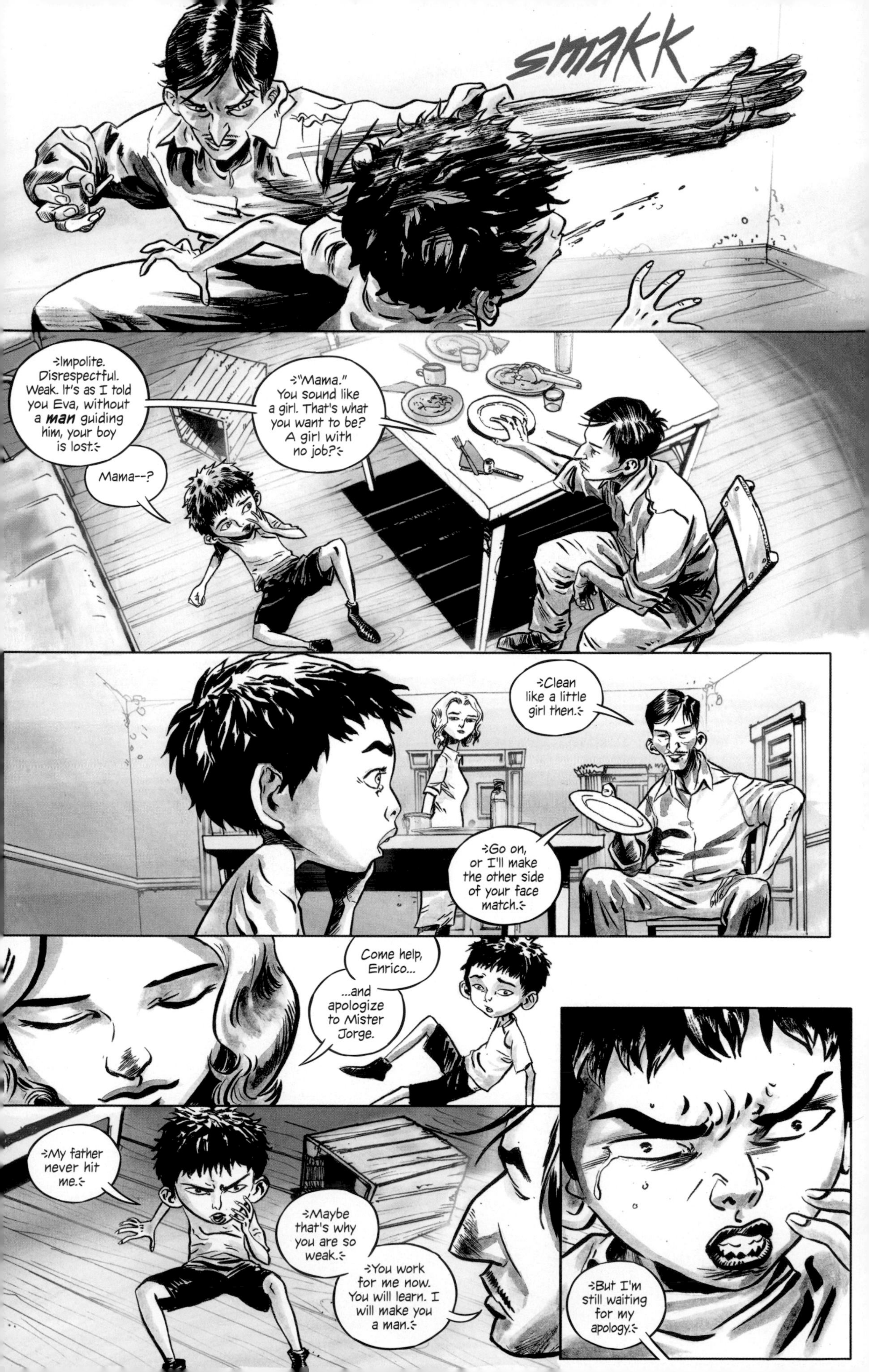
smakk
Impolite. Disrespectful. Weak. It's as I told you Eva, without a ***man*** guiding him, your boy is lost.
"Mama." You sound like a girl. That's what you want to be? A girl with no job?
Mama--?
Clean like a little girl then.
Go on, or I'll make the other side of your face match.
Come help, Enrico...
...and apologize to Mister Jorge.
My father never hit me.
Maybe that's why you are so weak.
You work for me now. You will learn. I will make you a man.
But I'm still waiting for my apology.

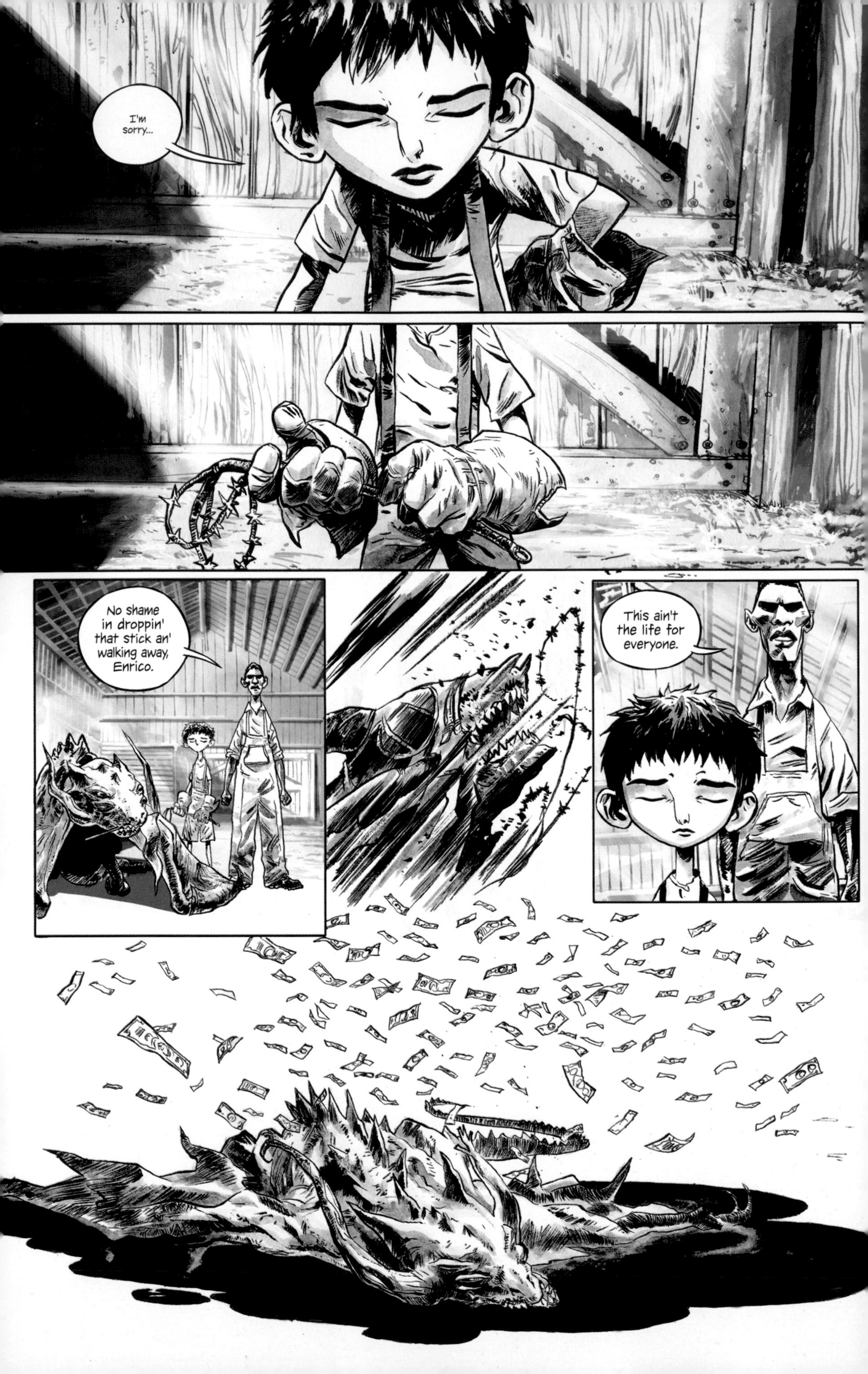
I'm sorry...
No shame in droppin' that stick an' walking away, Enrico.
This ain't the life for everyone.

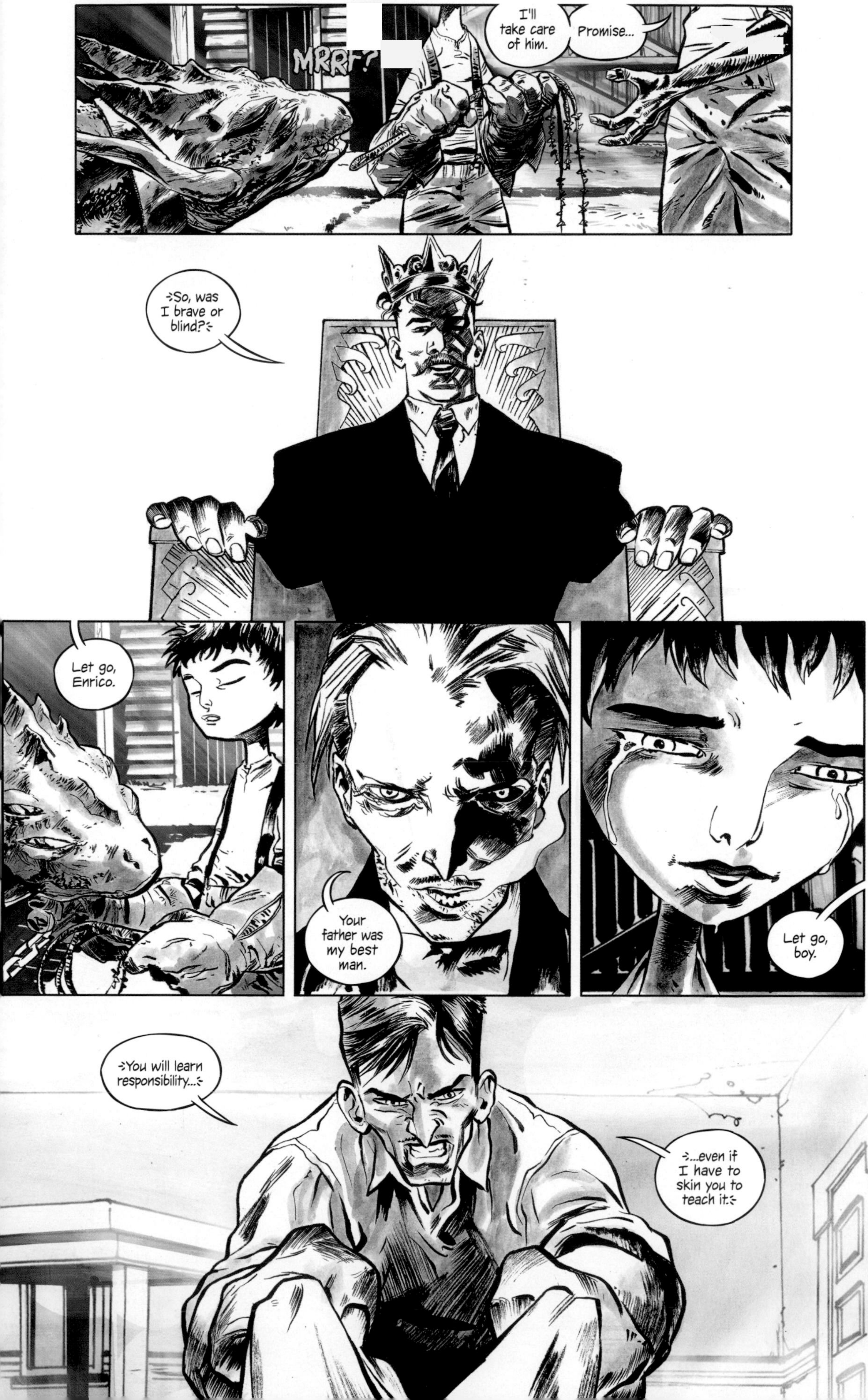
MRRF?
I'll take care of him.
Promise...
So, was I brave or blind?
Let go, Enrico.
Your father was my best man.
Let go, boy.
You will learn responsibility...
...even if I have to skin you to teach it.

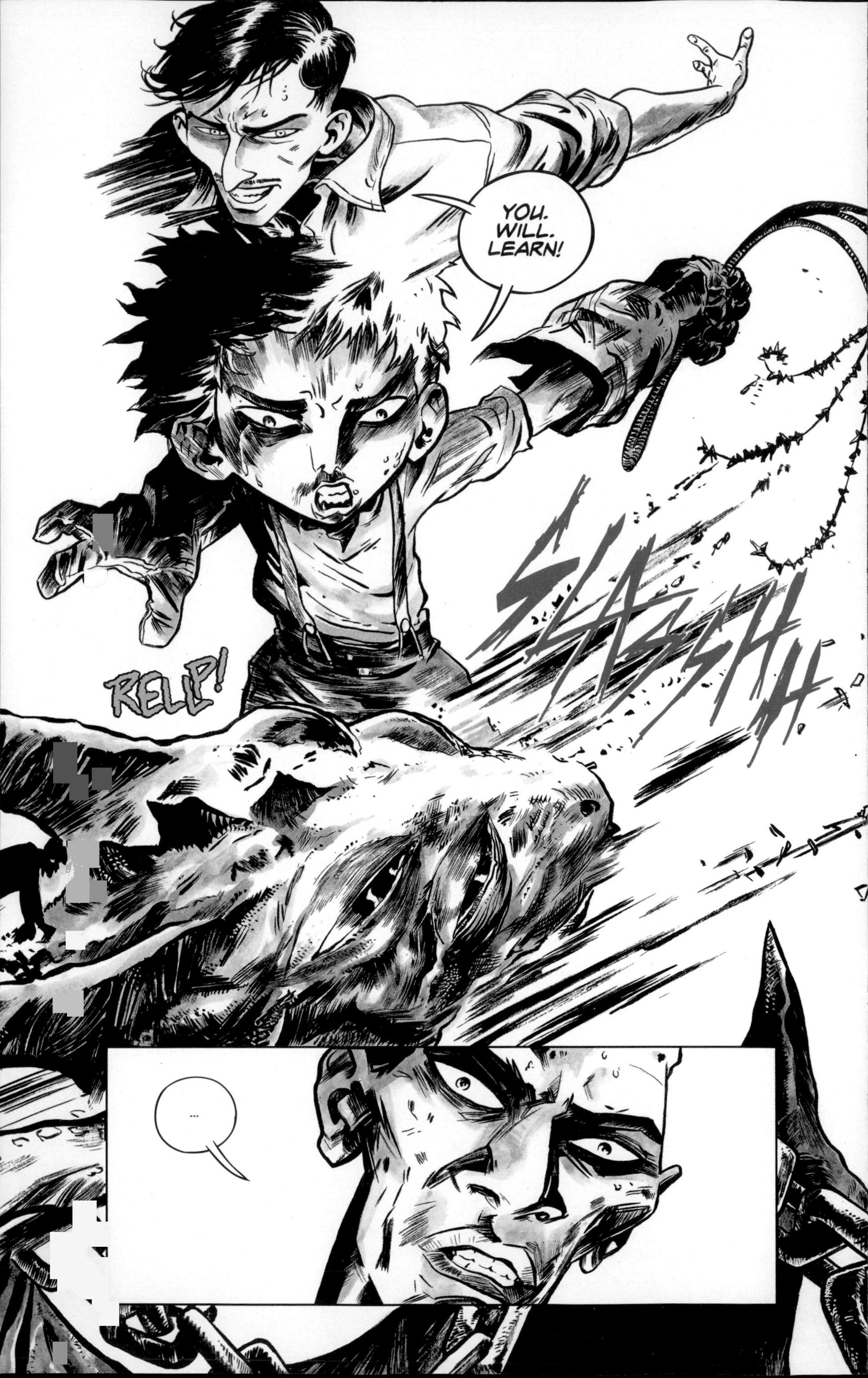

YOU. WILL. LEARN!
SLASSHH
RELLP!
...

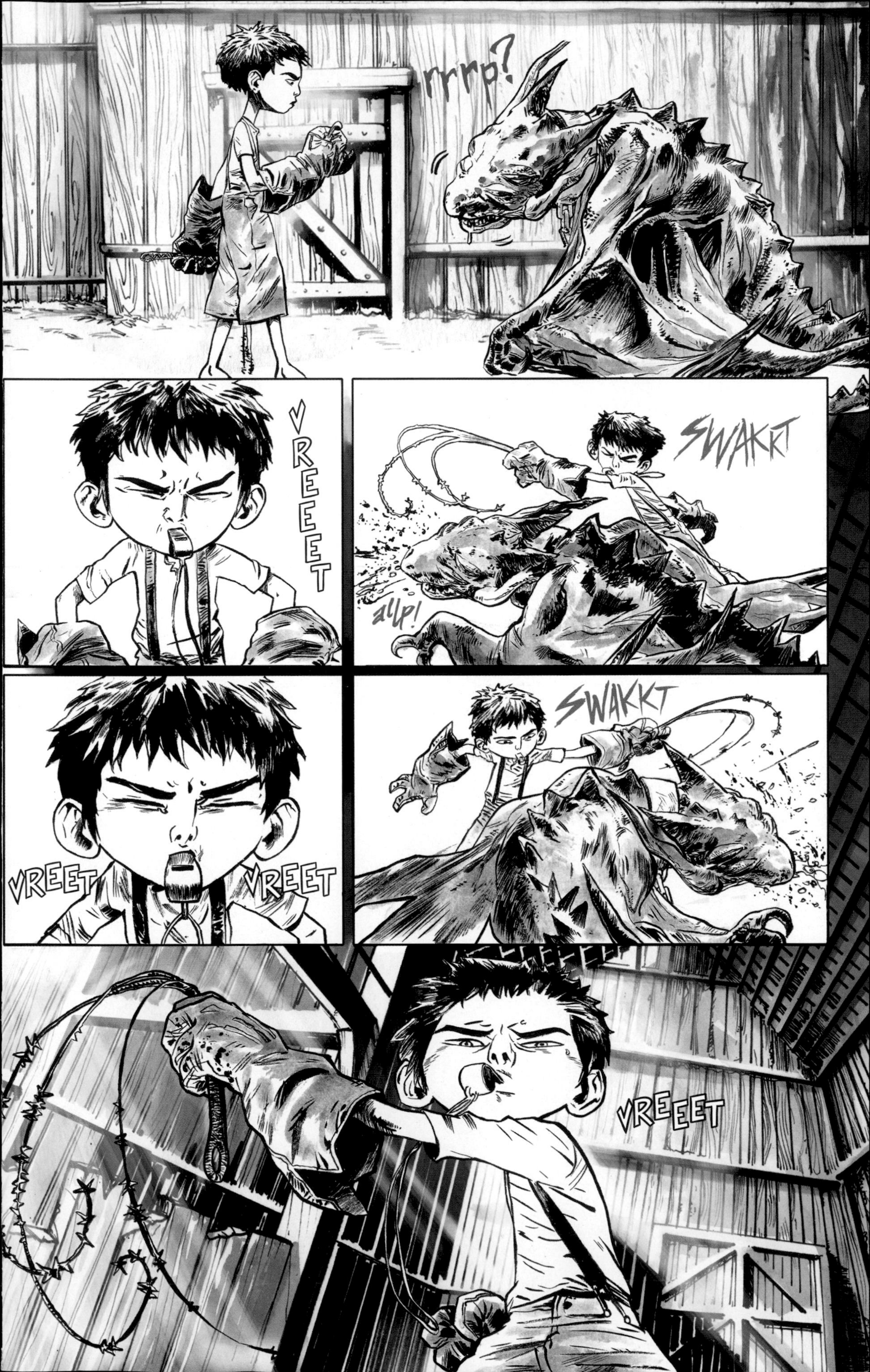
rrrp?
VREEET
SWAKKT
GULP!
VREET
VREET
SWAKKT
VREEET

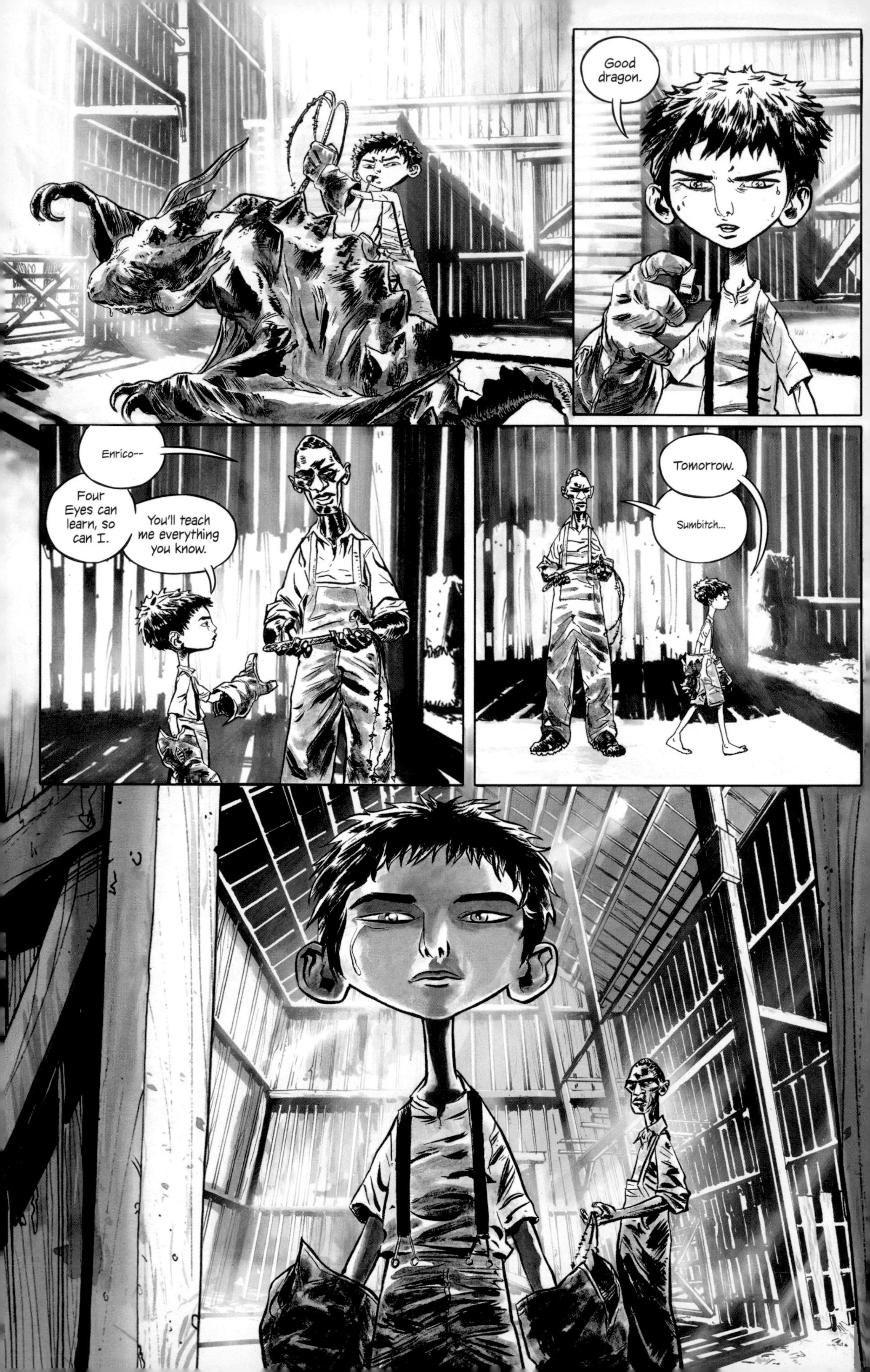
Good dragon.
Enrico--
Four Eyes can learn, so can I.
You'll teach me everything you know.
Tomorrow.
Sumbitch...

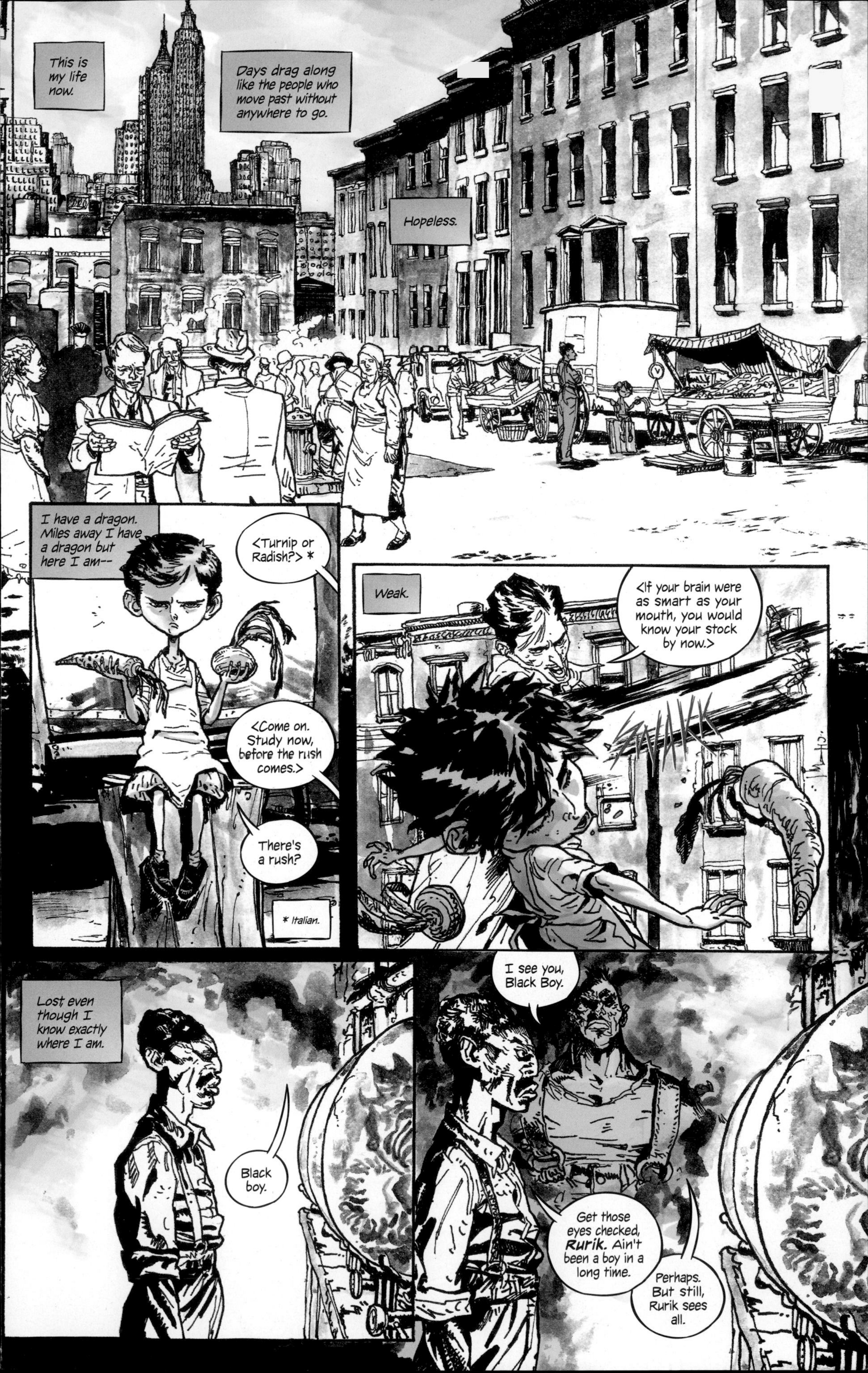
This is my life now.
Days drag along like the people who move past without anywhere to go.
Hopeless.
I have a dragon. Miles away I have a dragon but here I am--
<Turnip or Radish?> *
<Come on. Study now, before the rush comes.>
There's a rush?
* Italian.
Weak.
<If your brain were as smart as your mouth, you would know your stock by now.>
SNAKK
Lost even though I know exactly where I am.
Black boy.
I see you, Black Boy.
Get those eyes checked, **Rurik.** Ain't been a boy in a long time.
Perhaps. But still, Rurik sees all.

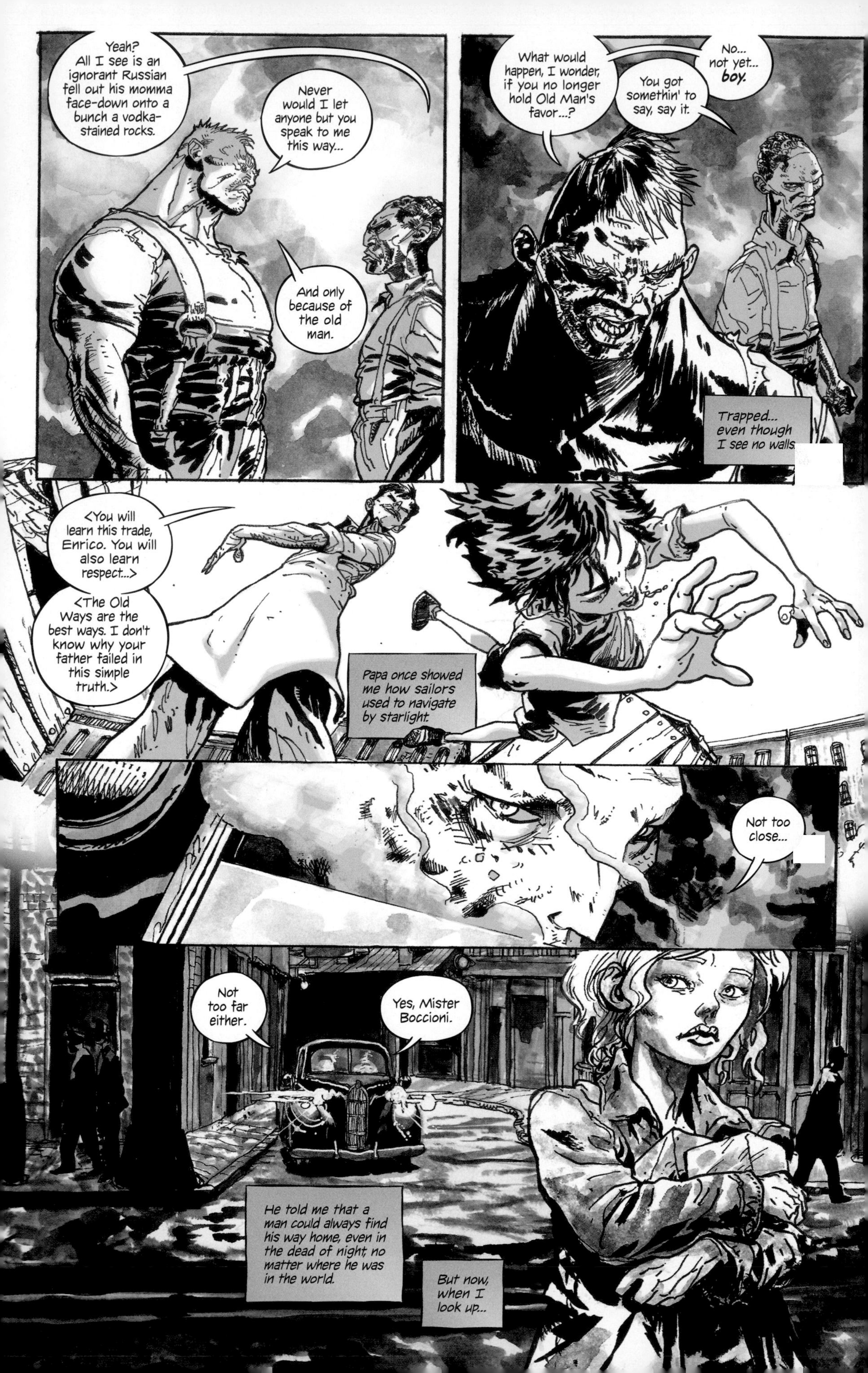

Yeah? All I see is an ignorant Russian fell out his momma face-down onto a bunch a vodka-stained rocks.
Never would I let anyone but you speak to me this way...
And only because of the old man.
What would happen, I wonder, if you no longer hold Old Man's favor...?
No... not yet... **boy.**
You got somethin' to say, say it.
Trapped... even though I see no walls.
<You will learn this trade, Enrico. You will also learn respect...>
<The Old Ways are the best ways. I don't know why your father failed in this simple truth.>
Papa once showed me how sailors used to navigate by starlight.
Not too close...
Not too far either.
Yes, Mister Boccioni.
He told me that a man could always find his way home, even in the dead of night, no matter where he was in the world.
But now, when I look up...

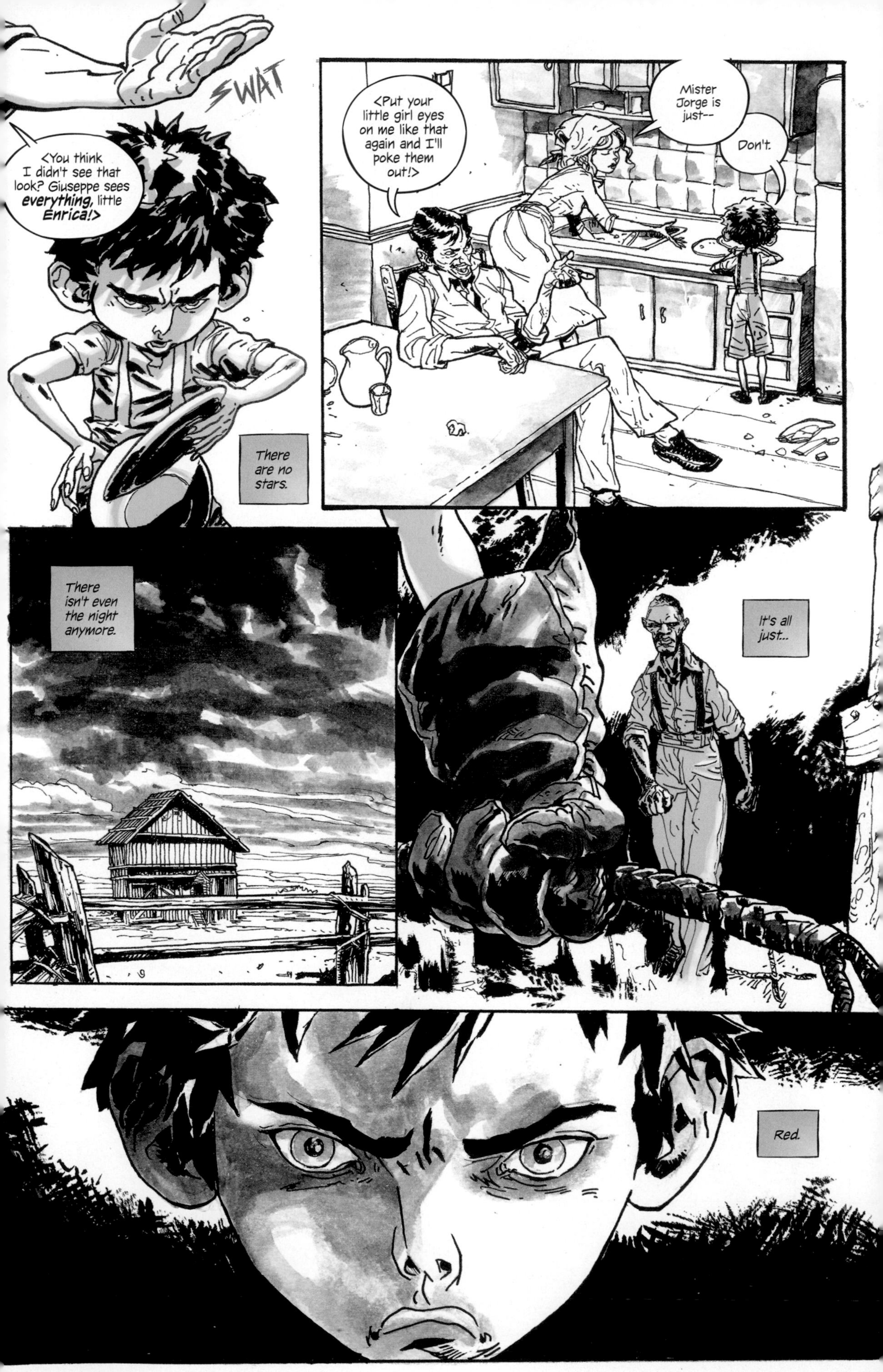
SWAT
<You think I didn't see that look? Giuseppe sees **everything**, little **Enrica!**>
There are no stars.
<Put your little girl eyes on me like that again and I'll poke them out!>
Mister Jorge is just--
Don't.
There isn't even the night anymore.
It's all just...
Red.

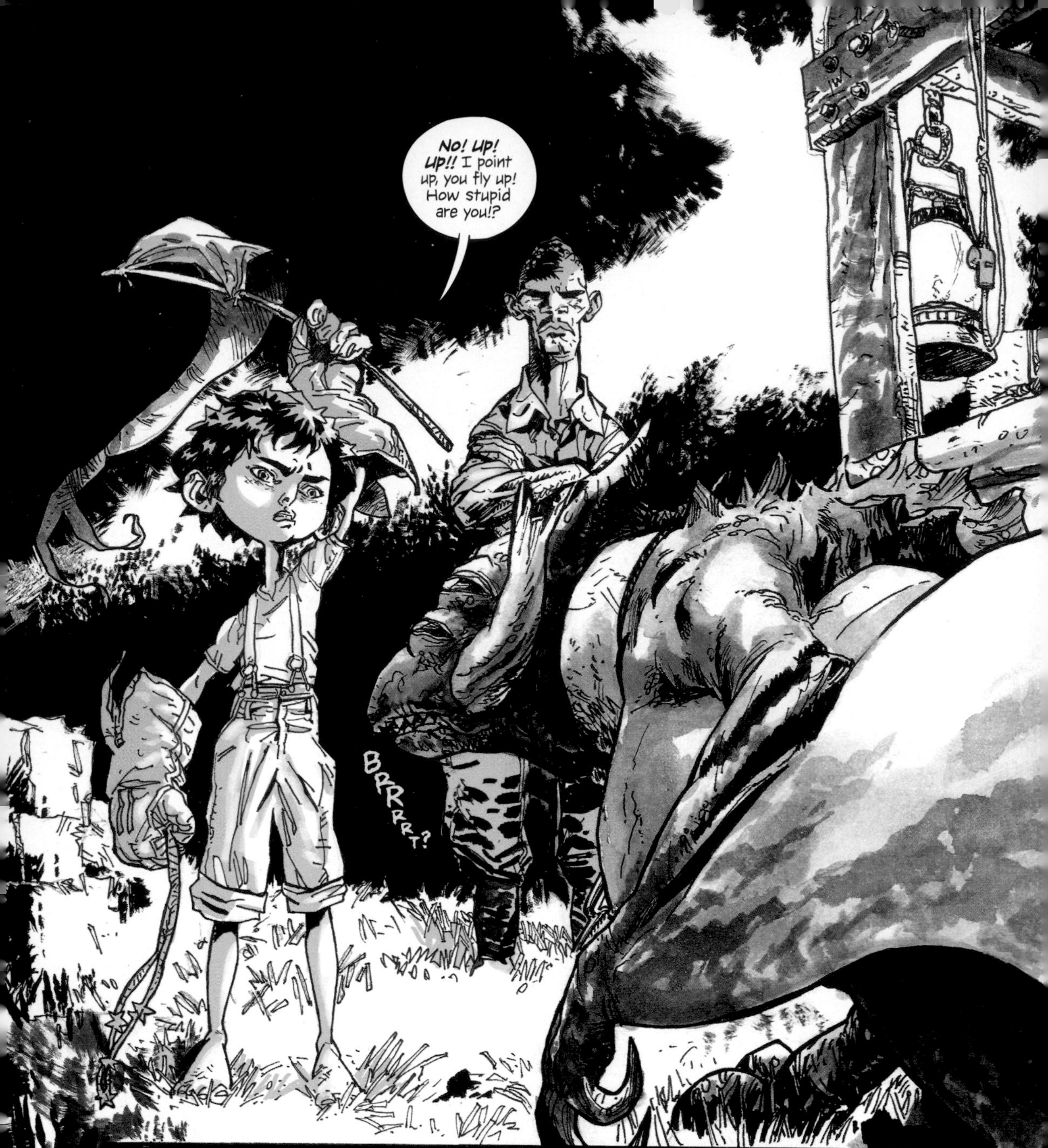
No! Up! Up!! I point up, you fly up! How stupid are you!?
BRRRRT?

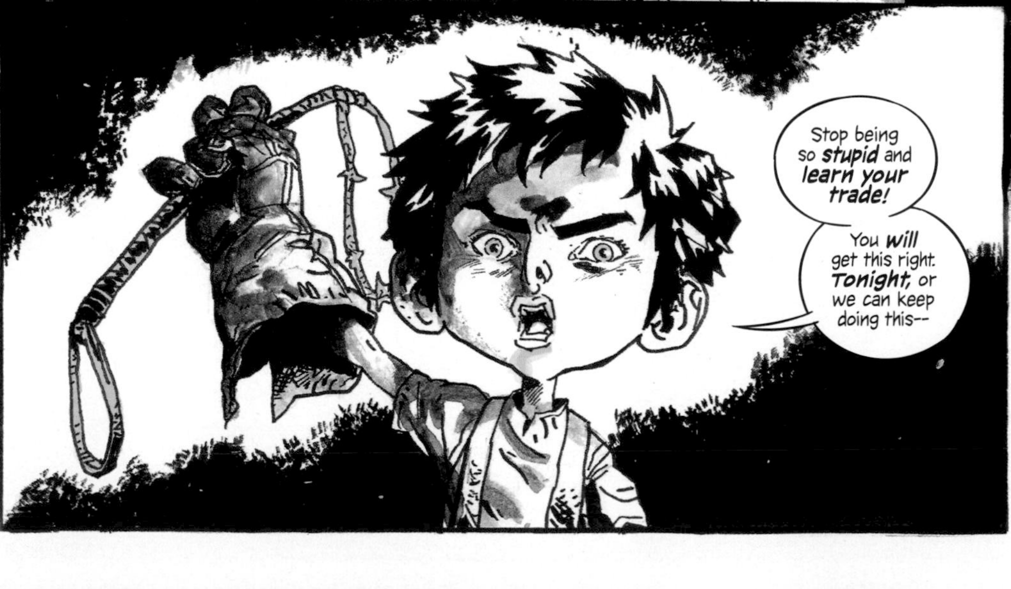
Stop being so stupid and learn your trade!
You will get this right. Tonight, or we can keep doing this--

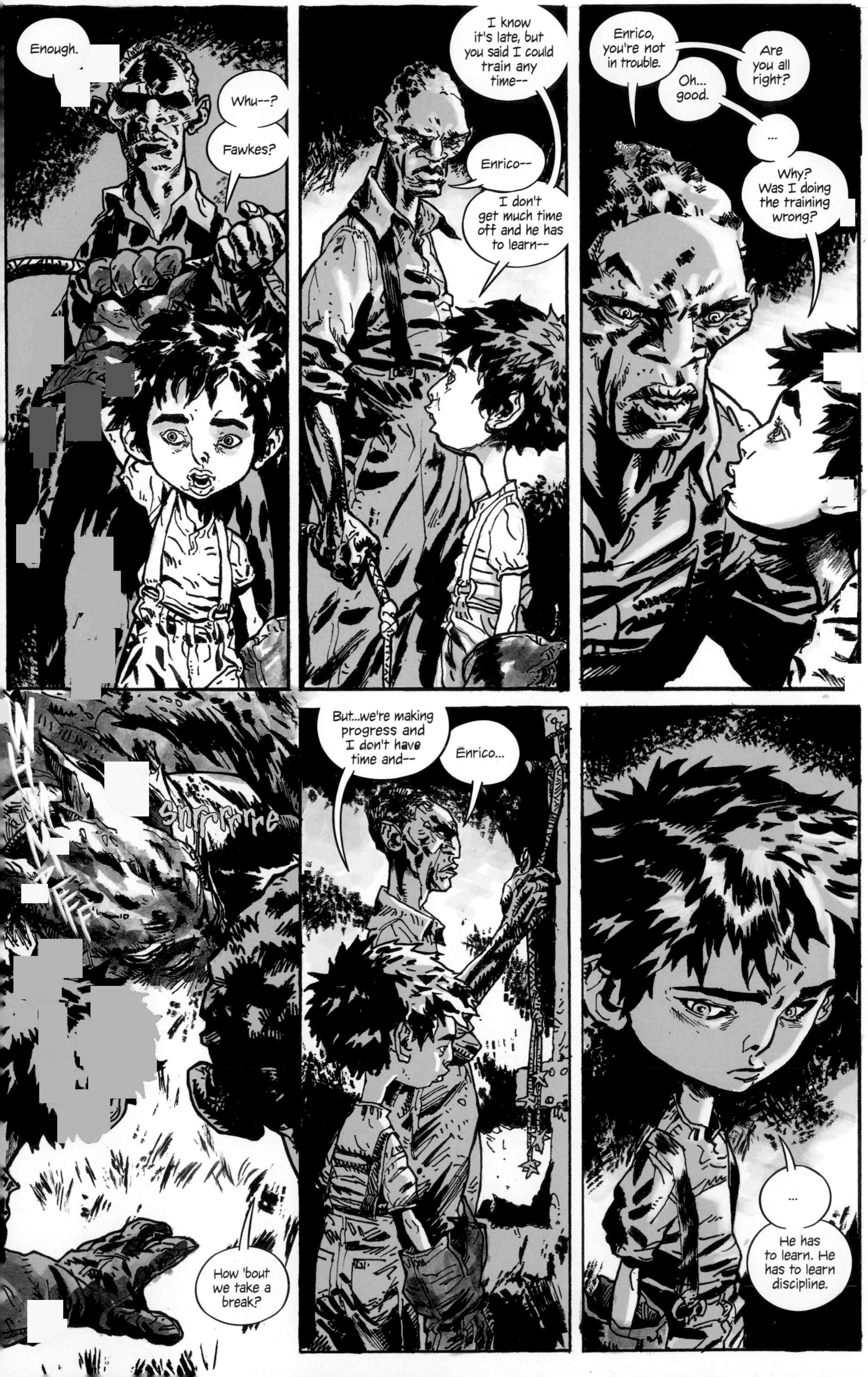
Enough.
Whu--?
Fawkes?
I know it's late, but you said I could train any time--
Enrico--
I don't get much time off and he has to learn--
Enrico, you're not in trouble.
Are you all right?
Oh... good.
...
Why? Was I doing the training wrong?
snrrrrre
How 'bout we take a break?
But...we're making progress and I don't have time and--
Enrico...
...
He has to learn. He has to learn discipline.

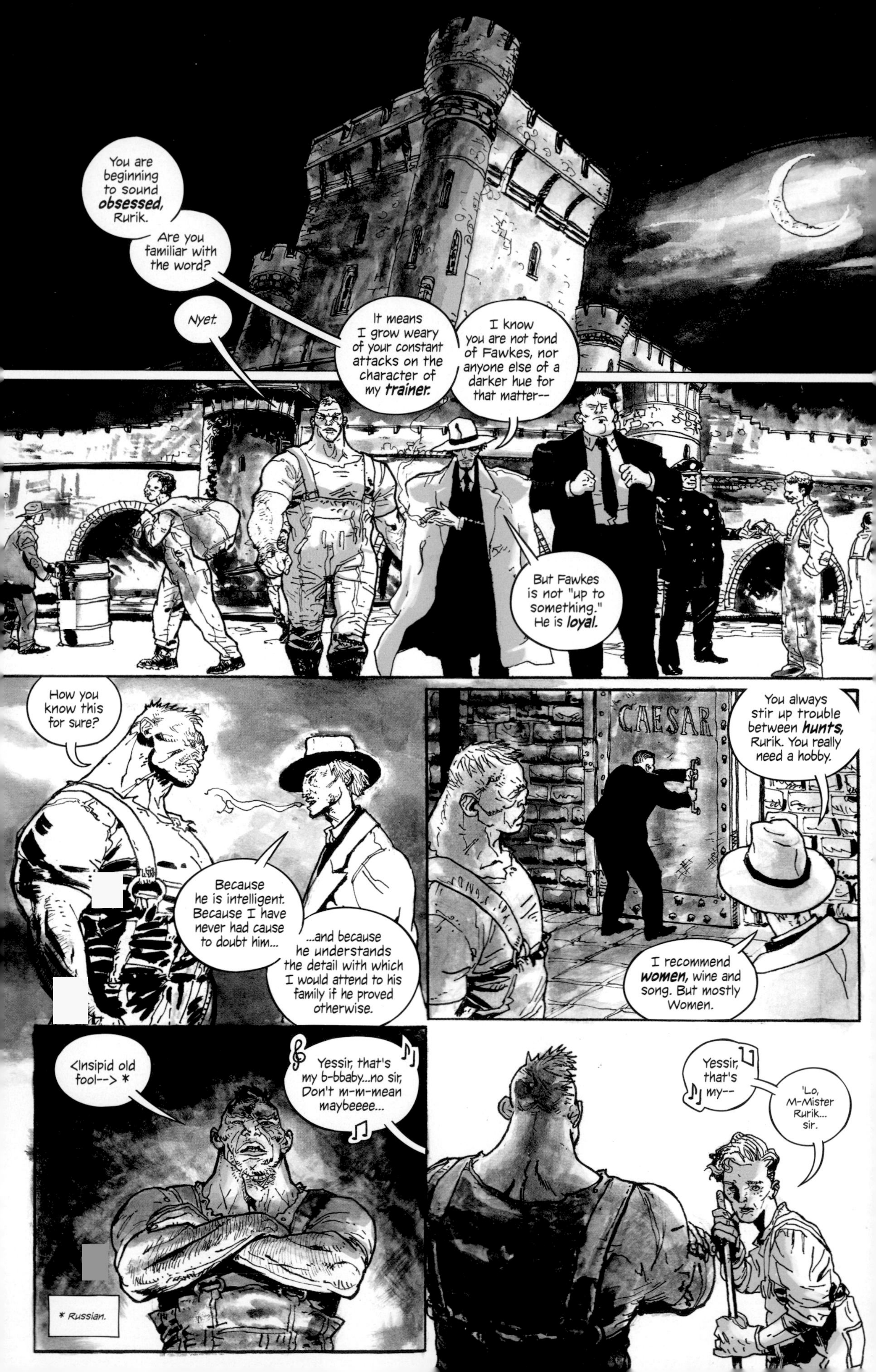

You are beginning to sound **obsessed,** Rurik.
Are you familiar with the word?
Nyet.
It means I grow weary of your constant attacks on the character of my **trainer.**
I know you are not fond of Fawkes, nor anyone else of a darker hue for that matter--
But Fawkes is not "up to something." He is **loyal.**
How you know this for sure?
Because he is intelligent. Because I have never had cause to doubt him...
...and because he understands the detail with which I would attend to his family if he proved otherwise.
CAESAR
You always stir up trouble between **hunts,** Rurik. You really need a hobby.
I recommend **women,** wine and song. But mostly Women.
<Insipid old fool--> *
Yessir, that's my b-bbaby...no sir, Don't m-m-mean maybeee...
Yessir, that's my--
'Lo, M-Mister Rurik... sir.
* Russian.

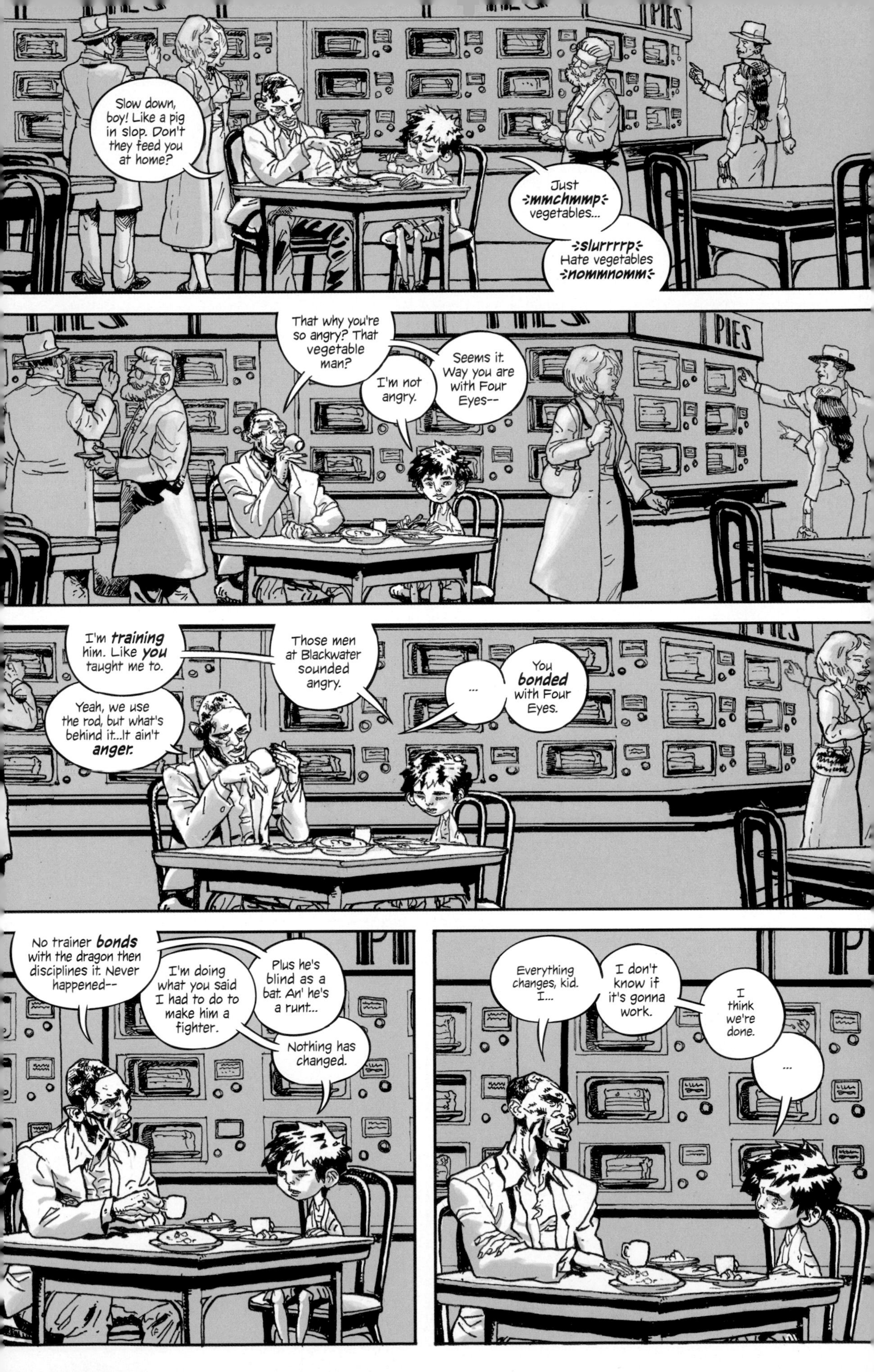

PIES
Slow down, boy! Like a pig in slop. Don't they feed you at home?
Just mmchmmp vegetables...
slurrrrp Hate vegetables nommnomm
That why you're so angry? That vegetable man?
I'm not angry.
Seems it. Way you are with Four Eyes--
I'm training him. Like you taught me to.
Yeah, we use the rod, but what's behind it...It ain't anger.
Those men at Blackwater sounded angry.
...
You bonded with Four Eyes.
No trainer bonds with the dragon then disciplines it. Never happened--
I'm doing what you said I had to do to make him a fighter.
Plus he's blind as a bat. An' he's a runt...
Nothing has changed.
Everything changes, kid. I...
I don't know if it's gonna work.
I think we're done.
...

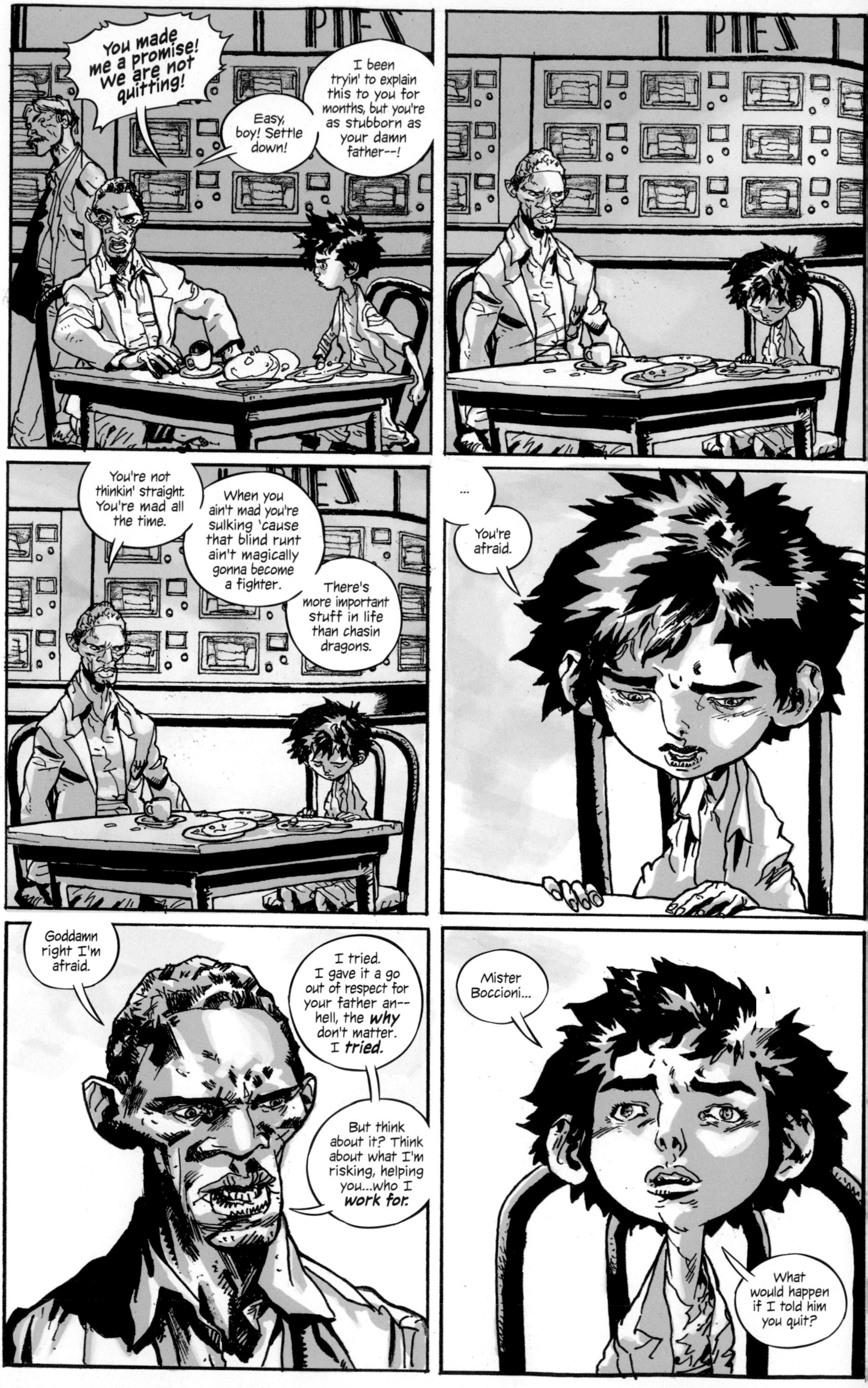

You made me a promise! We are not quitting!
Easy, boy! Settle down!
I been tryin' to explain this to you for months, but you're as stubborn as your damn father--!
You're not thinkin' straight. You're mad all the time.
When you ain't mad you're sulking 'cause that blind runt ain't magically gonna become a fighter.
There's more important stuff in life than chasin dragons.
...
You're afraid.
Goddamn right I'm afraid.
I tried. I gave it a go out of respect for your father an-- hell, the **why** don't matter. I **tried.**
But think about it? Think about what I'm risking, helping you...who I **work for.**
Mister Boccioni...
What would happen if I told him you quit?

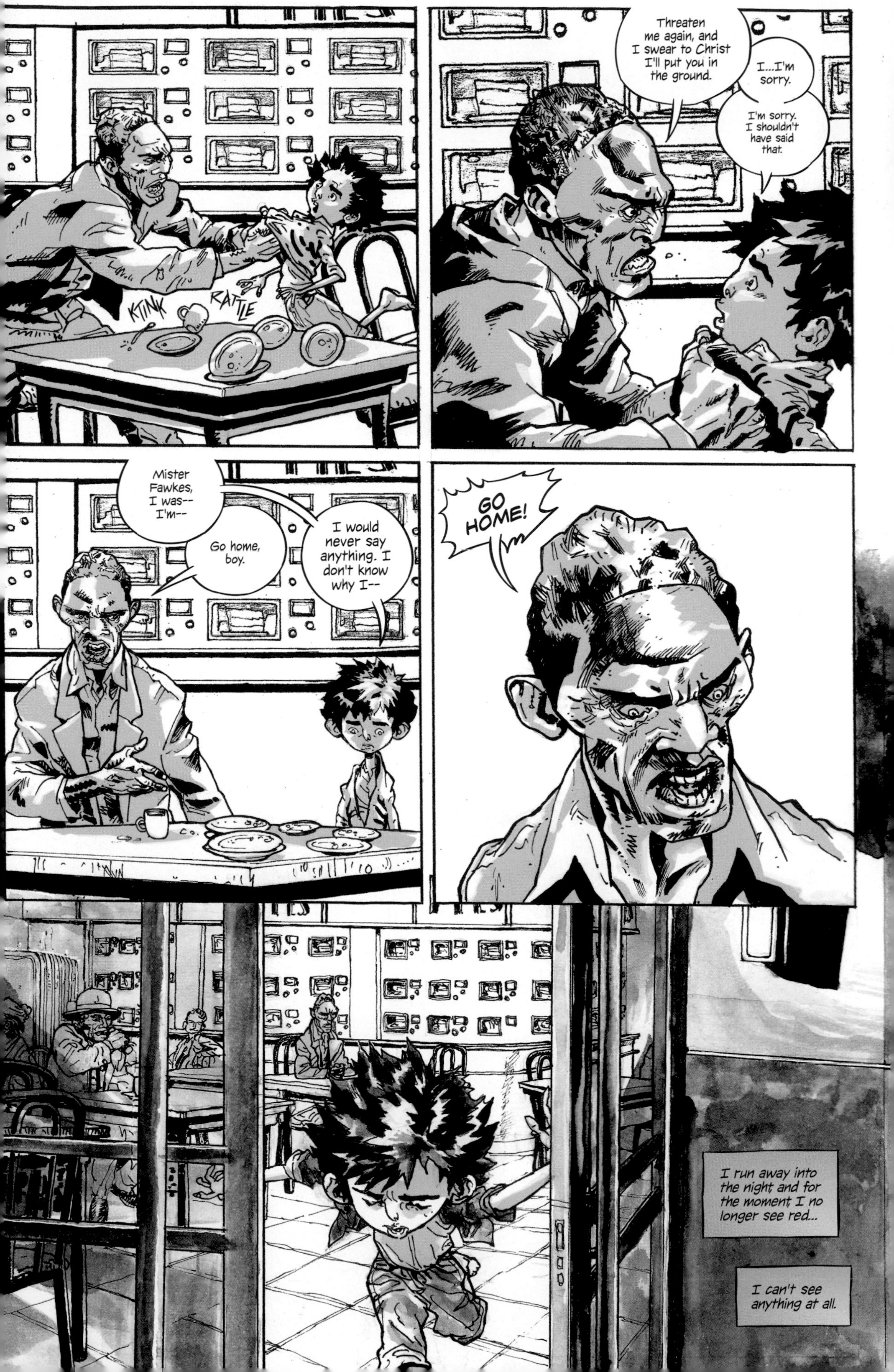
KTINK
RATTLE
Threaten me again, and I swear to Christ I'll put you in the ground.
I...I'm sorry.
I'm sorry. I shouldn't have said that.
Mister Fawkes, I was-- I'm--
Go home, boy.
I would never say anything. I don't know why I--
GO HOME!
I run away into the night and for the moment I no longer see red...
I can't see anything at all.

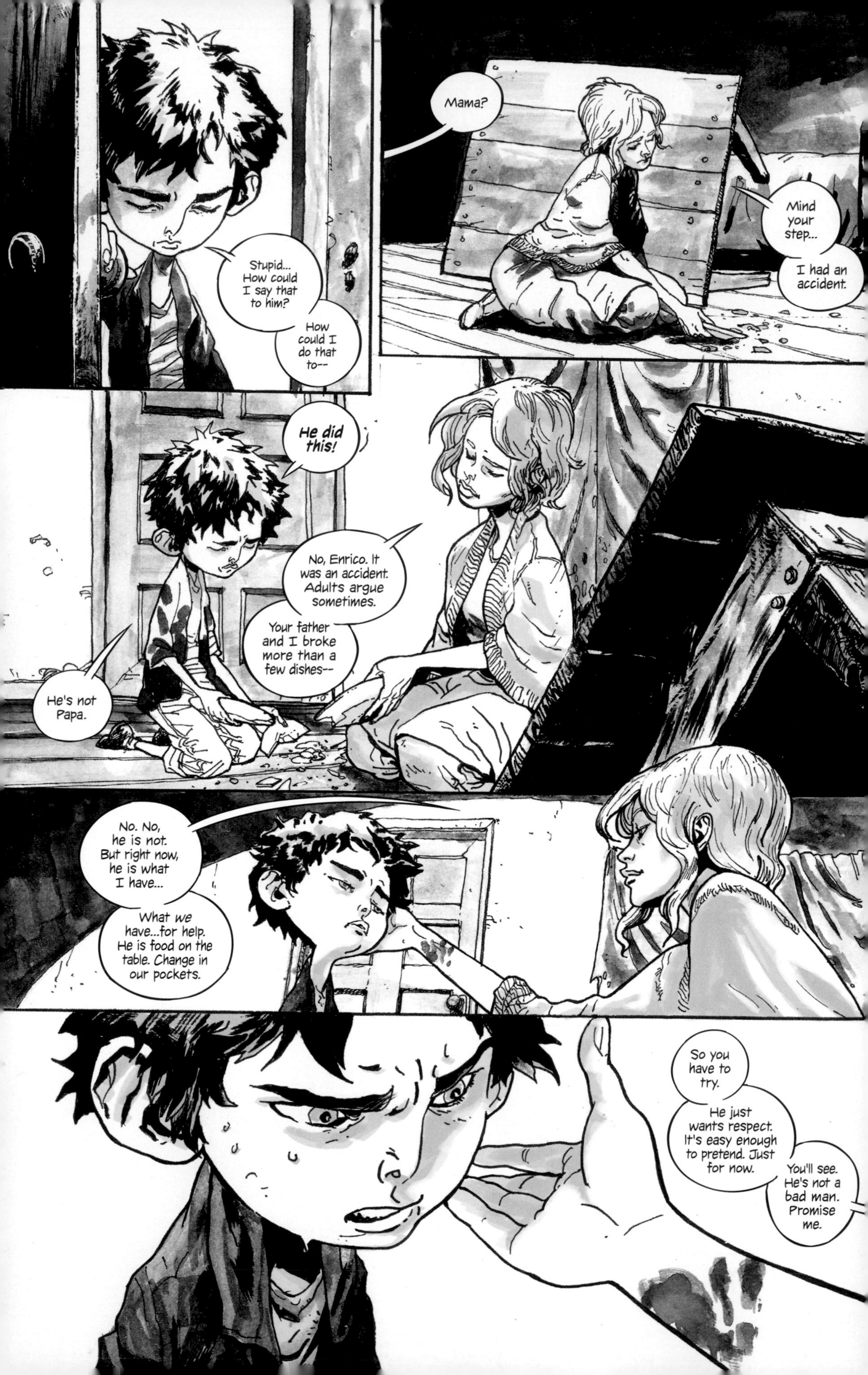

Stupid... How could I say that to him?
How could I do that to--
Mama?
Mind your step...
I had an accident.
He did this!
No, Enrico. It was an accident. Adults argue sometimes.
Your father and I broke more than a few dishes--
He's not Papa.
No. No, he is not. But right now, he is what I have...
What we have...for help. He is food on the table. Change in our pockets.
So you have to try.
He just wants respect. It's easy enough to pretend. Just for now.
You'll see. He's not a bad man. Promise me.

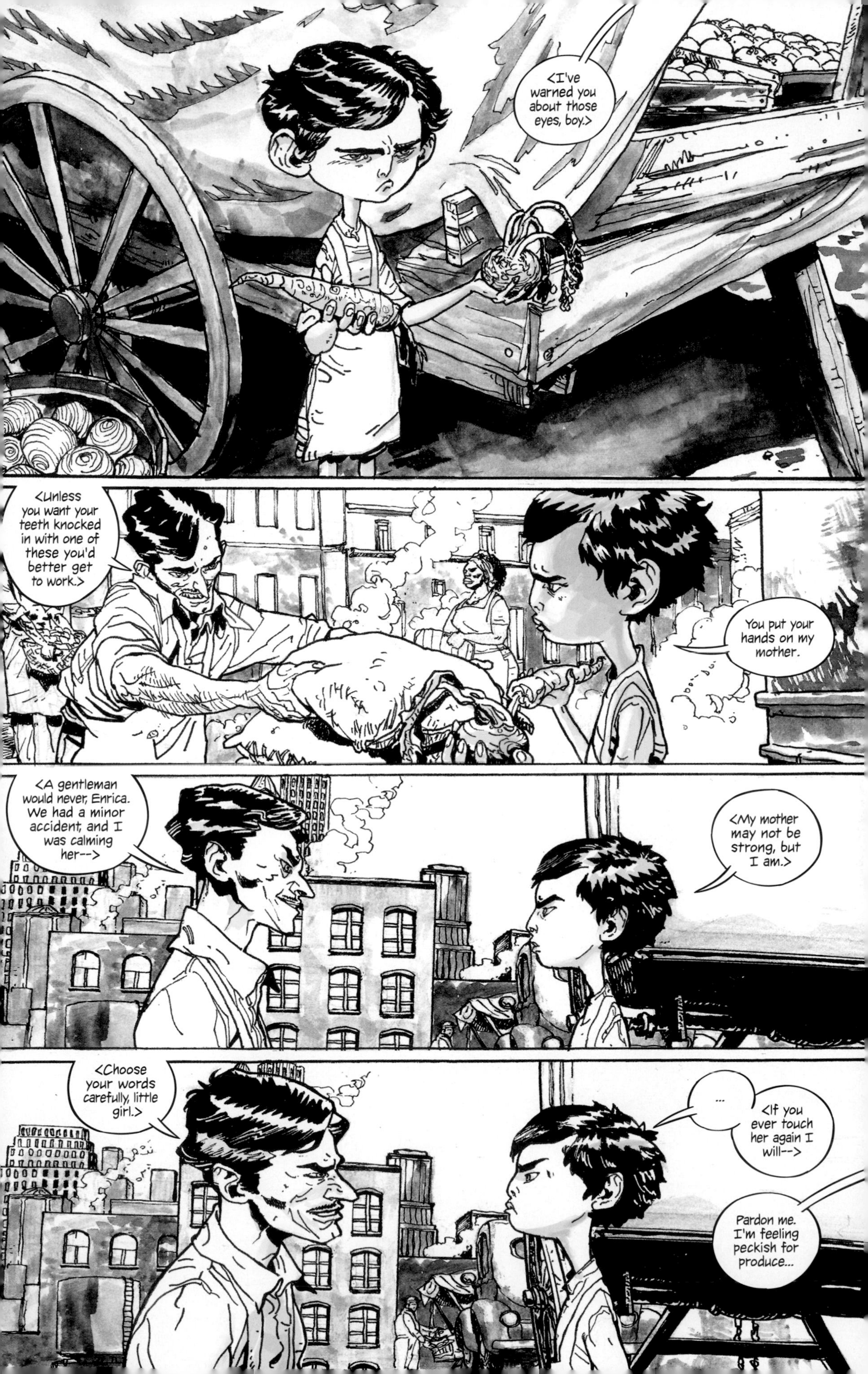
<I've warned you about those eyes, boy.>
<Unless you want your teeth knocked in with one of these you'd better get to work.>
You put your hands on my mother.
<A gentleman would never, Enrica. We had a minor accident, and I was calming her-->
<My mother may not be strong, but I am.>
<Choose your words carefully, little girl.>
...
<If you ever touch her again I will-->
Pardon me. I'm feeling peckish for produce...

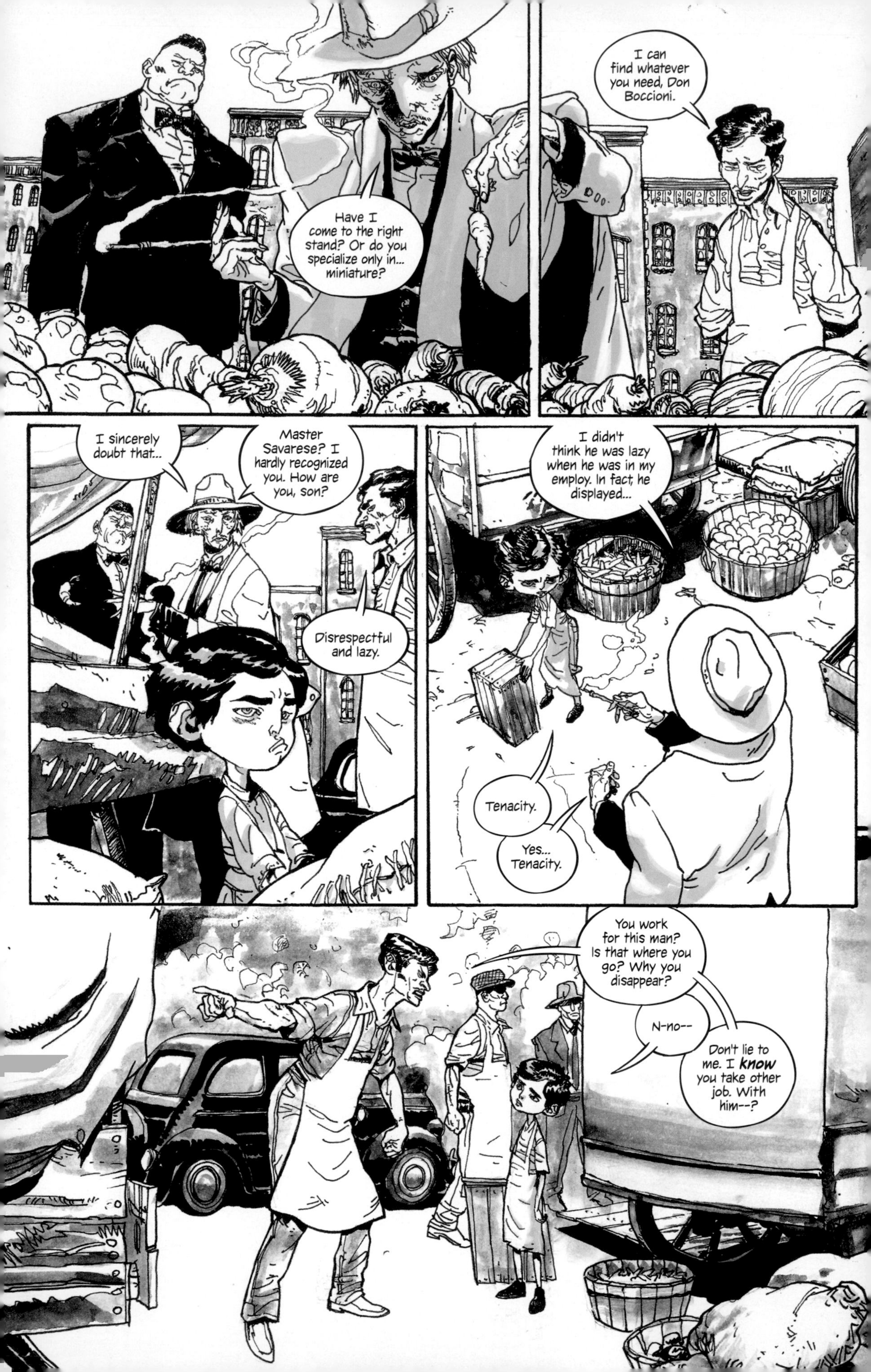
Have I come to the right stand? Or do you specialize only in... miniature?
I can find whatever you need, Don Boccioni.
I sincerely doubt that...
Master Savarese? I hardly recognized you. How are you, son?
Disrespectful and lazy.
I didn't think he was lazy when he was in my employ. In fact, he displayed...
Tenacity.
Yes... Tenacity.
You work for this man? Is that where you go? Why you disappear?
N-no--
Don't lie to me. I **know** you take other job. With him--?

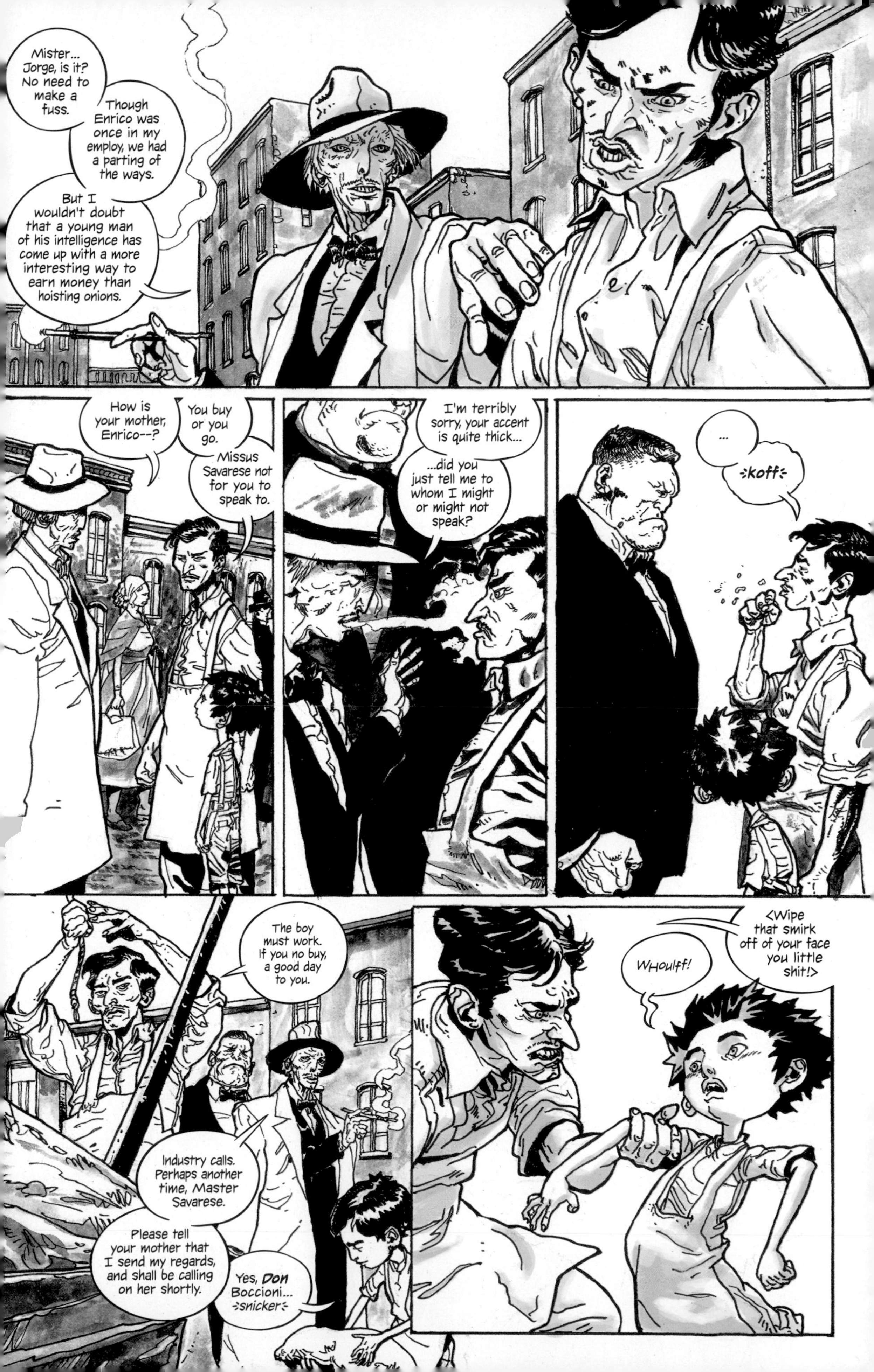
Mister... Jorge, is it? No need to make a fuss.
Though Enrico was once in my employ, we had a parting of the ways.
But I wouldn't doubt that a young man of his intelligence has come up with a more interesting way to earn money than hoisting onions.
How is your mother, Enrico--?
You buy or you go.
Missus Savarese not for you to speak to.
I'm terribly sorry, your accent is quite thick...
...did you just tell me to whom I might or might not speak?
...
koff
The boy must work. If you no buy, a good day to you.
Industry calls. Perhaps another time, Master Savarese.
Please tell your mother that I send my regards, and shall be calling on her shortly.
Yes, ***Don*** Boccioni... snicker
<Wipe that smirk off of your face you little shit!>
WHoulf!

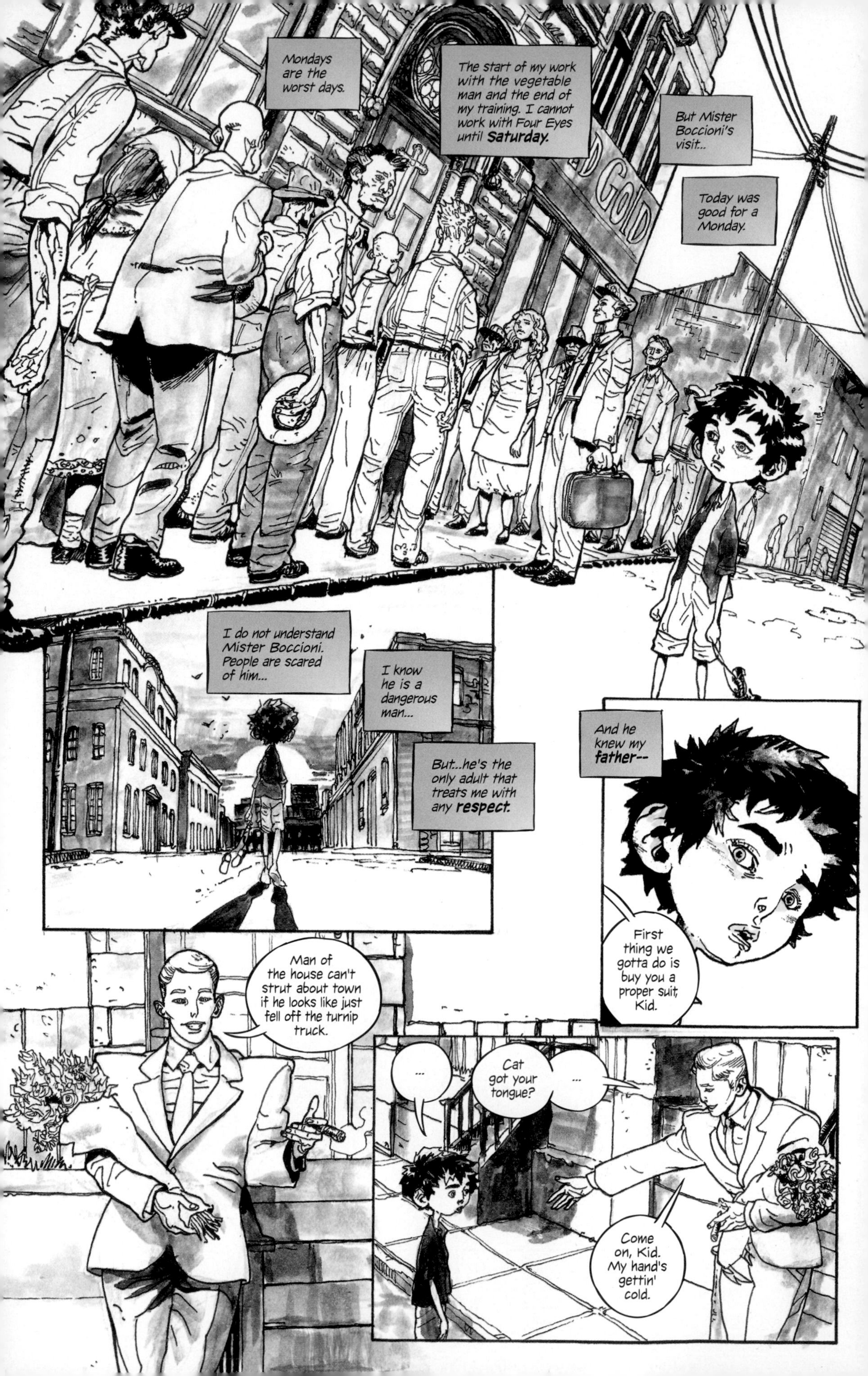

Mondays are the worst days.
The start of my work with the vegetable man and the end of my training. I cannot work with Four Eyes until **Saturday.**
But Mister Boccioni's visit...
Today was good for a Monday.
GOLD
I do not understand Mister Boccioni. People are scared of him...
I know he is a dangerous man...
But...he's the only adult that treats me with any **respect.**
And he knew my **father--**
First thing we gotta do is buy you a proper suit, Kid.
Man of the house can't strut about town if he looks like just fell off the turnip truck.
...
Cat got your tongue?
...
Come on, Kid. My hand's gettin' cold.

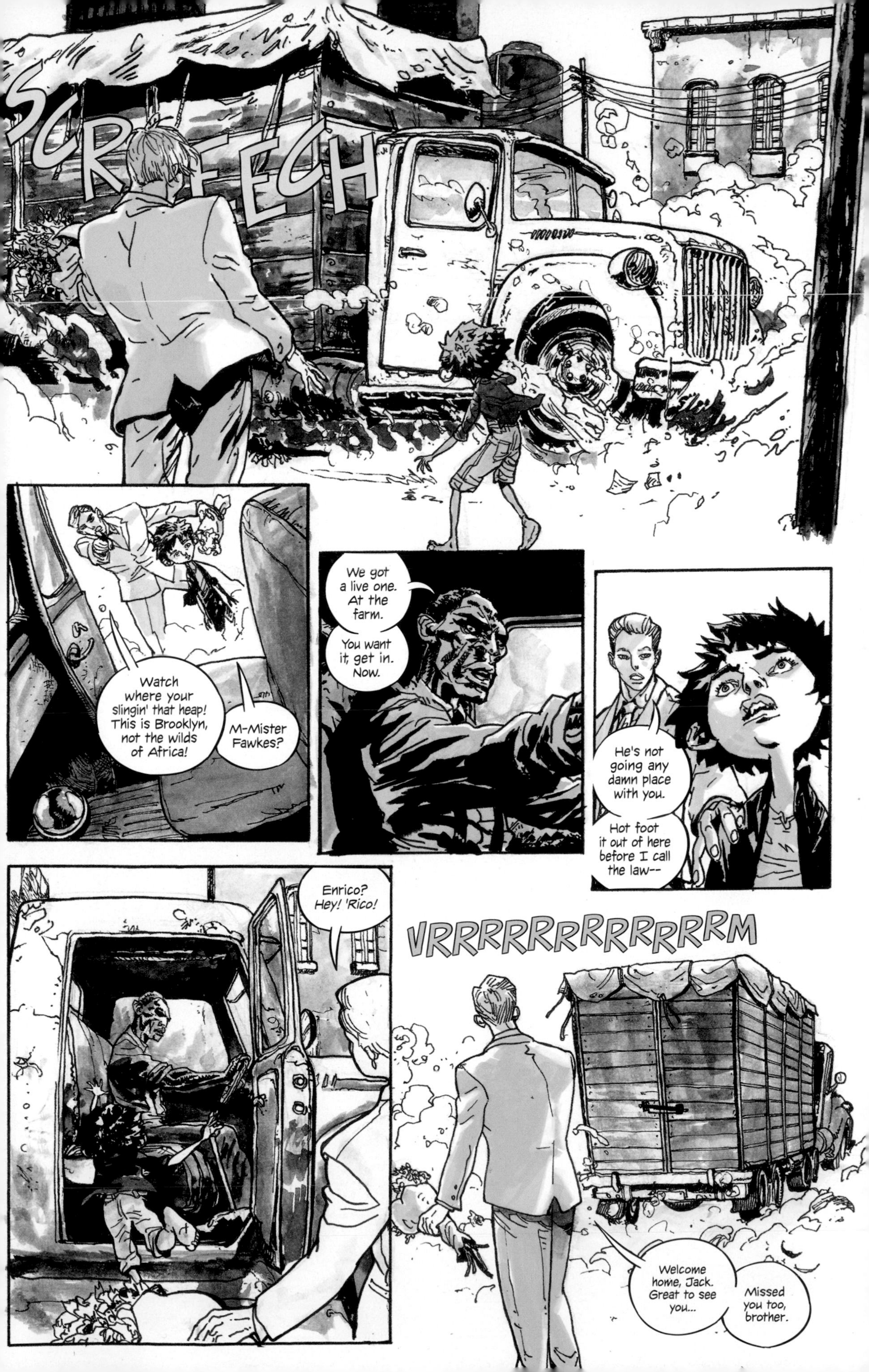

SCREECH
Watch where your slingin' that heap! This is Brooklyn, not the wilds of Africa!
M-Mister Fawkes?
We got a live one. At the farm.
You want it, get in. Now.
He's not going any damn place with you.
Hot foot it out of here before I call the law--
Enrico? Hey! 'Rico!
VRRRRRRRRRRRRM
Welcome home, Jack. Great to see you...
Missed you too, brother.

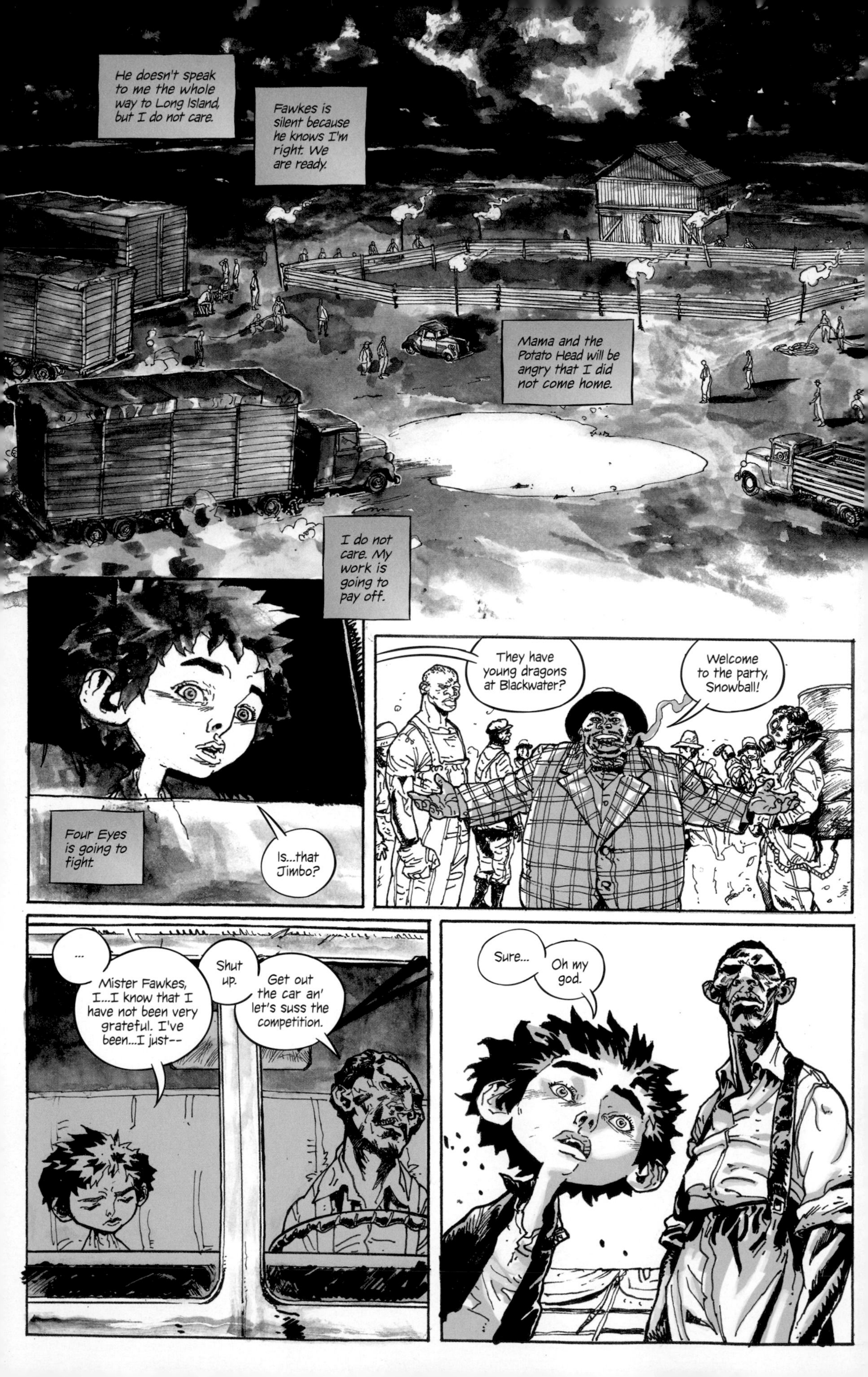

He doesn't speak to me the whole way to Long Island, but I do not care.
Fawkes is silent because he knows I'm right. We are ready.
Mama and the Potato Head will be angry that I did not come home.
I do not care. My work is going to pay off.
Four Eyes is going to fight.
Is...that Jimbo?
They have young dragons at Blackwater?
Welcome to the party, Snowball!
...
Mister Fawkes, I...I know that I have not been very grateful. I've been...I just--
Shut up.
Get out the car an' let's suss the competition.
Sure...
Oh my god.

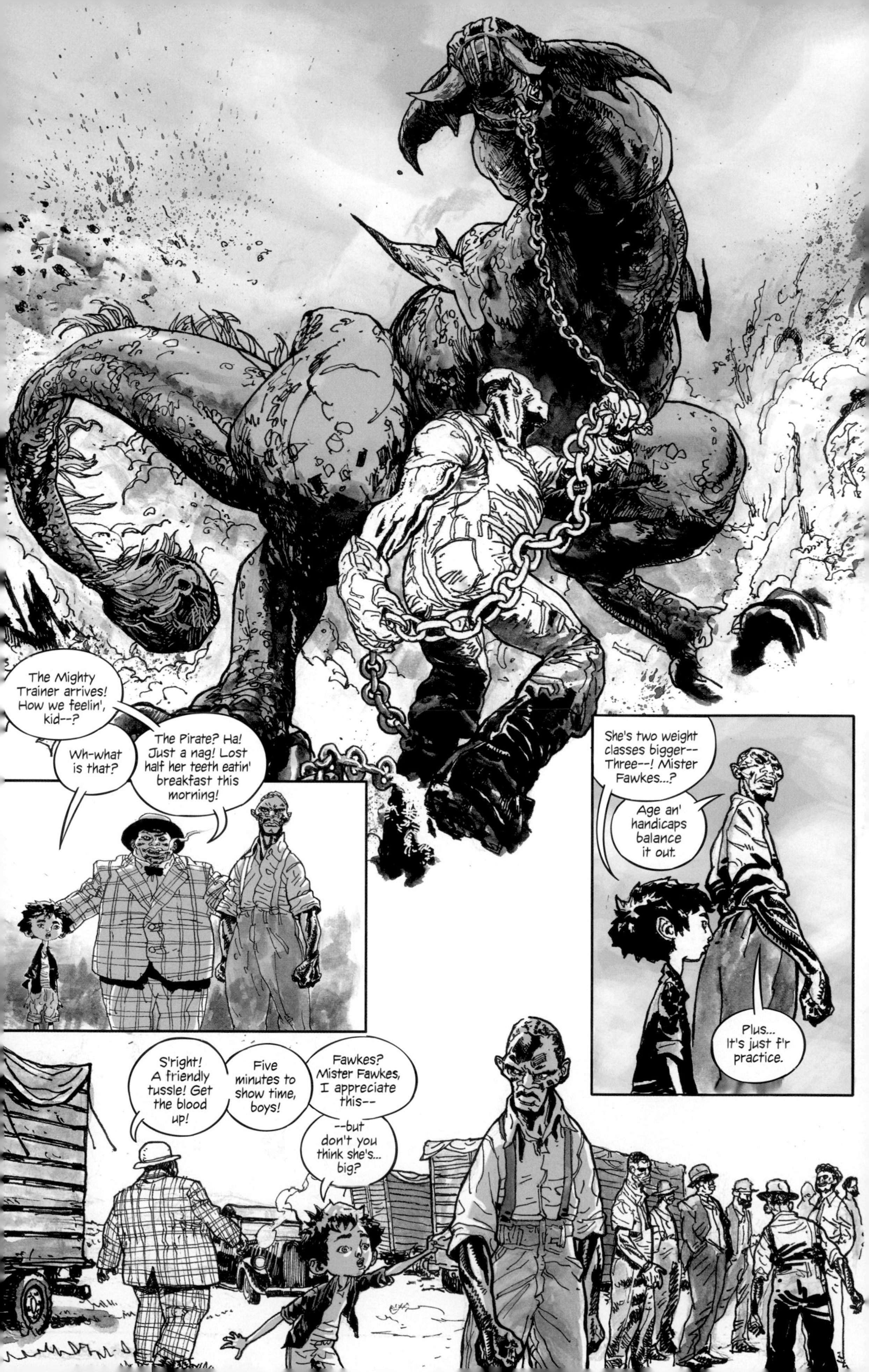
The Mighty Trainer arrives! How we feelin', kid--?
Wh-what is that?
The Pirate? Ha! Just a nag! Lost half her teeth eatin' breakfast this morning!
She's two weight classes bigger-- Three--! Mister Fawkes...?
Age an' handicaps balance it out.
Plus... It's just f'r practice.
S'right! A friendly tussle! Get the blood up!
Five minutes to show time, boys!
Fawkes? Mister Fawkes, I appreciate this--
--but don't you think she's... big?

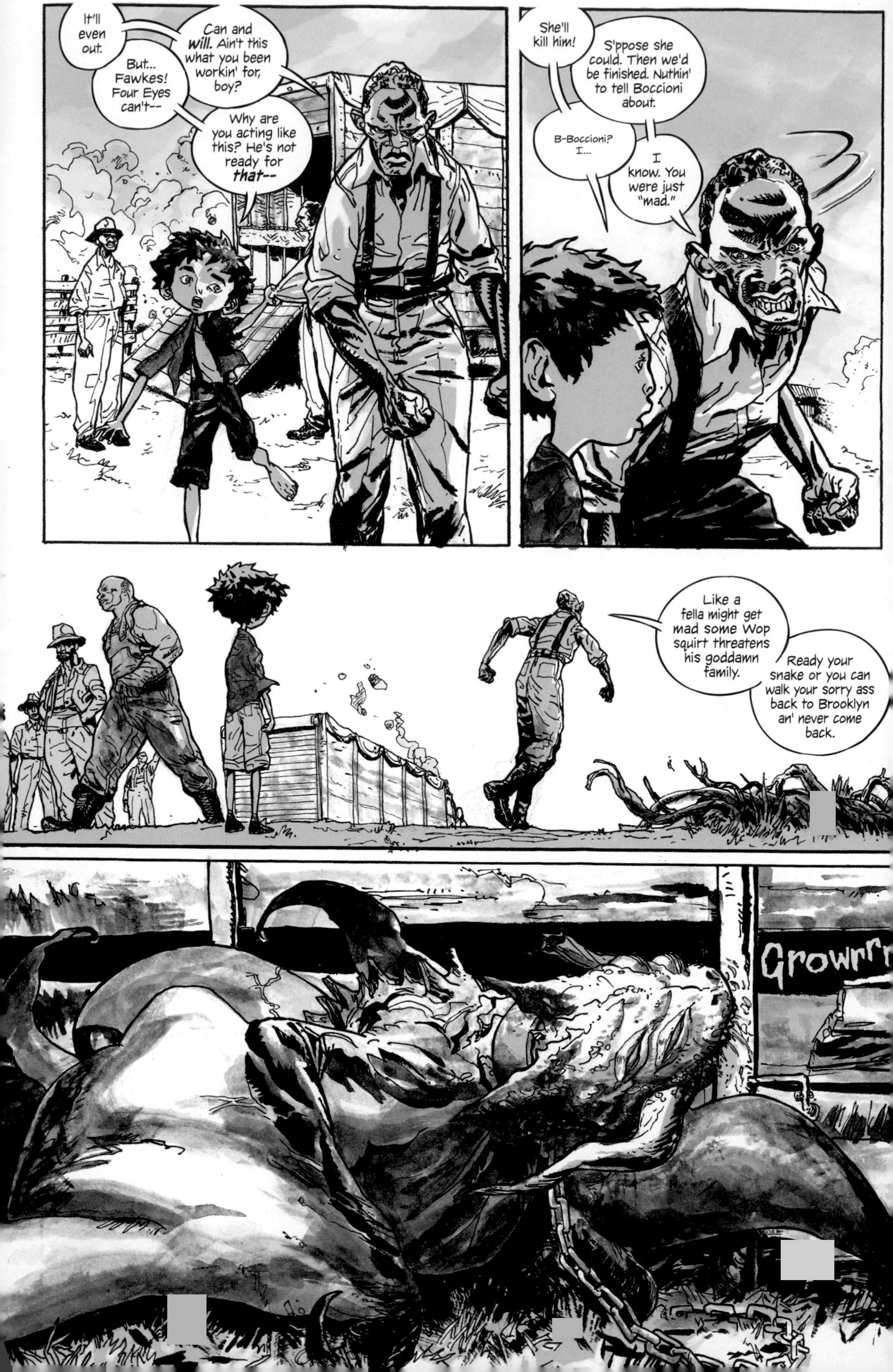
It'll even out.
But... Fawkes! Four Eyes can't--
Can and *will.* Ain't this what you been workin' for, boy?
Why are you acting like this? He's not ready for ***that--***
She'll kill him!
S'ppose she could. Then we'd be finished. Nuthin' to tell Boccioni about.
B-Boccioni? I...
I know. You were just "mad."
Like a fella might get mad some Wop squirt threatens his goddamn family.
Ready your snake or you can walk your sorry ass back to Brooklyn an' never come back.
Growrr

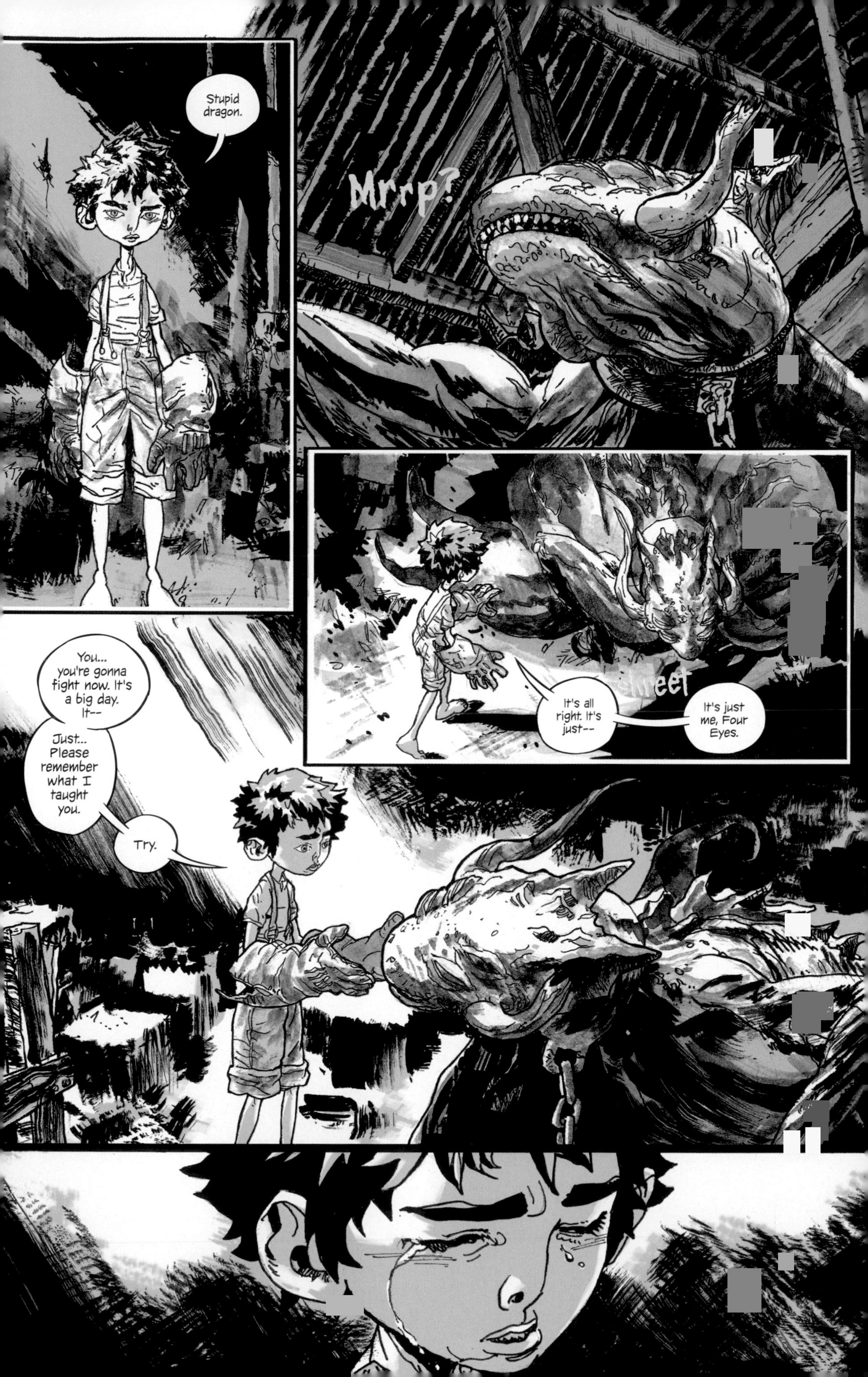
Stupid dragon.
Mrrp?
shreet
It's all right. It's just--
It's just me, Four Eyes.
You... you're gonna fight now. It's a big day. It--
Just... Please remember what I taught you.
Try.

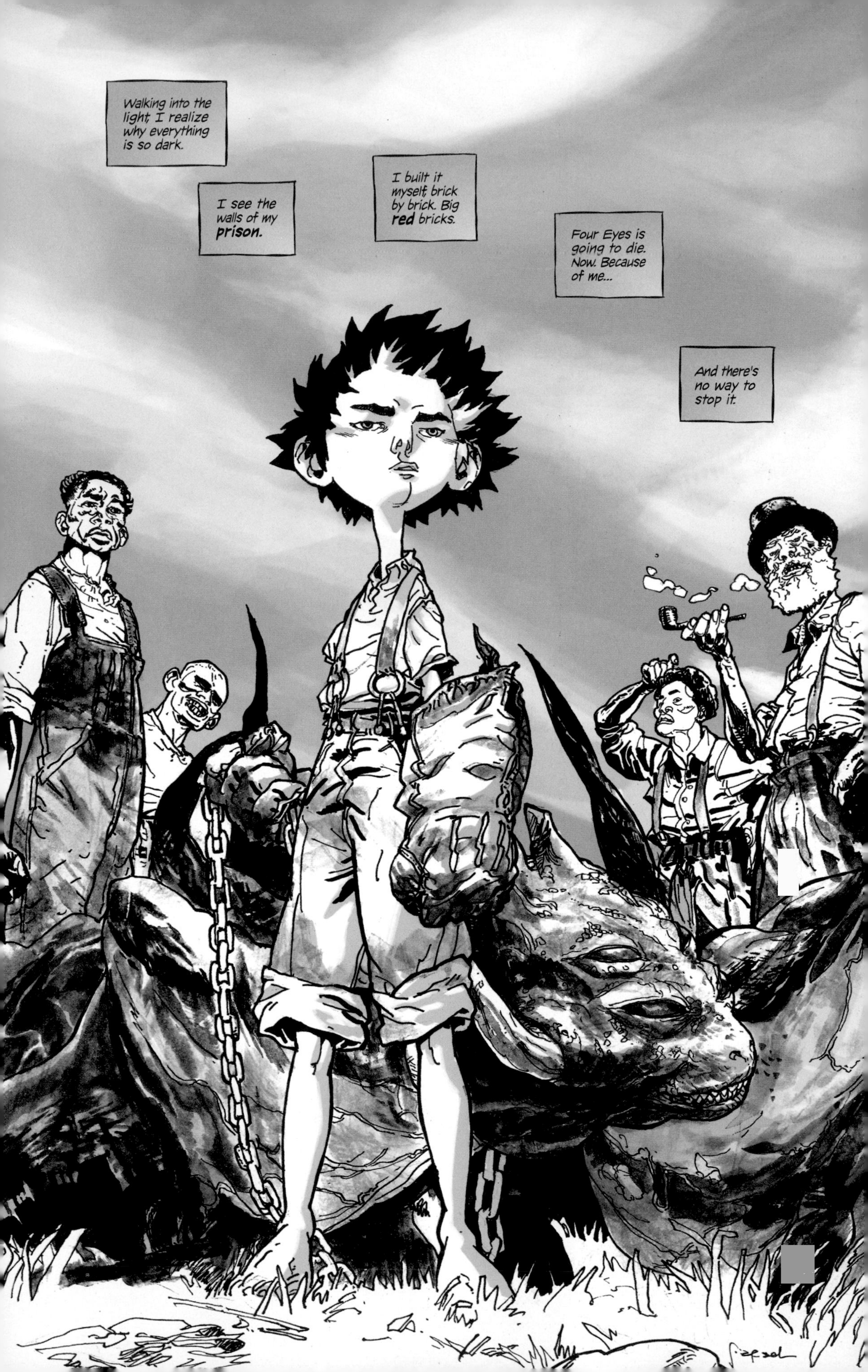
Walking into the light, I realize why everything is so dark.
I see the walls of my **prison.**
I built it myself, brick by brick. Big **red** bricks.
Four Eyes is going to die. Now. Because of me...
And there's no way to stop it.

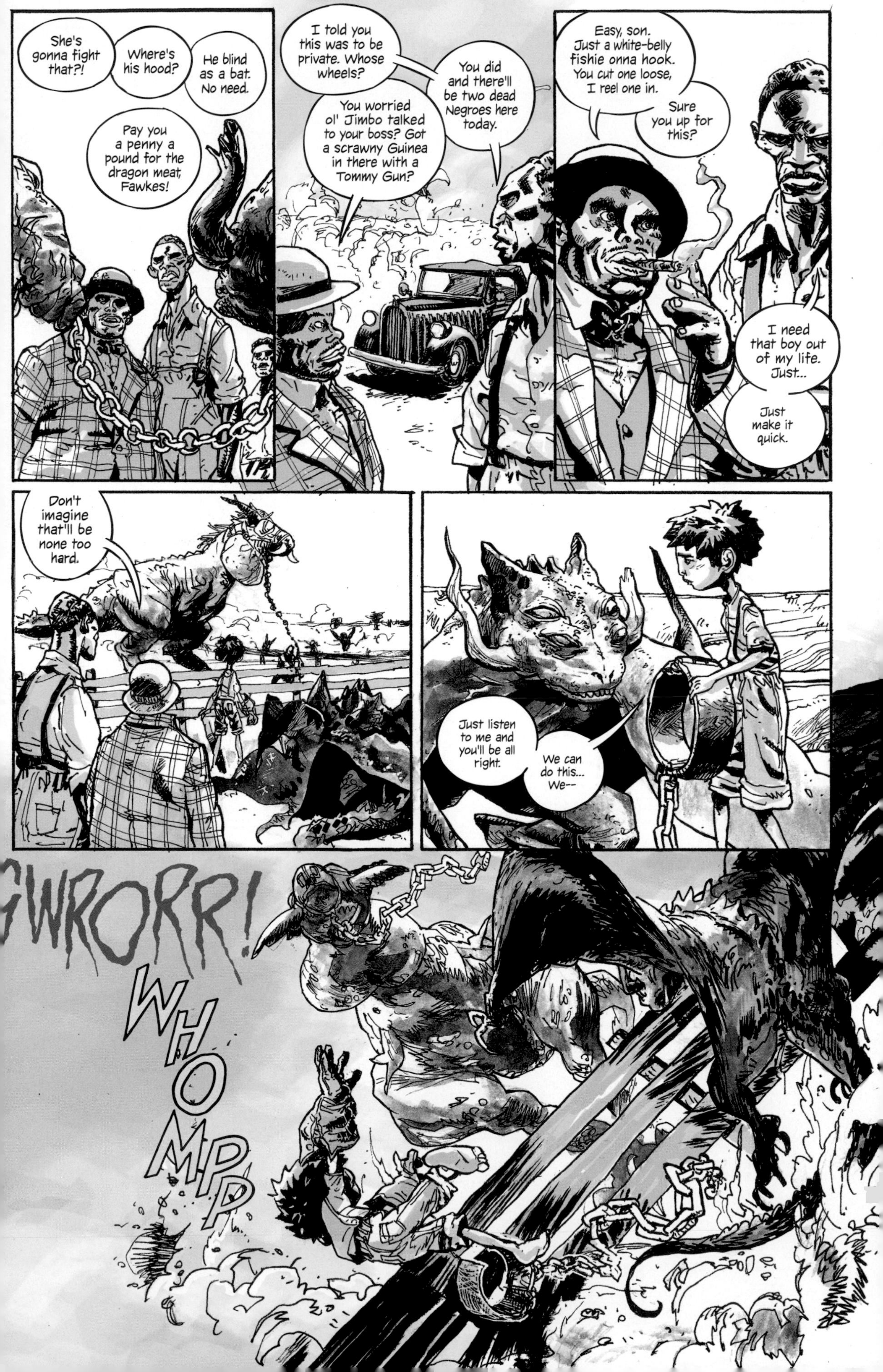

She's gonna fight that?!
Where's his hood?
He blind as a bat. No need.
Pay you a penny a pound for the dragon meat, Fawkes!
I told you this was to be private. Whose wheels?
You did and there'll be two dead Negroes here today.
You worried ol' Jimbo talked to your boss? Got a scrawny Guinea in there with a Tommy Gun?
Easy, son. Just a white-belly fishie onna hook. You cut one loose, I reel one in.
Sure you up for this?
I need that boy out of my life. Just...
Just make it quick.
Don't imagine that'll be none too hard.
Just listen to me and you'll be all right.
We can do this... We--
GWRORR!
WHOMPP

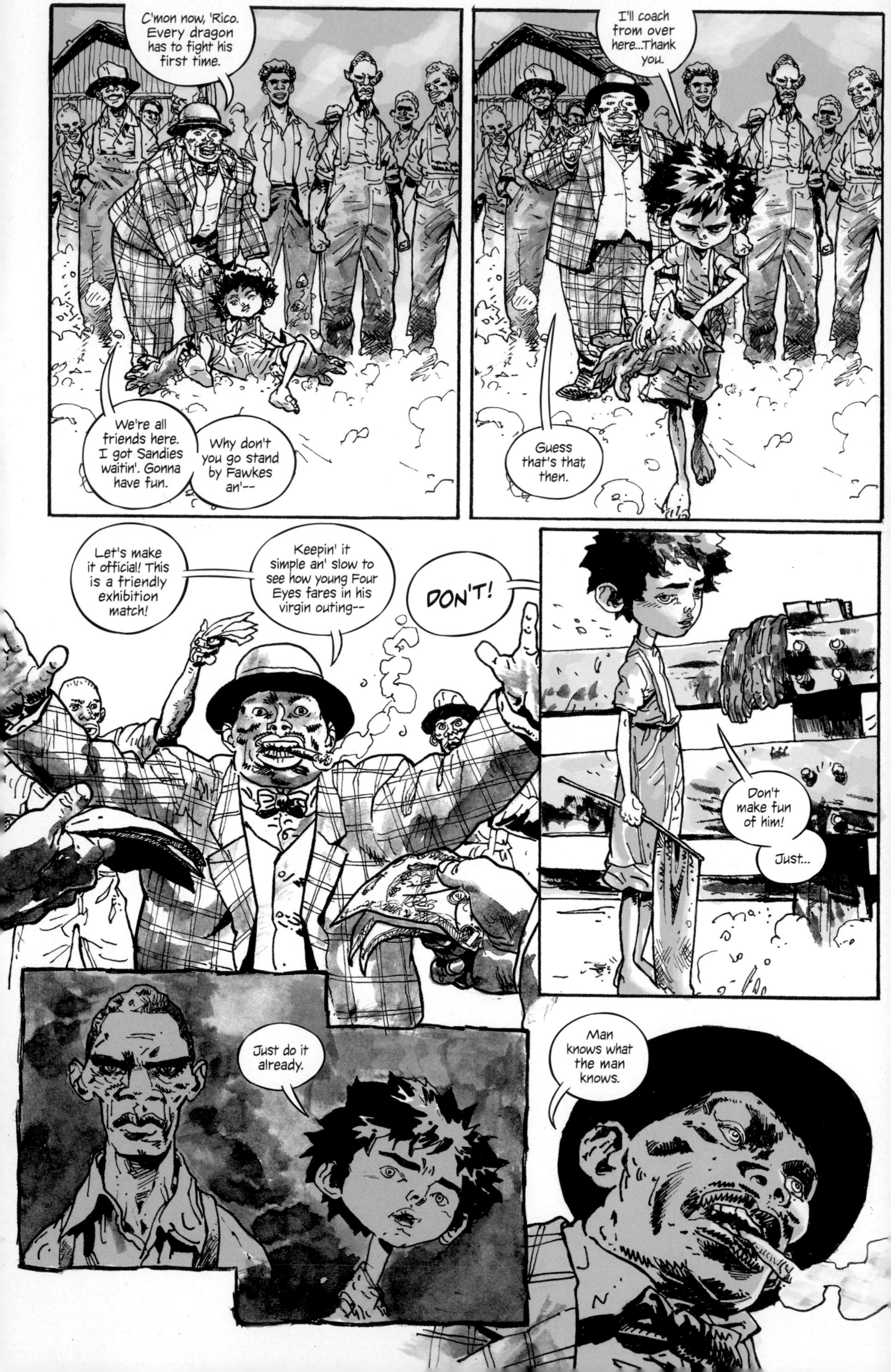
C'mon now, 'Rico. Every dragon has to fight his first time.
We're all friends here. I got Sandies waitin'. Gonna have fun.
Why don't you go stand by Fawkes an'--
I'll coach from over here...Thank you.
Guess that's that, then.
Let's make it official! This is a friendly exhibition match!
Keepin' it simple an' slow to see how young Four Eyes fares in his virgin outing--
DON'T!
Don't make fun of him!
Just...
Just do it already.
Man knows what the man knows.

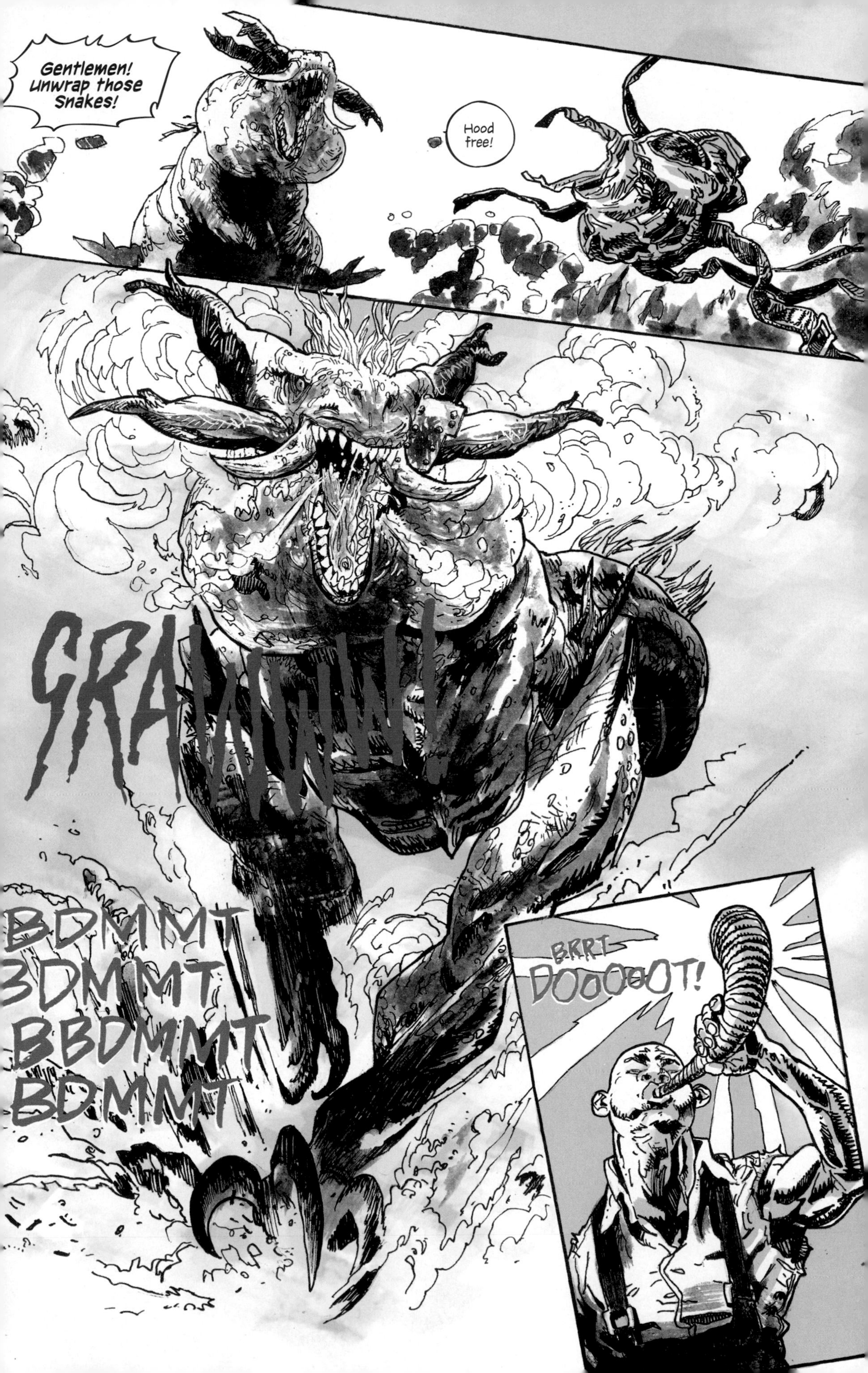
Gentlemen! Unwrap those Snakes!
Hood free!
GRAWWWW!
BDMMT
BDMMT
BBDMMT
BDMMT
BRRT
DOOOOOOT!

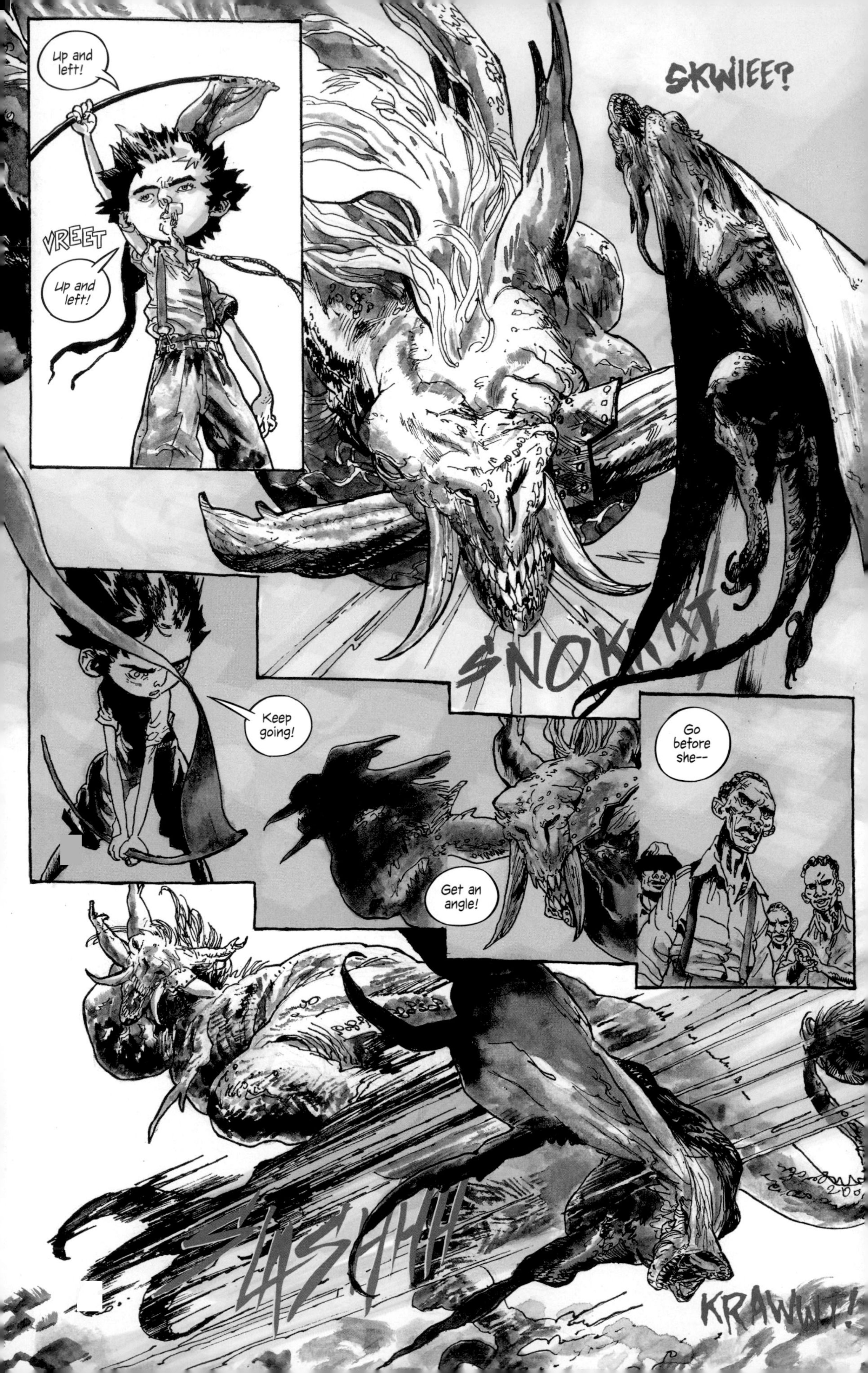
Up and left!
VREET
Up and left!
SKWIEE?
SNOKKKT
Keep going!
Go before she--
Get an angle!
SLASHHH
KRAWWT!

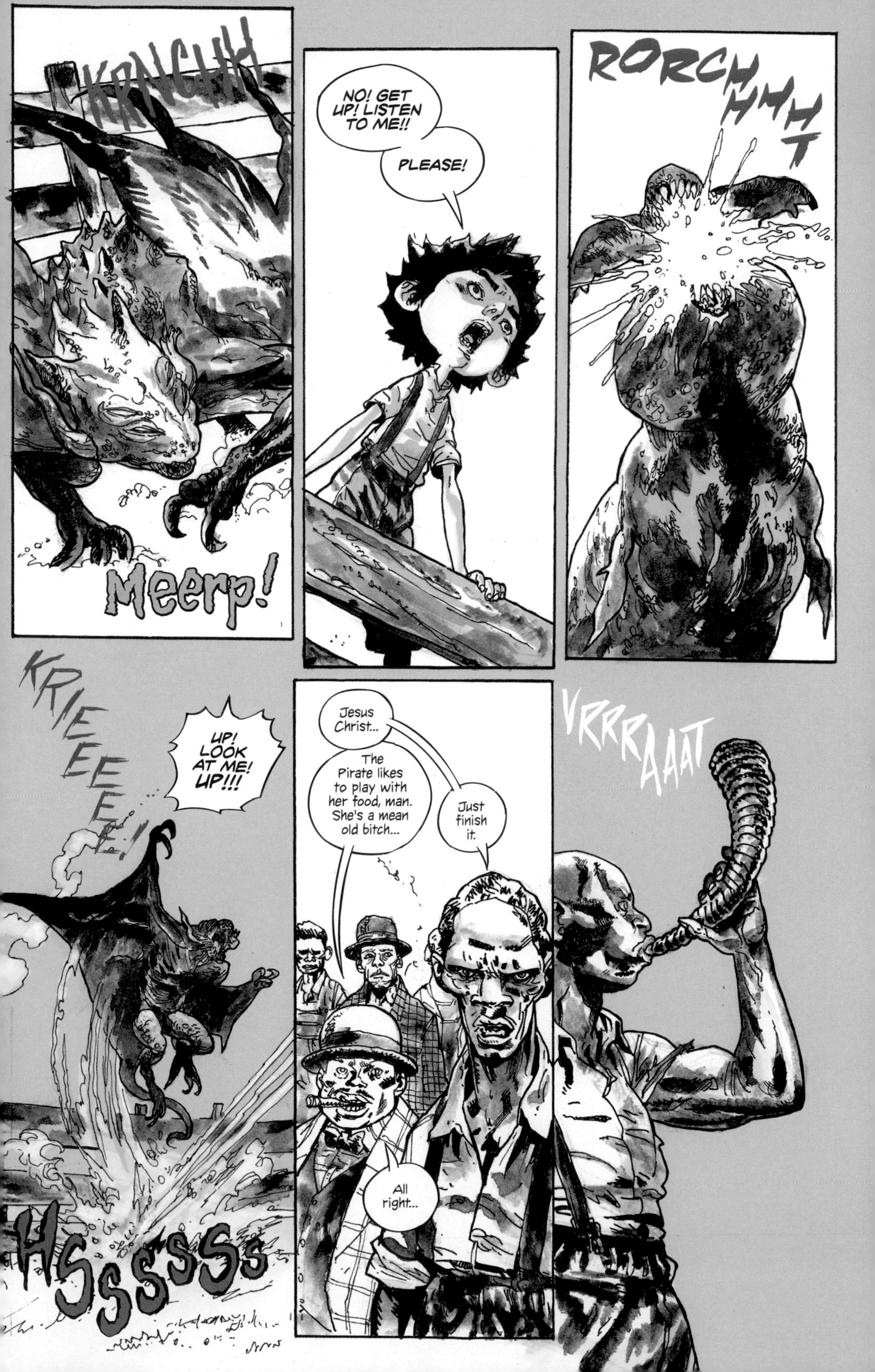
KRNCHH
Meerp!
NO! GET UP! LISTEN TO ME!!
PLEASE!
RORCHHMHT
KRIEEEEEE!
UP! LOOK AT ME! UP!!!
HSSSSSSS
Jesus Christ...
The Pirate likes to play with her food, man. She's a mean old bitch...
Just finish it.
All right...
VRRRAAAT

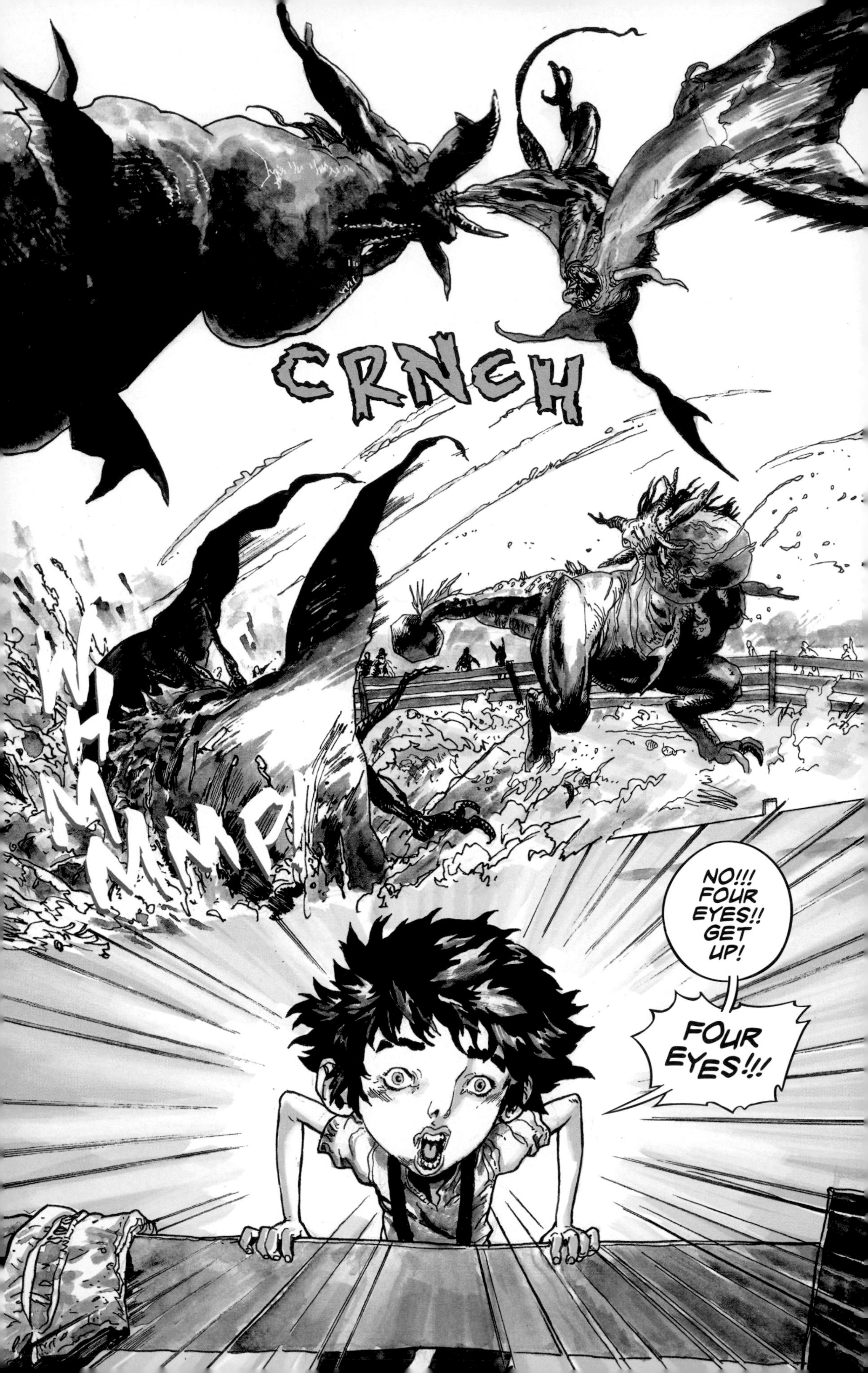
CRNCH
WHMMMP!
NO!!! FOUR EYES!! GET UP!
FOUR EYES!!!

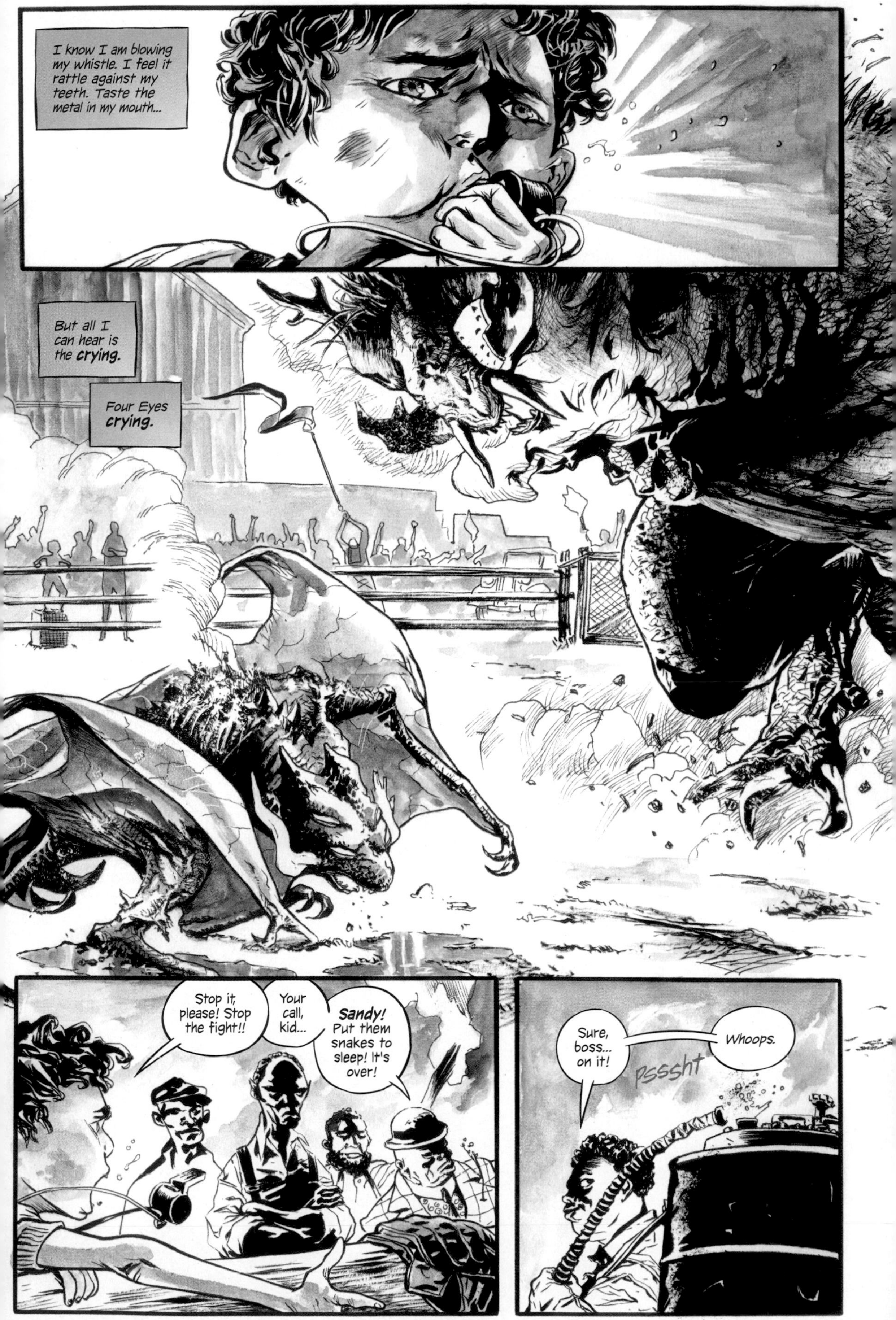
I know I am blowing my whistle. I feel it rattle against my teeth. Taste the metal in my mouth...
But all I can hear is the **crying.**
Four Eyes **crying.**
Stop it, please! Stop the fight!!
Your call, kid...
Sandy! Put them snakes to sleep! It's over!
Sure, boss... on it!
PSSSHT
Whoops.

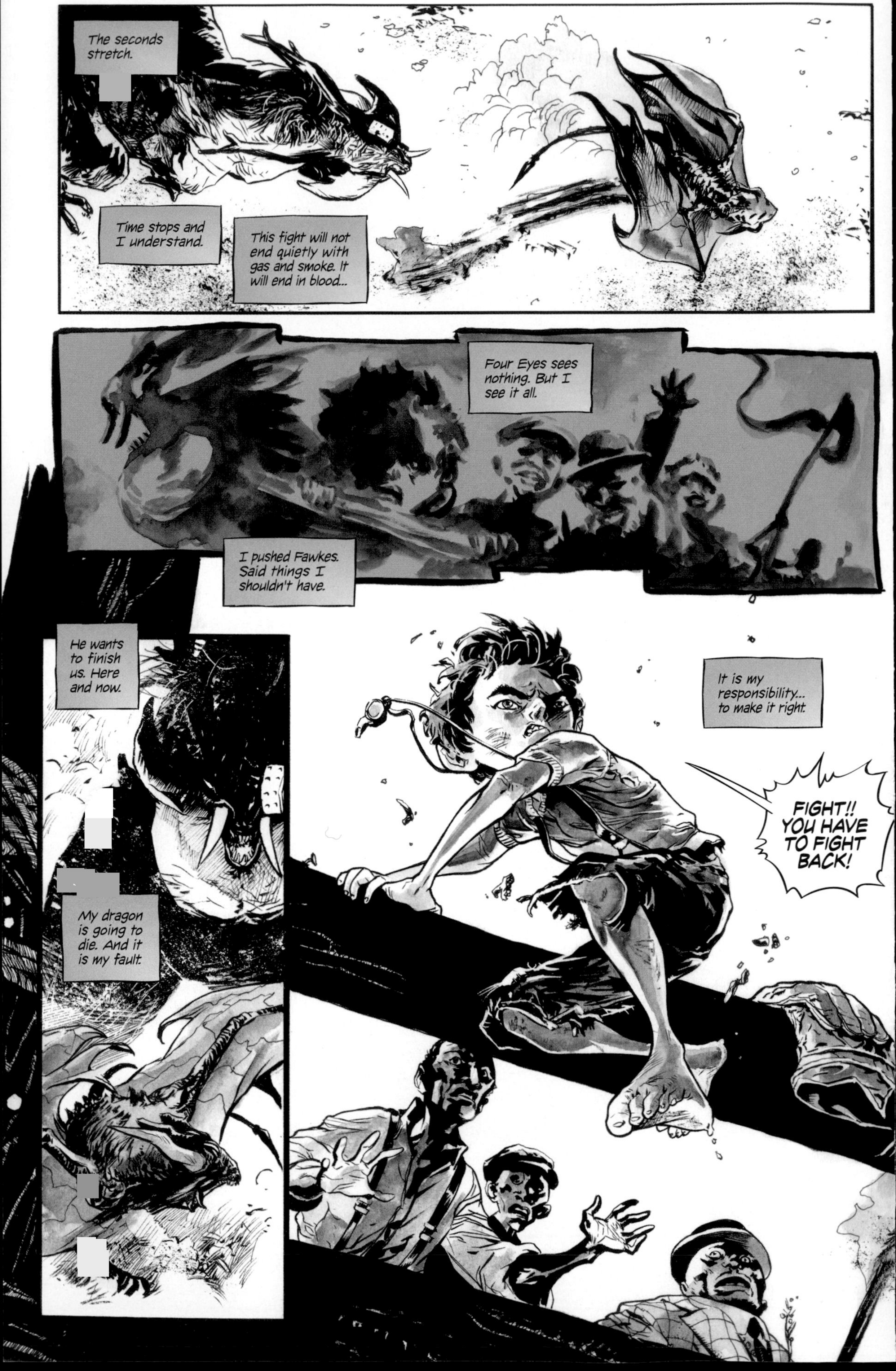
The seconds stretch.
Time stops and I understand.
This fight will not end quietly with gas and smoke. It will end in blood...
Four Eyes sees nothing. But I see it all.
I pushed Fawkes. Said things I shouldn't have.
He wants to finish us. Here and now.
My dragon is going to die. And it is my fault.
It is my responsibility... to make it right.
FIGHT!! YOU HAVE TO FIGHT BACK!

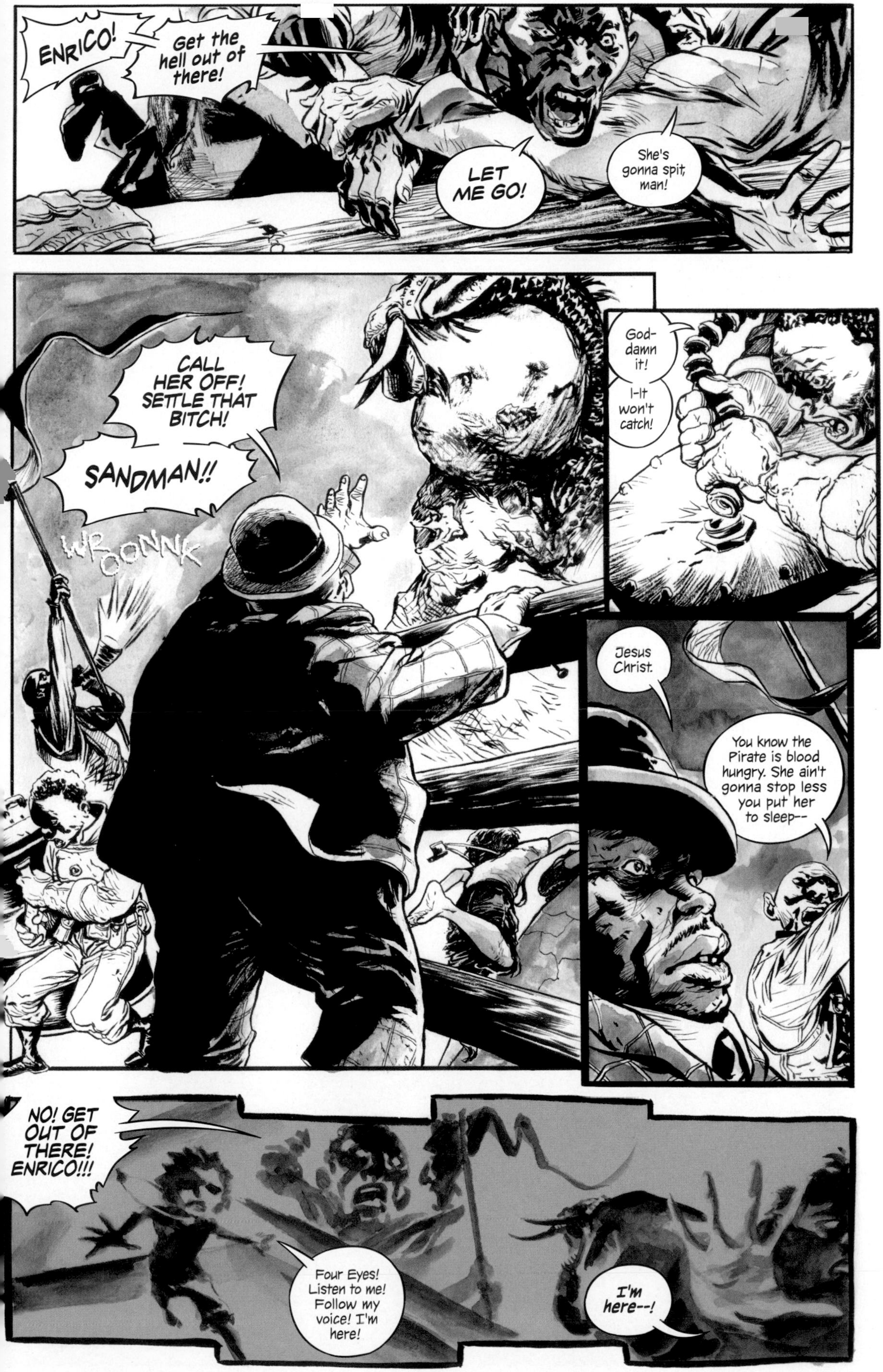
ENRICO!
Get the hell out of there!
LET ME GO!
She's gonna spit, man!
CALL HER OFF! SETTLE THAT BITCH!
SANDMAN!!
WROONNK
God-damn it!
I-It won't catch!
Jesus Christ.
You know the Pirate is blood hungry. She ain't gonna stop less you put her to sleep--
NO! GET OUT OF THERE! ENRICO!!!
Four Eyes! Listen to me! Follow my voice! I'm here!
I'm here--!

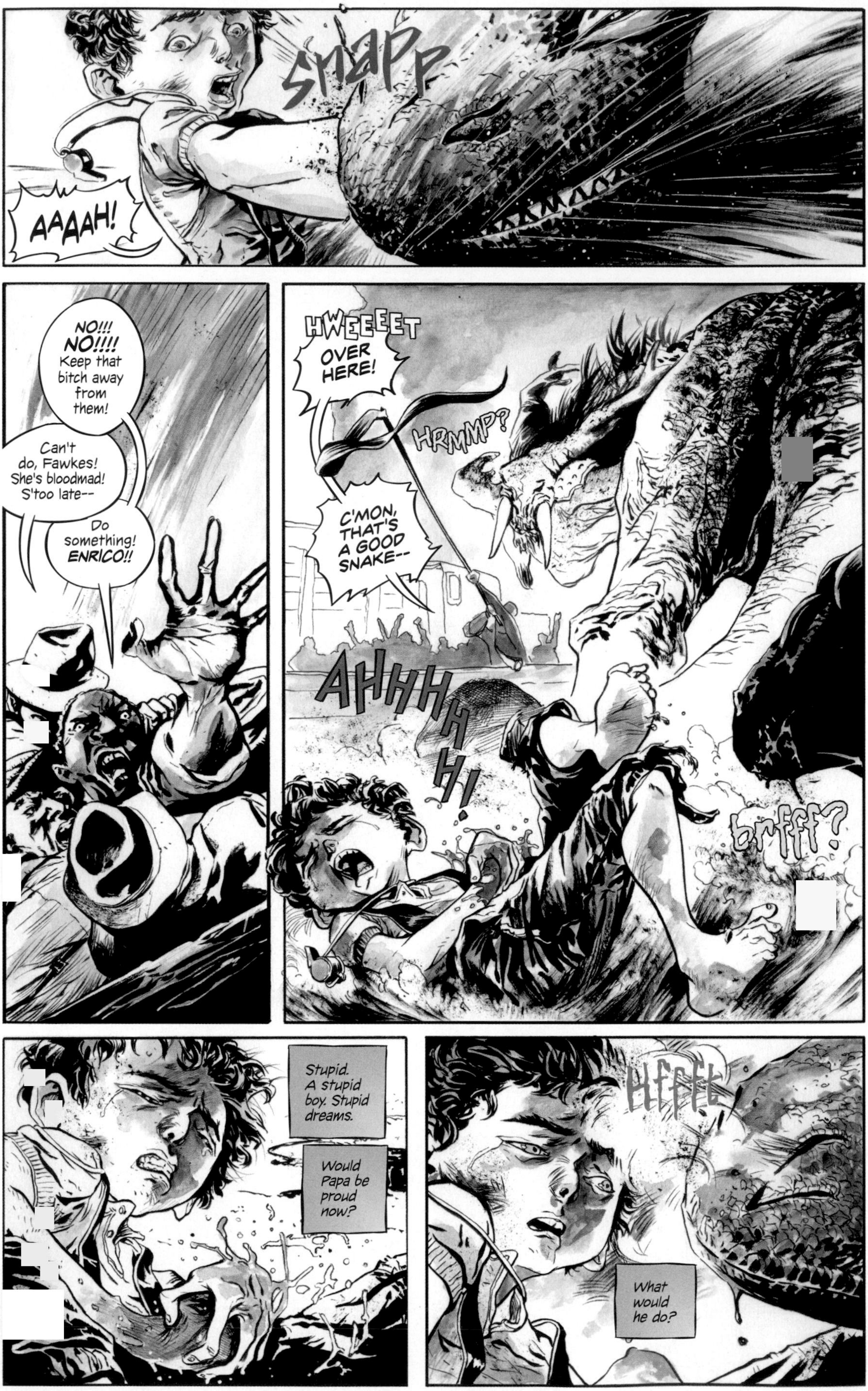

SNAPP
AAAAH!
NO!!! NO!!!! Keep that bitch away from them!
Can't do, Fawkes! She's bloodmad! S'too late--
Do something! ENRICO!!
HWEEEEET
OVER HERE!
HRMMP?
C'MON, THAT'S A GOOD SNAKE--
AHHHHHH!
brfff?
Stupid. A stupid boy. Stupid dreams.
Would Papa be proud now?
HFFFT
What would he do?

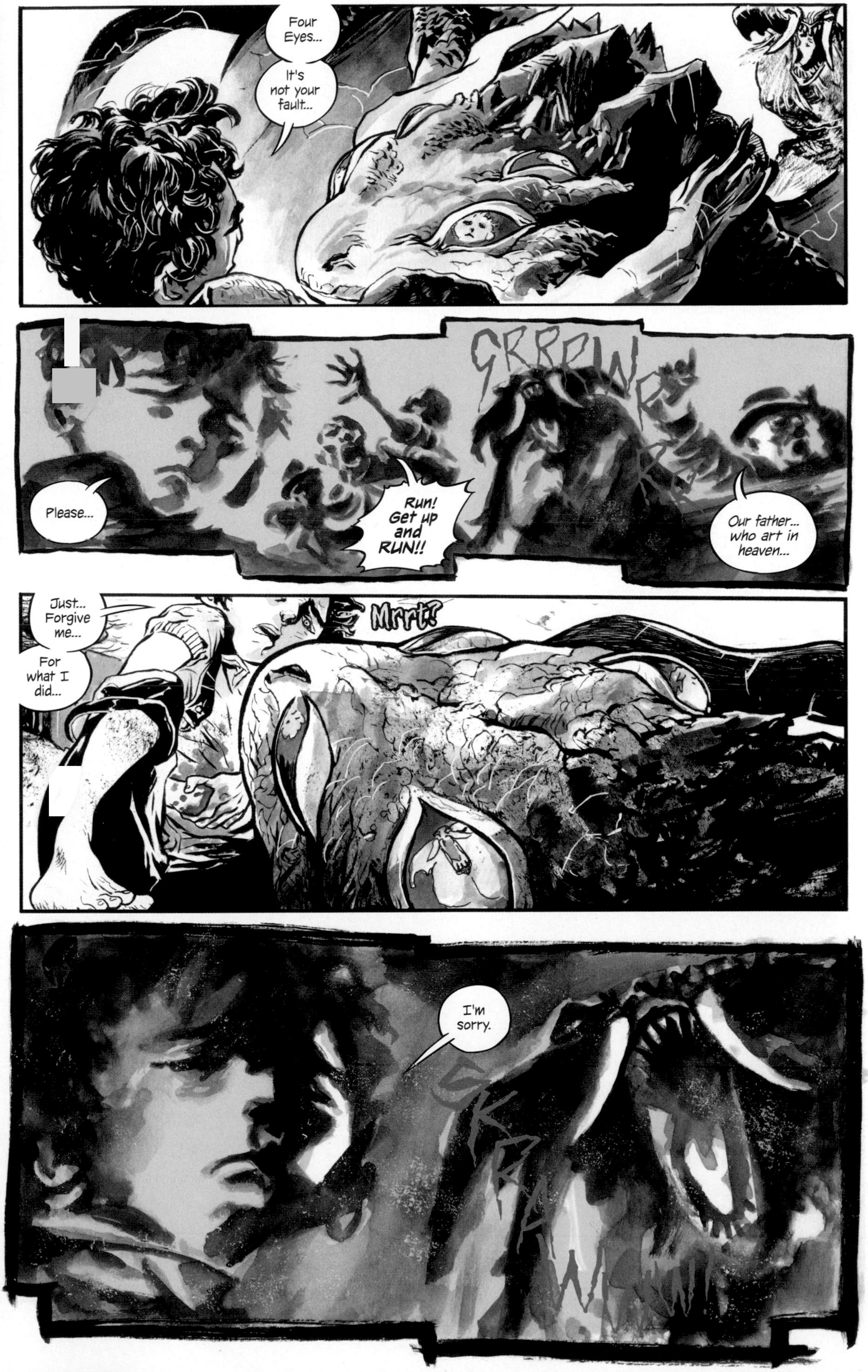
Four Eyes...
It's not your fault...
GRRRWR
Please...
Run! Get up and RUN!!
Our father... who art in heaven...
Just... Forgive me...
For what I did...
Mrrt?
I'm sorry.
SKRAW

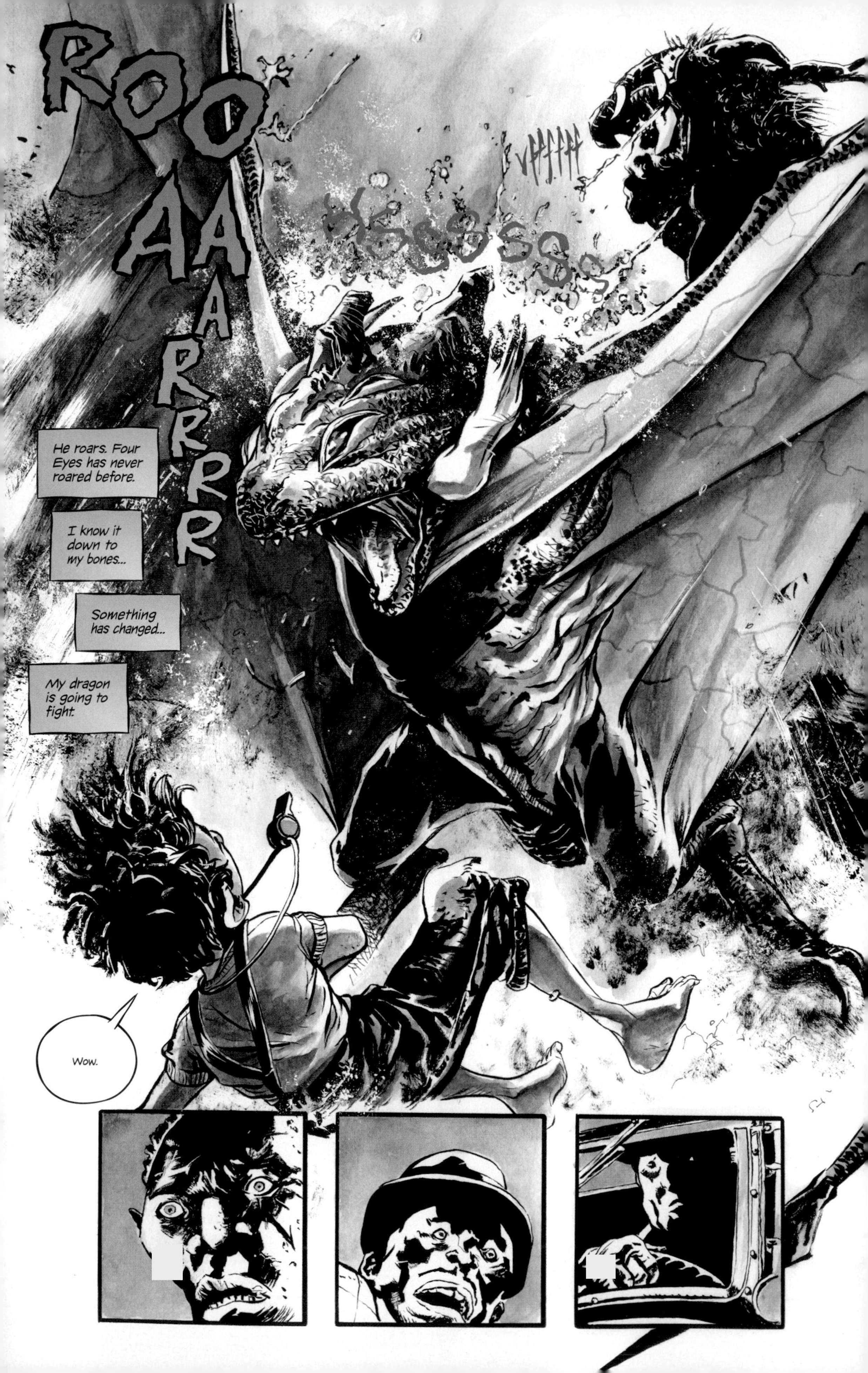
ROOAAARRRR
VFFFFF
HSSSSSS
He roars. Four Eyes has never roared before.
I know it down to my bones...
Something has changed...
My dragon is going to fight.
Wow.

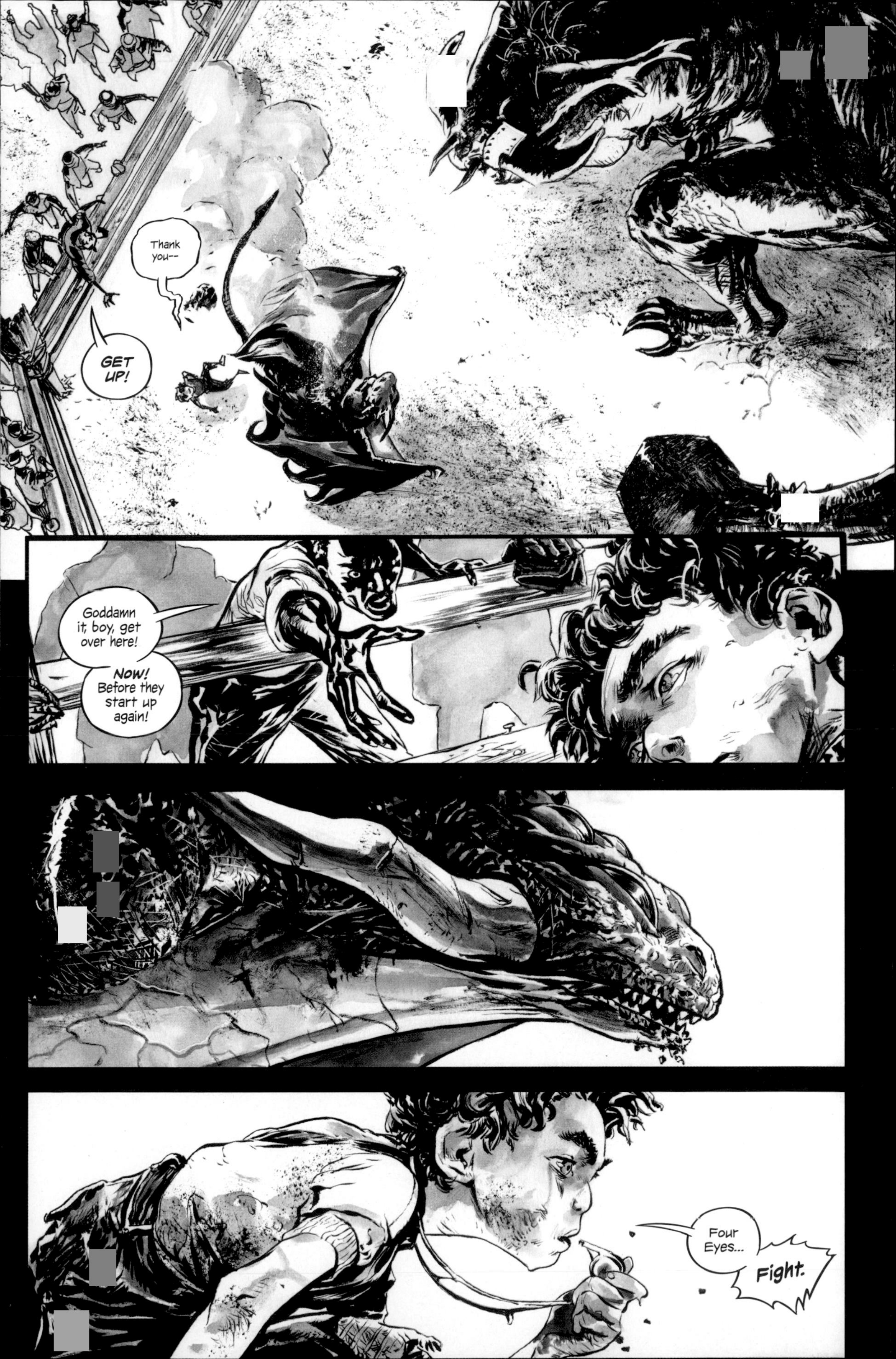
Thank you--
GET UP!
Goddamn it, boy, get over here!
NOW! Before they start up again!
Four Eyes...
Fight.

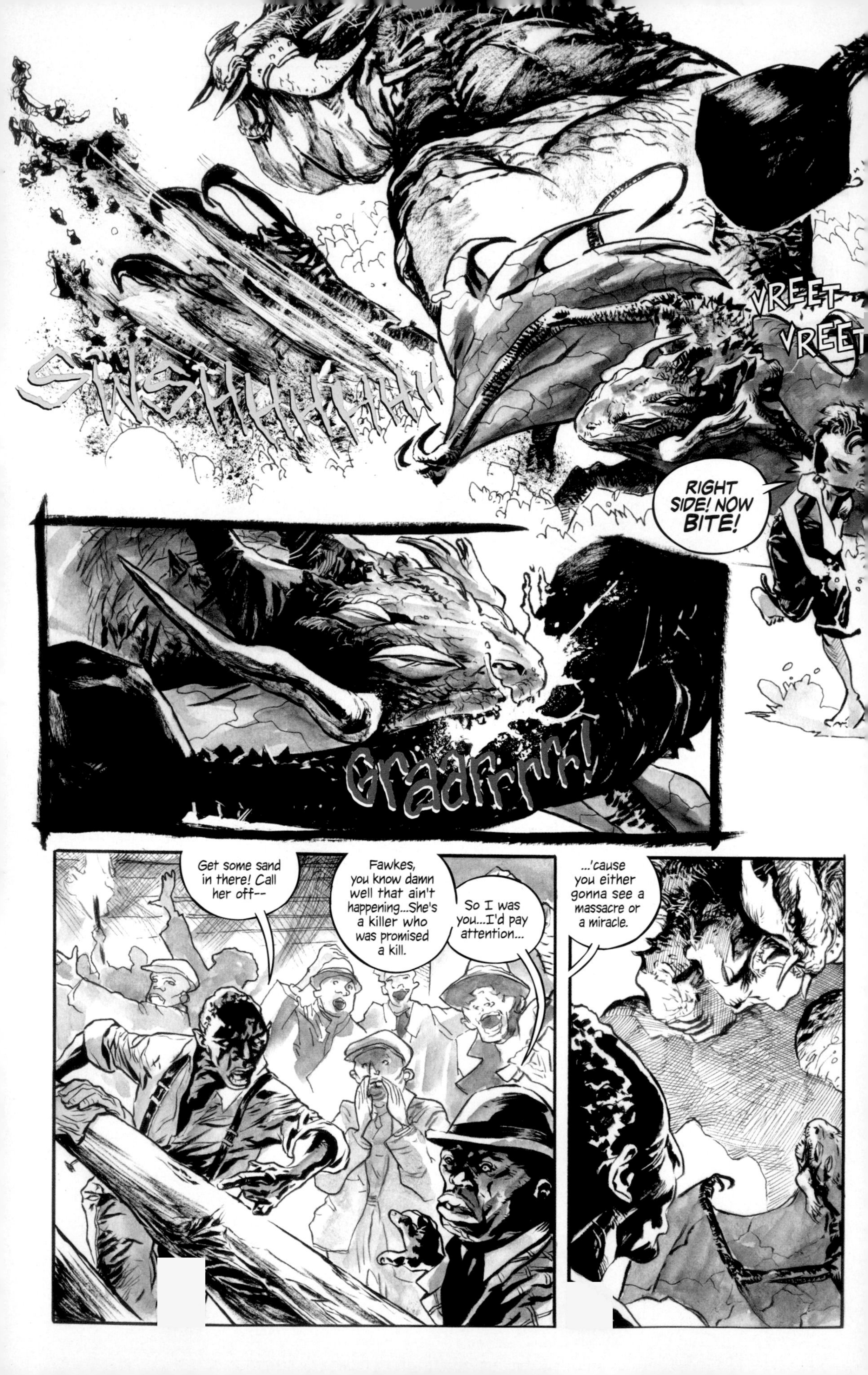
VREET VREET
SWSHHHHHH
RIGHT SIDE! NOW BITE!
Graarrrrr!
Get some sand in there! Call her off--
Fawkes, you know damn well that ain't happening...She's a killer who was promised a kill.
So I was you...I'd pay attention...
...'cause you either gonna see a massacre or a miracle.

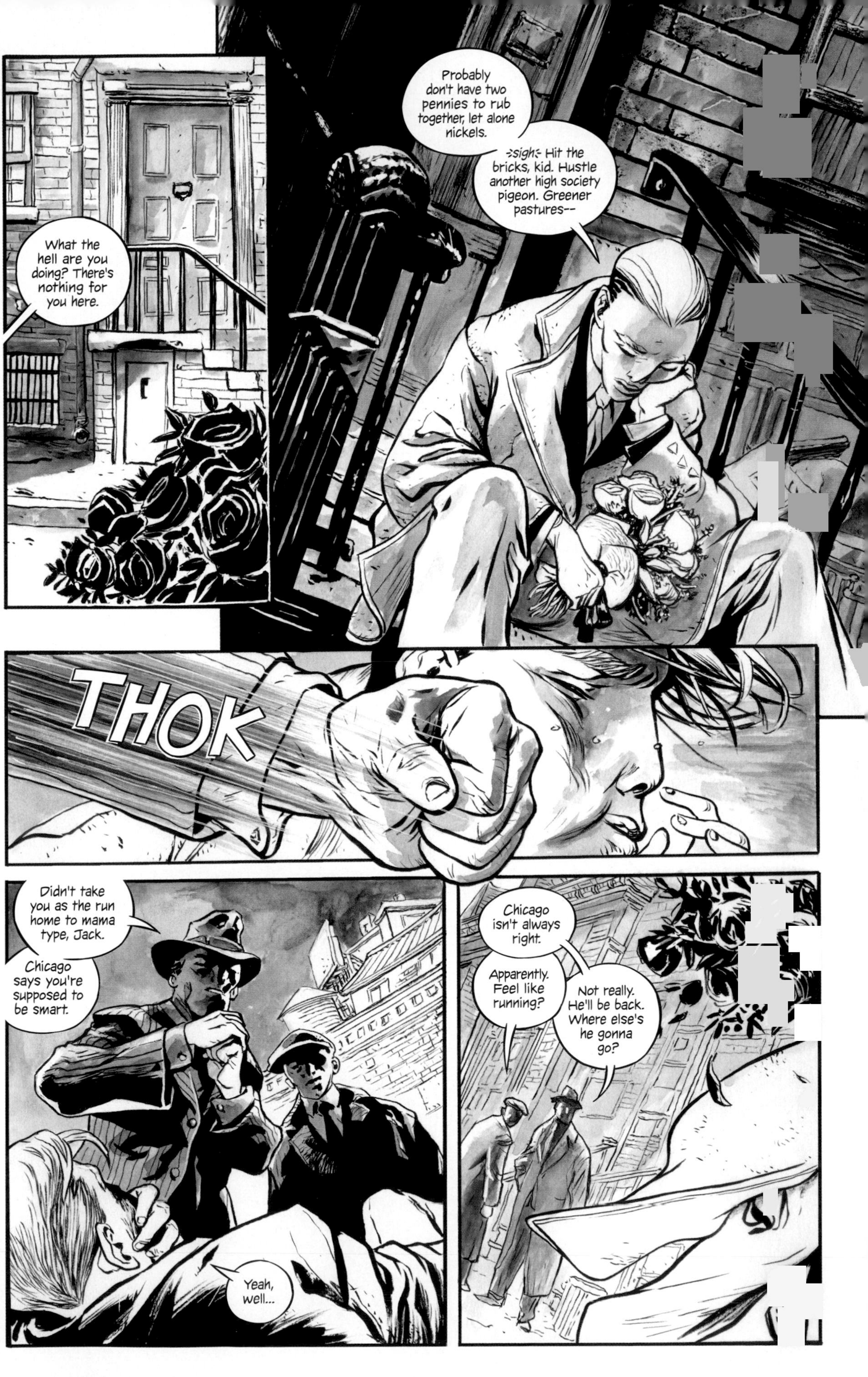
What the hell are you doing? There's nothing for you here.
Probably don't have two pennies to rub together, let alone nickels.
sigh Hit the bricks, kid. Hustle another high society pigeon. Greener pastures--
THOK
Didn't take you as the run home to mama type, Jack.
Chicago says you're supposed to be smart.
Yeah, well...
Chicago isn't always right.
Apparently. Feel like running?
Not really. He'll be back. Where else's he gonna go?

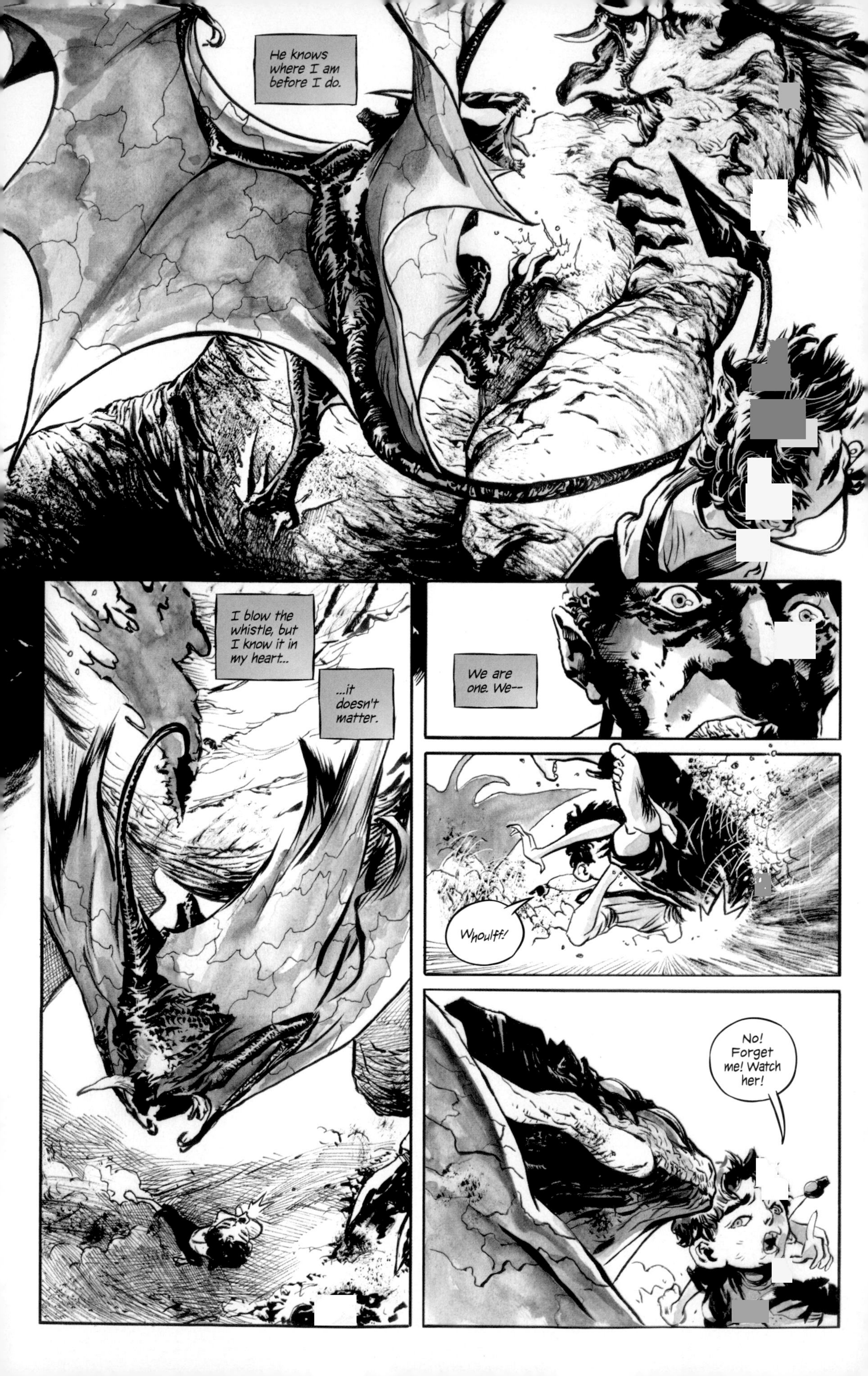
He knows where I am before I do.
I blow the whistle, but I know it in my heart...
...it doesn't matter.
We are one. We--
Whoulff!
No! Forget me! Watch her!

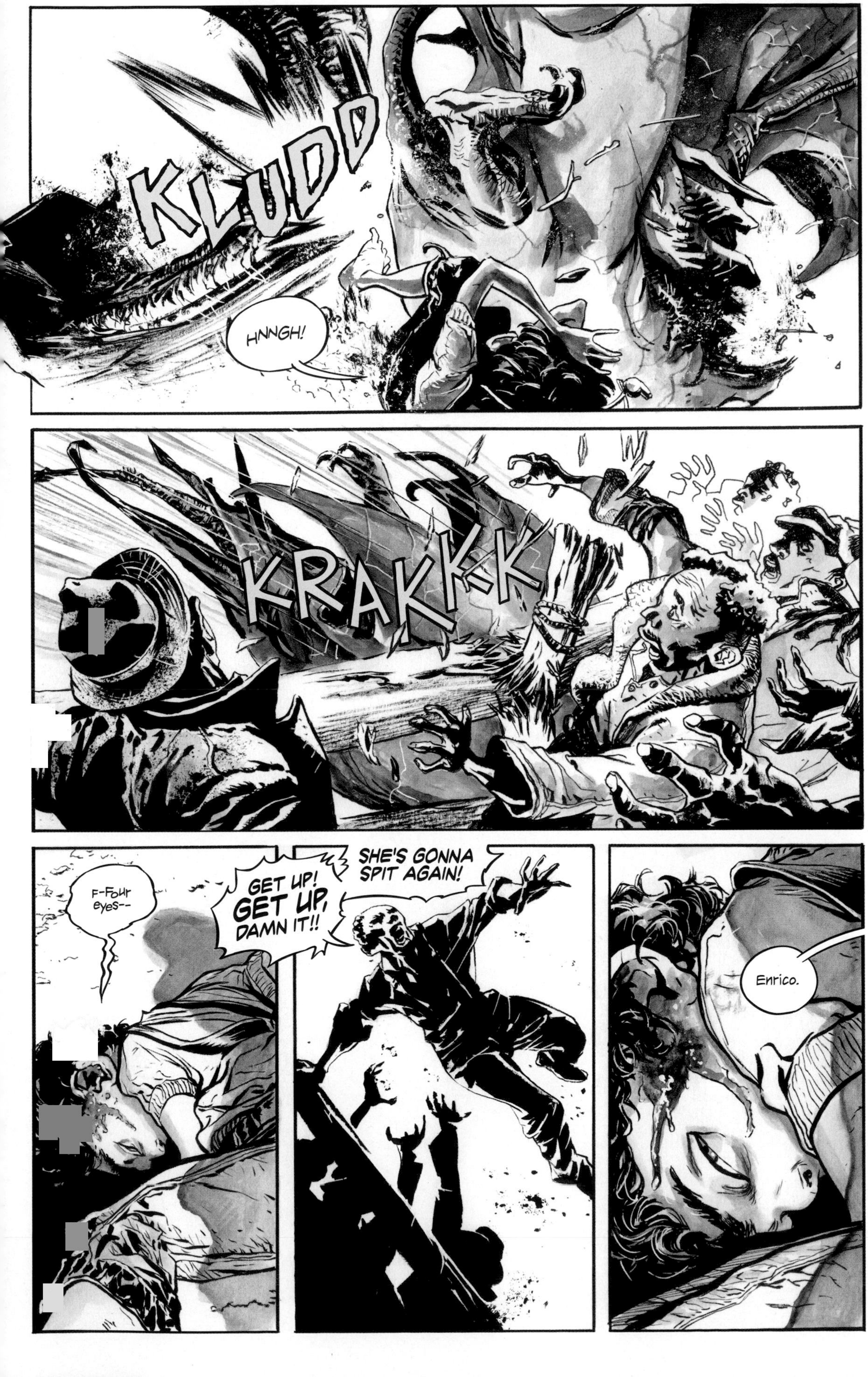
KLUDD
HNNGH!
KRAKK-K
F-Four eyes--
SHE'S GONNA SPIT AGAIN!
GET UP! GET UP, DAMN IT!!
Enrico.

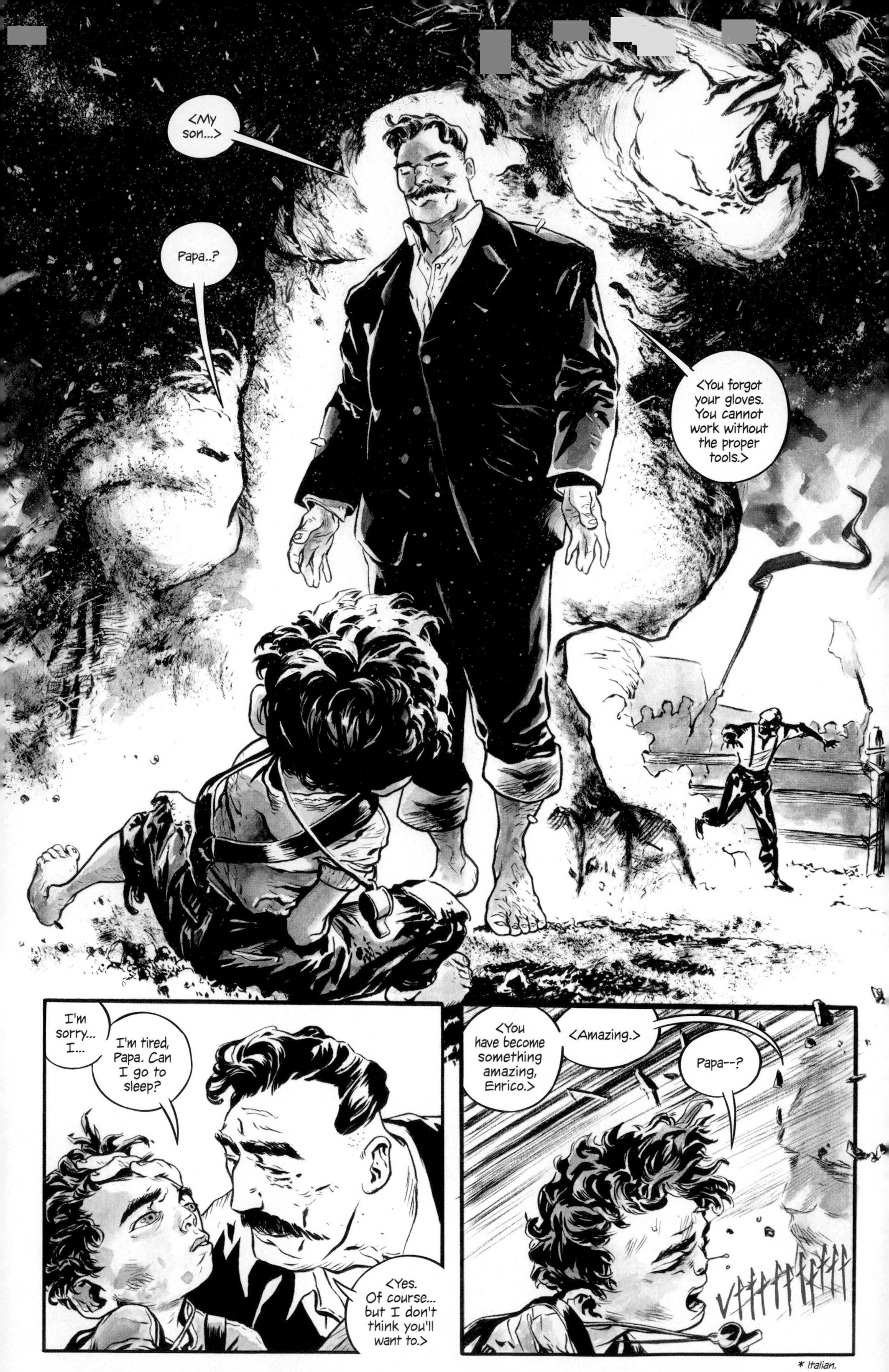
<My son...>
Papa..?
<You forgot your gloves. You cannot work without the proper tools.>
I'm sorry... I...
I'm tired, Papa. Can I go to sleep?
<Yes. Of course... but I don't think you'll want to.>
<You have become something amazing, Enrico.>
<Amazing.>
Papa--?

* Italian.

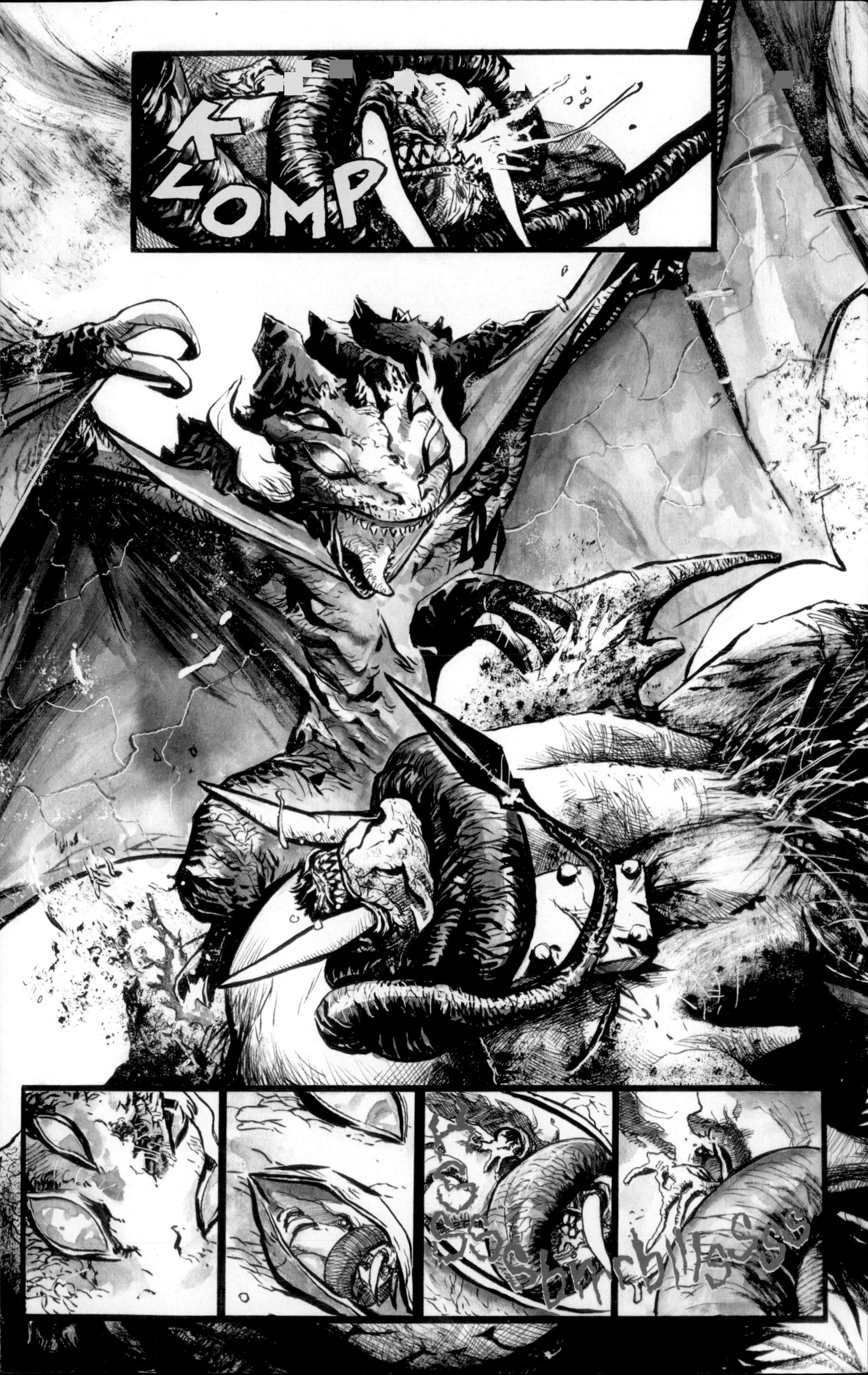
KLOMP

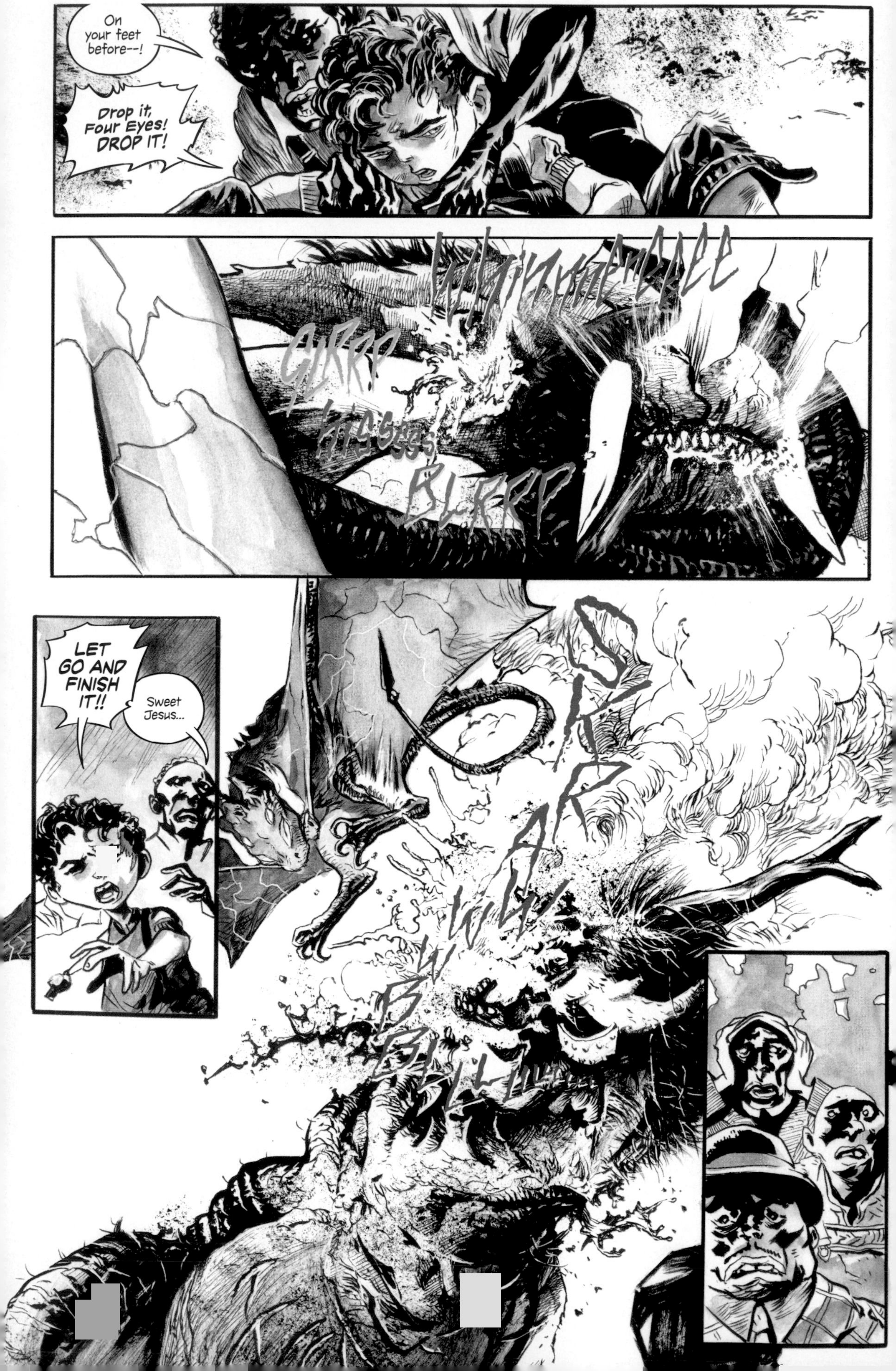
On your feet before--!
Drop it, Four Eyes! DROP IT!
Whiiyyuuueeeee
GLRRP
hissss
BLRRP
LET GO AND FINISH IT!!
Sweet Jesus...
SKRAAW

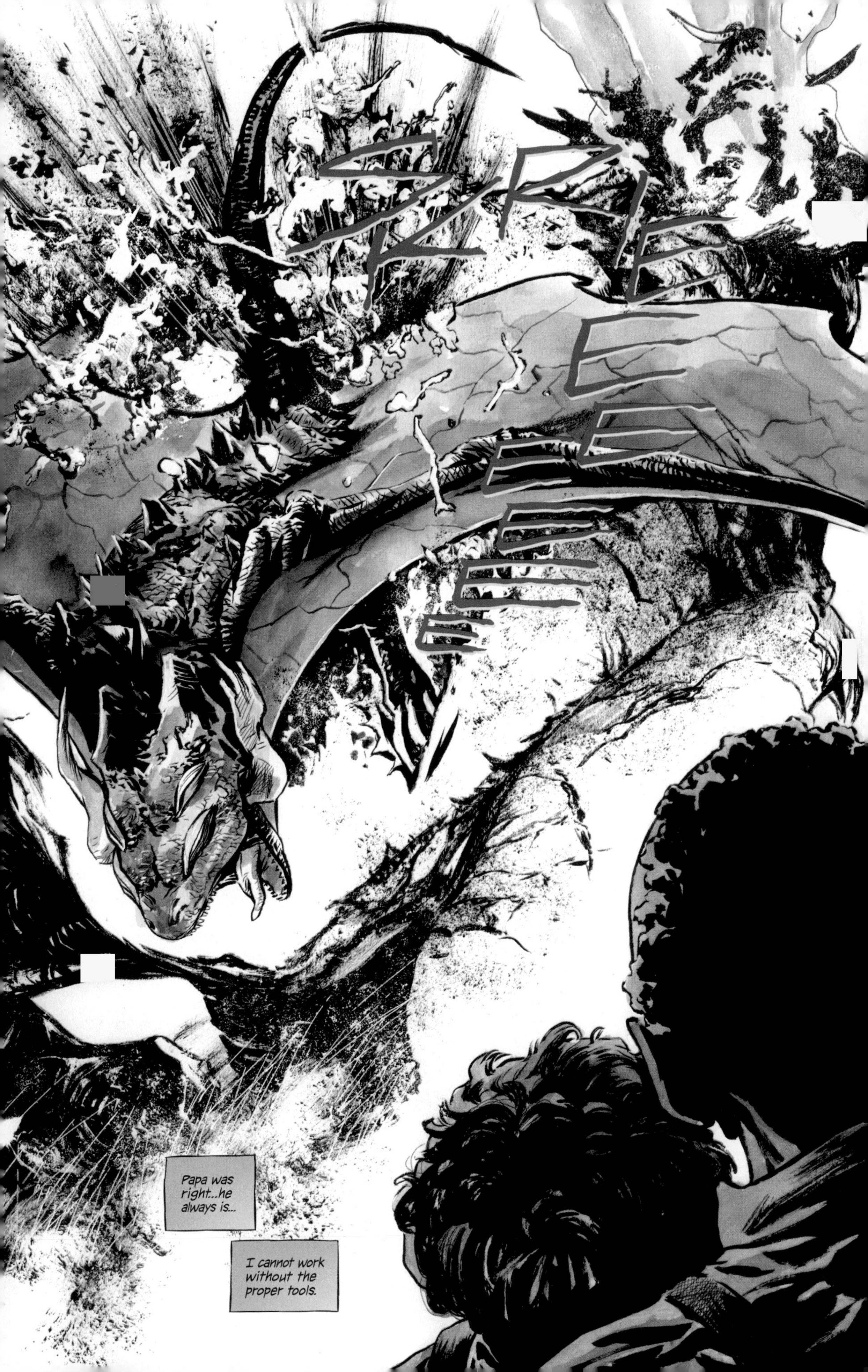
SKREEEEEEEEE
Papa was right...he always is...
I cannot work without the proper tools.

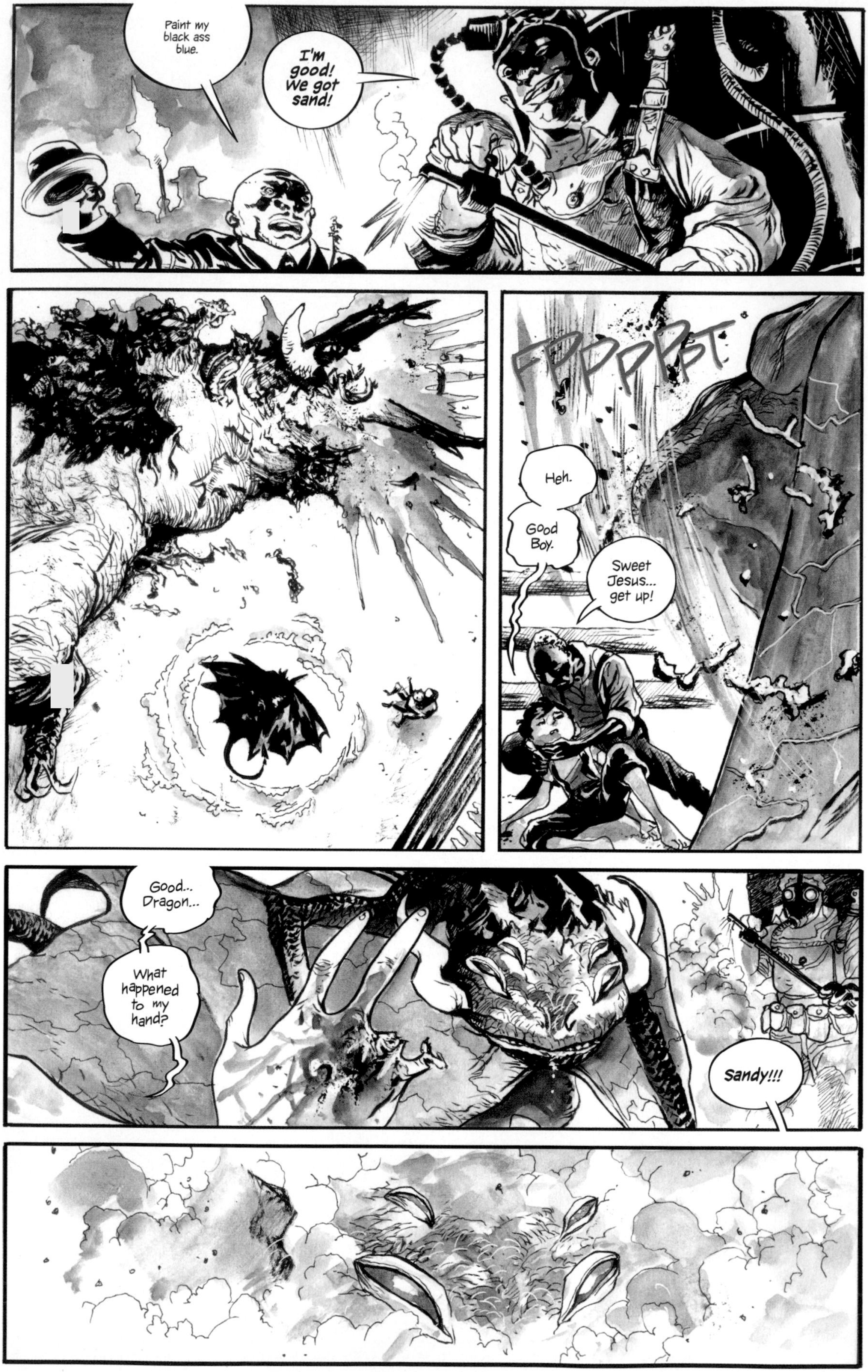
Paint my black ass blue.
I'm good! We got sand!
FPPPPPT
Heh.
Good Boy.
Sweet Jesus... get up!
Good.. Dragon...
What happened to my hand?
Sandy!!!

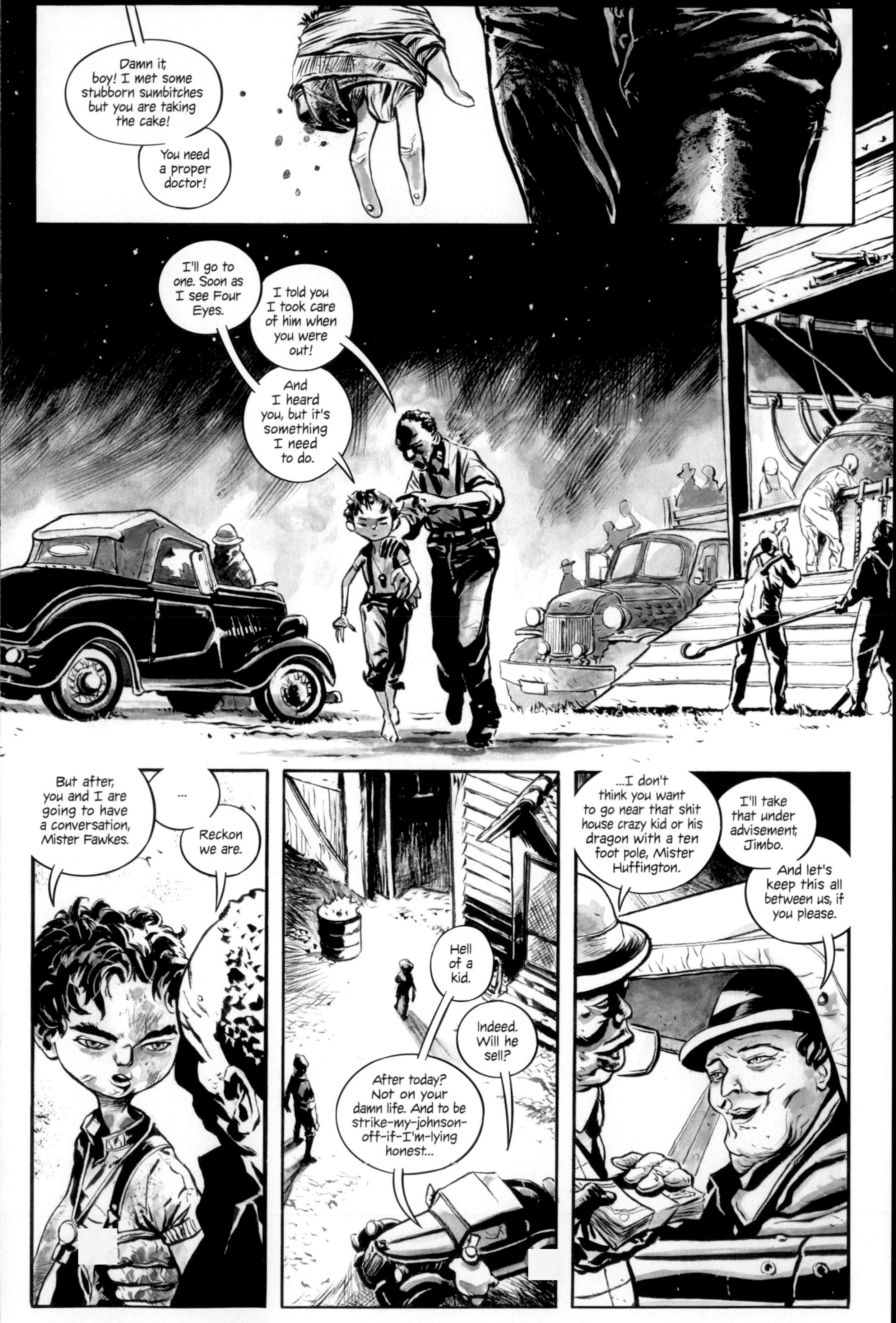

Damn it, boy! I met some stubborn sumbitches but you are taking the cake!
You need a proper doctor!
I'll go to one. Soon as I see Four Eyes.
I told you I took care of him when you were out!
And I heard you, but it's something I need to do.
But after, you and I are going to have a conversation, Mister Fawkes.
...
Reckon we are.
Hell of a kid.
Indeed. Will he sell?
After today? Not on your damn life. And to be strike-my-johnson-off-if-I'm-lying honest...
...I don't think you want to go near that shit house crazy kid or his dragon with a ten foot pole, Mister Huffington.
I'll take that under advisement, Jimbo.
And let's keep this all between us, if you please.

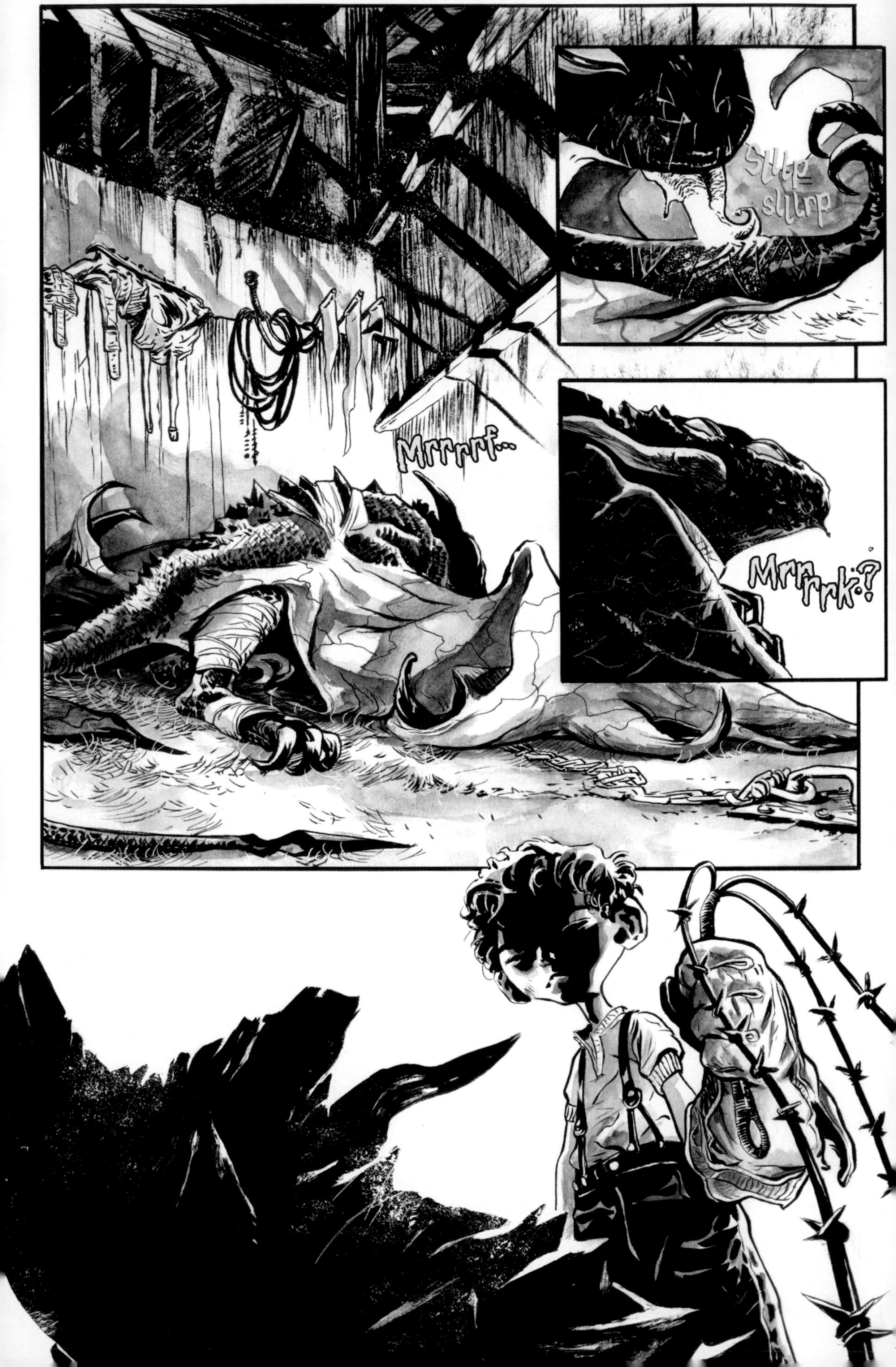
Mrrrrf...
sllrp sllrp
Mrrrrrk?

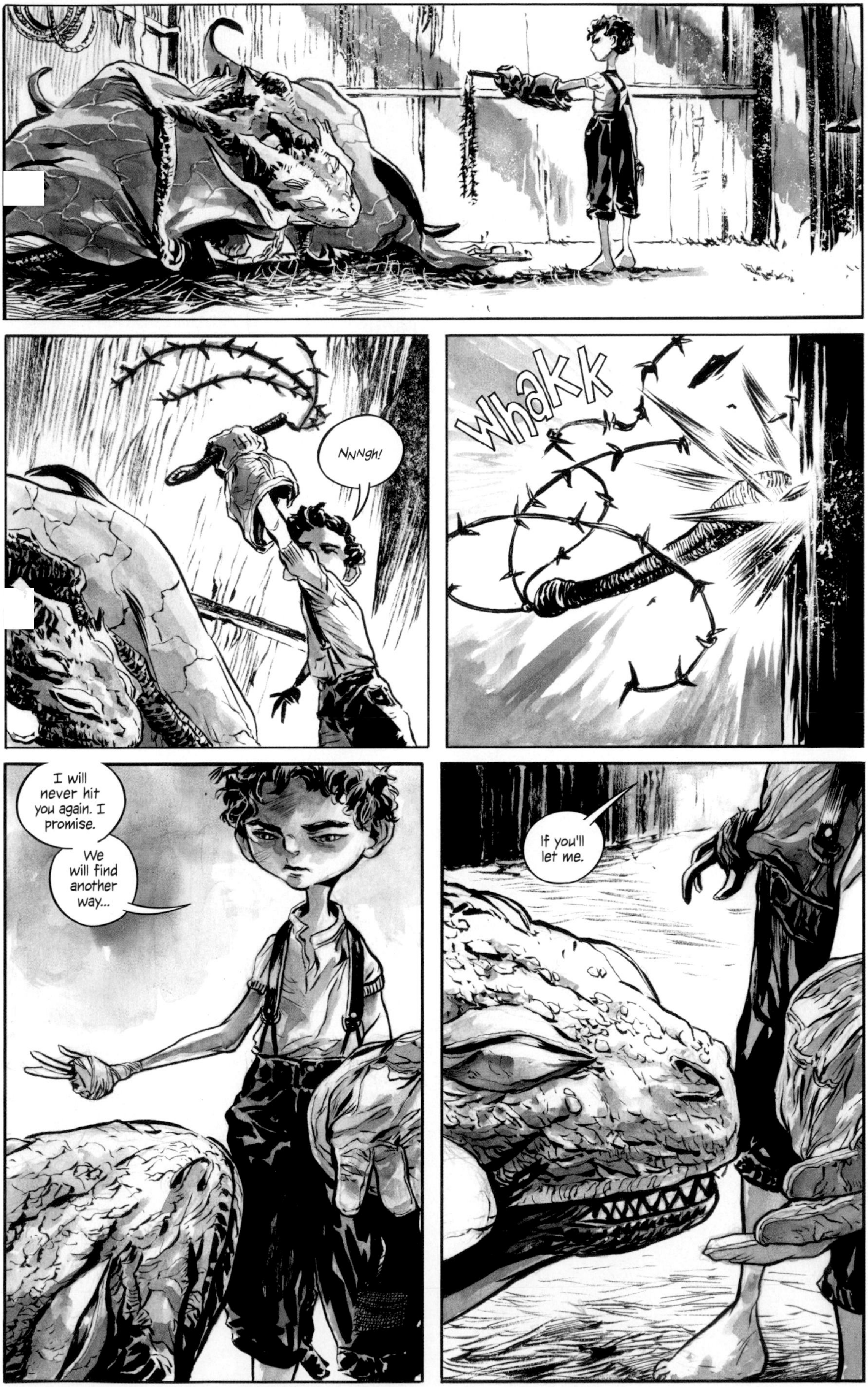
NNNgh!
WhaKK
I will never hit you again. I promise.
We will find another way...
If you'll let me.

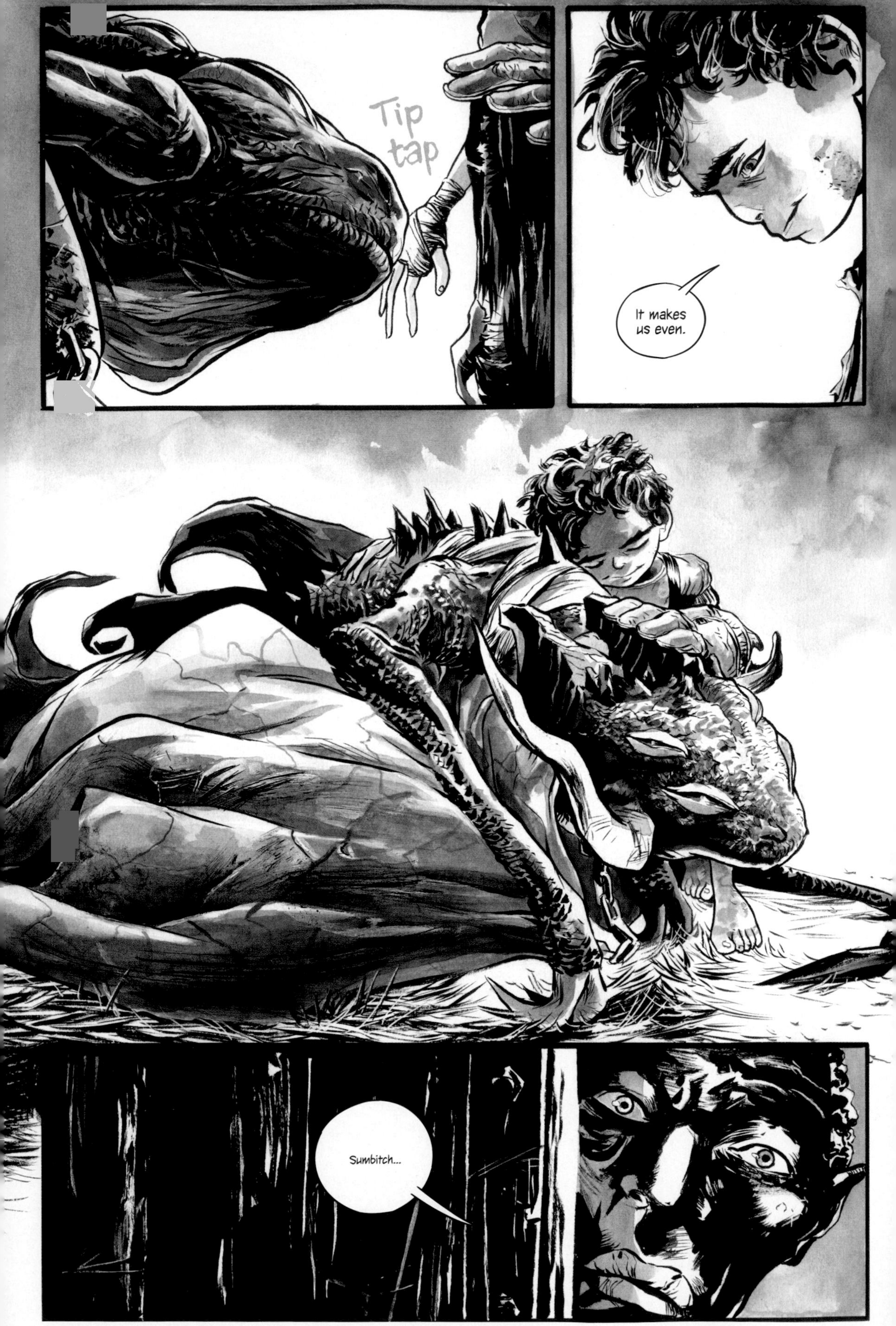
Tip tap
It makes us even.
Sumbitch...

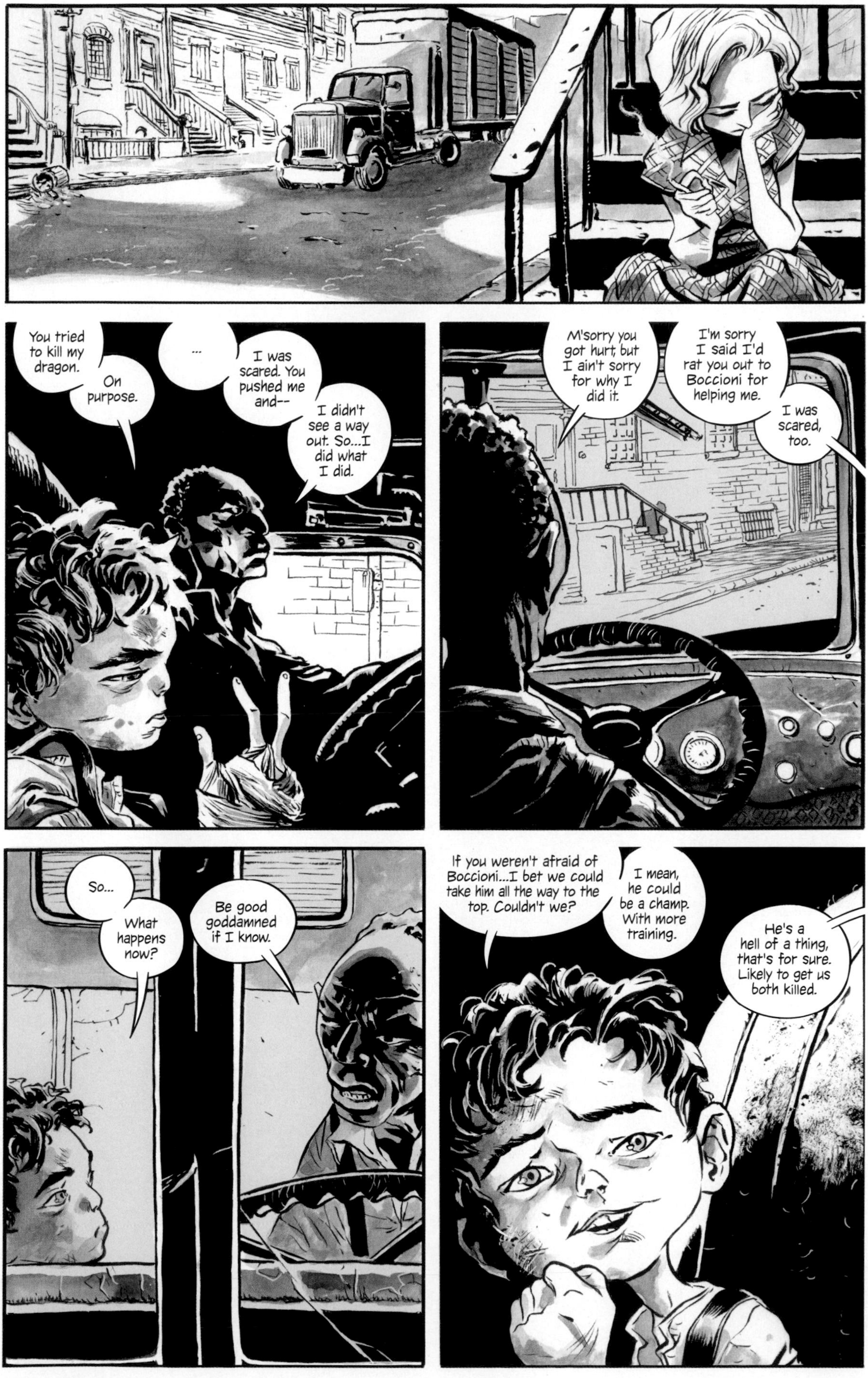

You tried to kill my dragon.
On purpose.
...
I was scared. You pushed me and--
I didn't see a way out. So...I did what I did.
M'sorry you got hurt, but I ain't sorry for why I did it.
I'm sorry I said I'd rat you out to Boccioni for helping me.
I was scared, too.
So...
What happens now?
Be good goddamned if I know.
If you weren't afraid of Boccioni...I bet we could take him all the way to the top. Couldn't we?
I mean, he could be a champ. With more training.
He's a hell of a thing, that's for sure. Likely to get us both killed.

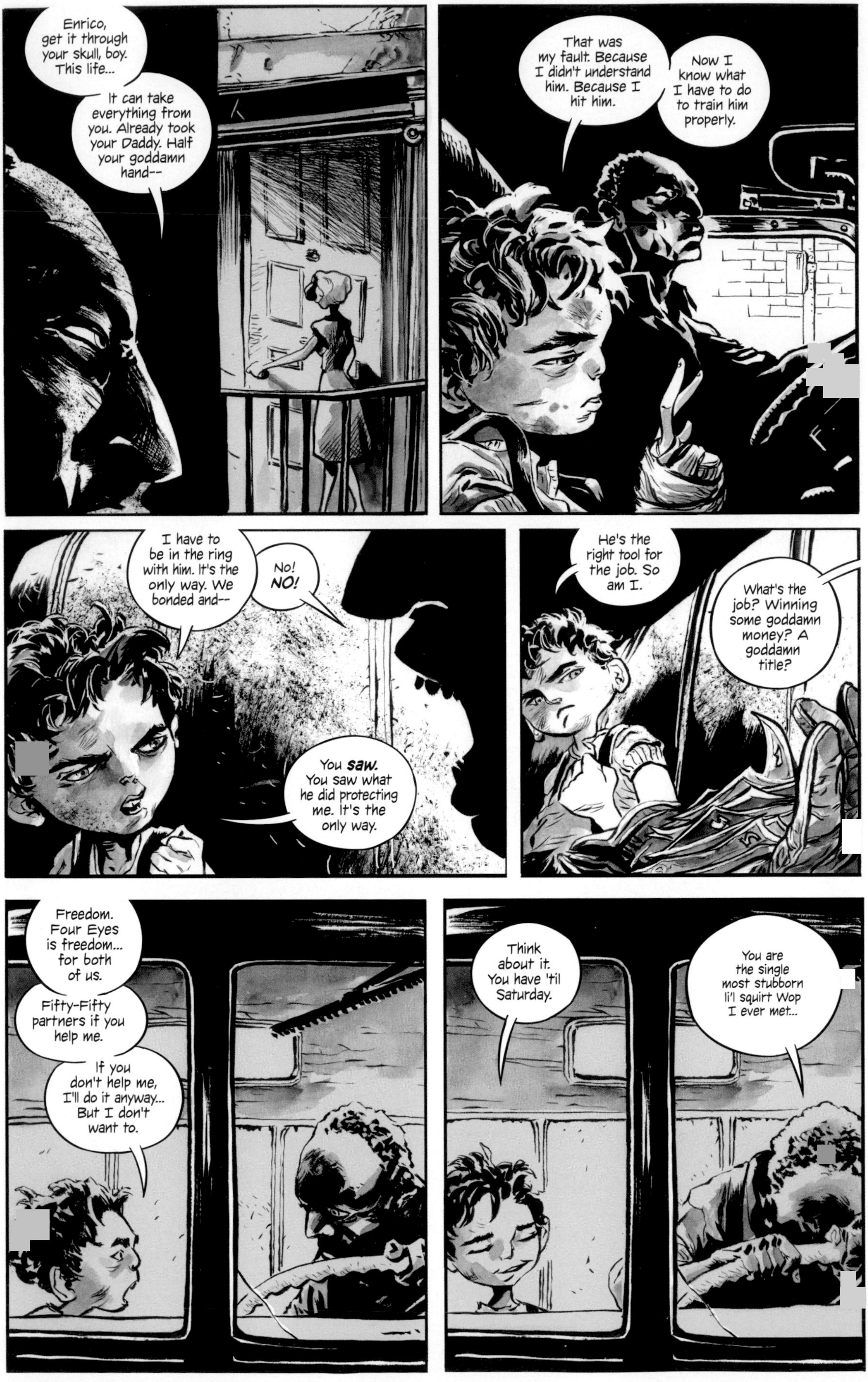
Enrico, get it through your skull, boy. This life...
It can take everything from you. Already took your Daddy. Half your goddamn hand--
That was my fault. Because I didn't understand him. Because I hit him.
Now I know what I have to do to train him properly.
I have to be in the ring with him. It's the only way. We bonded and--
No! NO!
You saw. You saw what he did protecting me. It's the only way.
He's the right tool for the job. So am I.
What's the job? Winning some goddamn money? A goddamn title?
Freedom. Four Eyes is freedom... for both of us.
Fifty-Fifty partners if you help me.
If you don't help me, I'll do it anyway... But I don't want to.
Think about it. You have 'til Saturday.
You are the single most stubborn li'l squirt Wop I ever met...

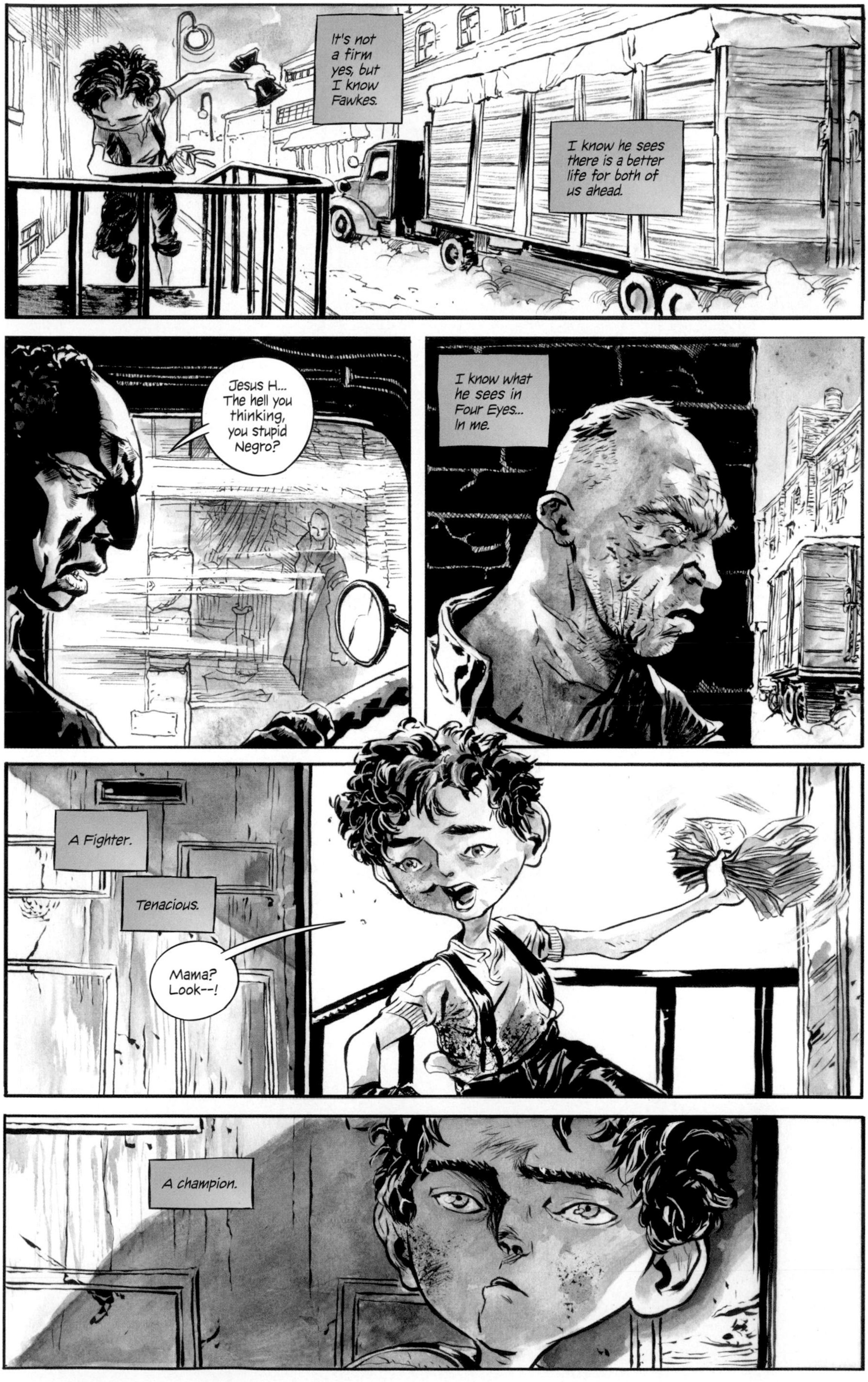
It's not a firm yes, but I know Fawkes.
I know he sees there is a better life for both of us ahead.
Jesus H... The hell you thinking, you stupid Negro?
I know what he sees in Four Eyes... In me.
A Fighter.
Tenacious.
Mama? Look--!
A champion.

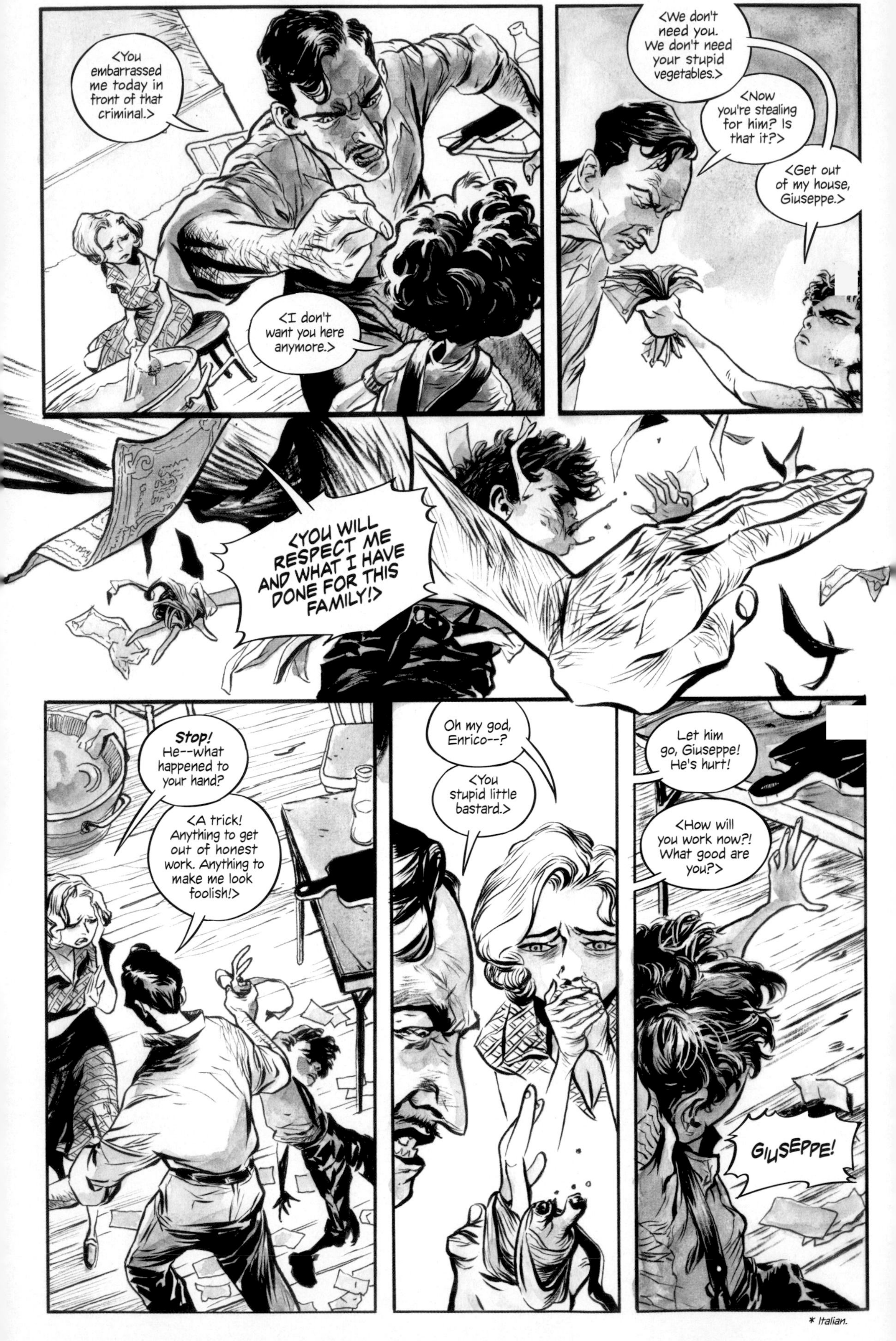

<You embarrassed me today in front of that criminal.>
<I don't want you here anymore.>
<We don't need you. We don't need your stupid vegetables.>
<Now you're stealing for him? Is that it?>
<Get out of my house, Giuseppe.>
<YOU WILL RESPECT ME AND WHAT I HAVE DONE FOR THIS FAMILY!>
Stop! He--what happened to your hand?
<A trick! Anything to get out of honest work. Anything to make me look foolish!>
Oh my god, Enrico--?
<You stupid little bastard.>
Let him go, Giuseppe! He's hurt!
<How will you work now?! What good are you?>
GIUSEPPE!

* Italian.

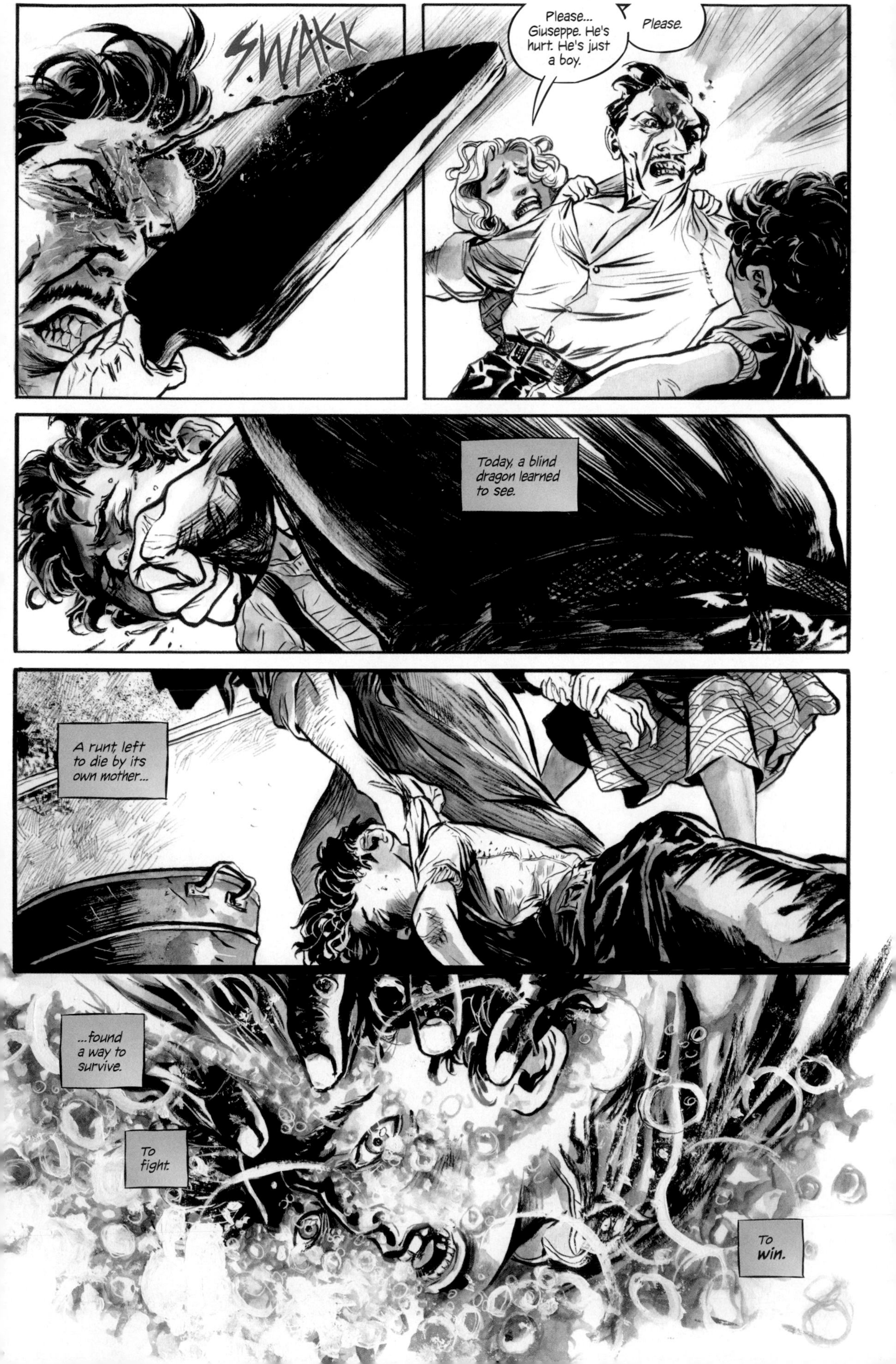
SWAKK
Please... Giuseppe. He's hurt. He's just a boy.
Please.
Today, a blind dragon learned to see.
A runt, left to die by its own mother...
...found a way to survive.
To fight.
To win.

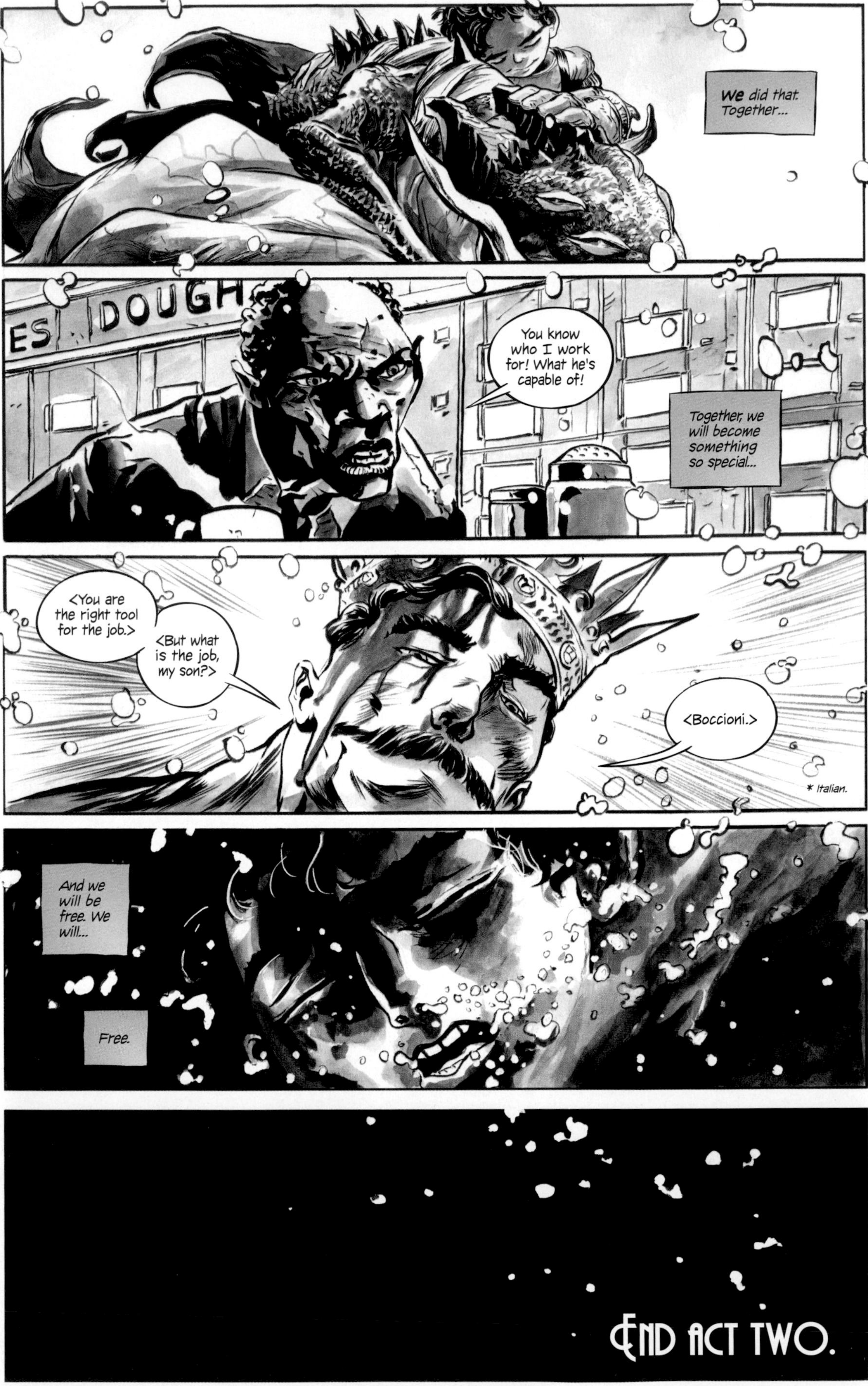
We did that. Together...
DOUGH
You know who I work for! What he's capable of!
Together, we will become something so special...
<You are the right tool for the job.>
<But what is the job, my son?>
<Boccioni.>
* Italian.
And we will be free. We will...
Free.
END ACT TWO.

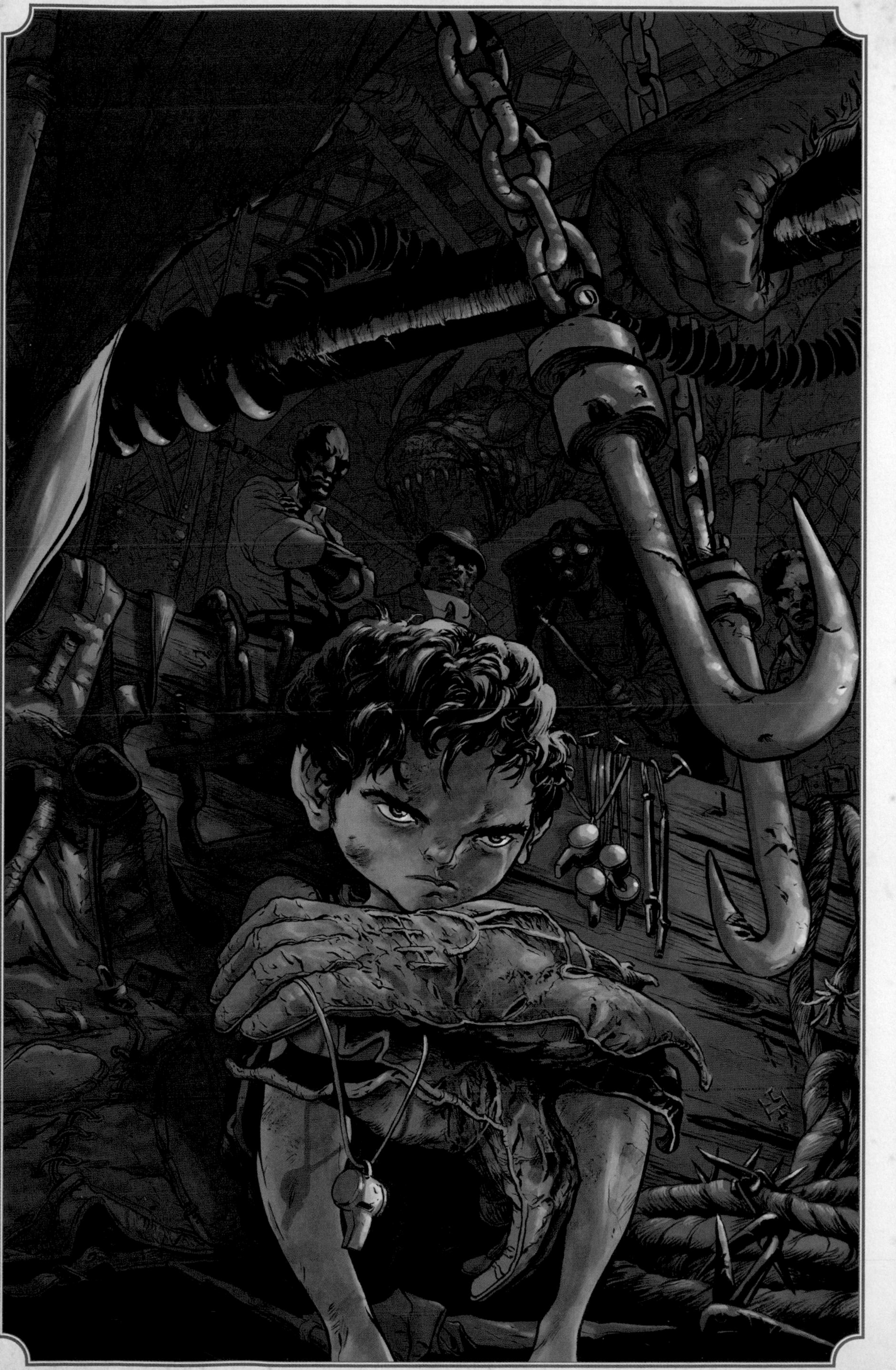

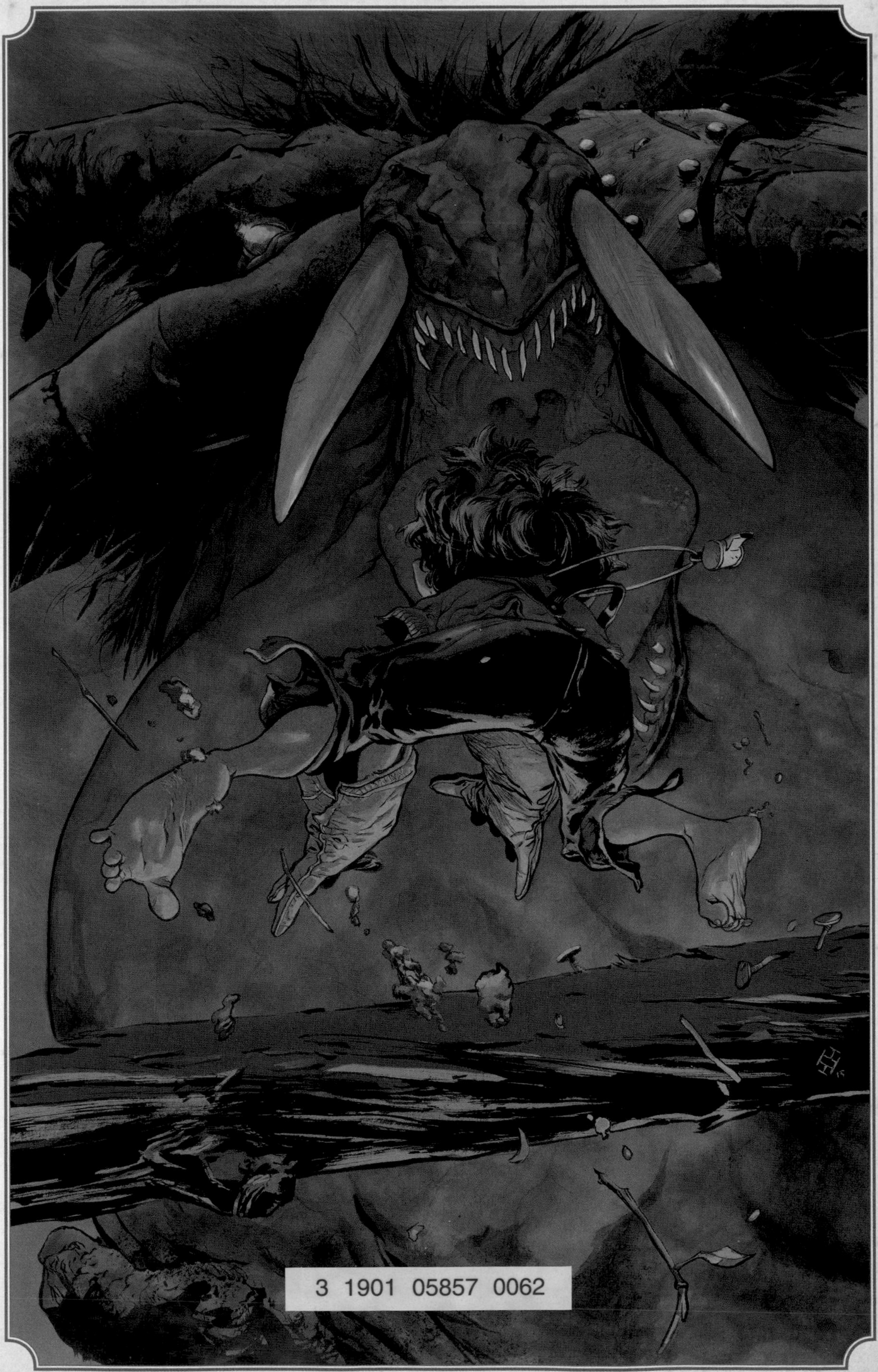